FICTION
Hall
Hall, Parnell.

Manslaughter : a Stanley
Hastings mystery /

MANSLAUGHTER

MANSLAUGHTER

A Stanley Hastings Mystery

Parnell Hall

CARROLL & GRAF PUBLISHERS
NEW YORK

MANSLAUGHTER
A Stanley Hastings Mystery

Carroll & Graf Publishers
An Imprint of Avalon Publishing Group Inc.
161 William St., 16th Floor
New York, NY 10038

Library of Congress Cataloging-in-Publication Data is available.

ISBN: 0-7867-1127-2

Book design by Simon M. Sullivan

Printed in the United States of America
Distributed by Publishers Group West

For Jim and Franny

MANSLAUGHTER

One

"I KILLED A MAN."

Uh-oh.

Not exactly what I wanted to hear. The man who graced my office first thing on a Monday morning was rather large. Still, he had a kindly face, a not-at-all hostile face, yet certainly not the type of face I'd like to have angry at me. Joe Balfour was a simpleminded but amiable lout, who obviously killed only at the behest of undesirable companions who led him into evil against his will.

Of course, I was making all that up. All I really knew about Mr. Balfour was he was an impediment I had to circumvent before setting out on my actual job, chasing ambulances for a negligence lawyer. I had three cases lined up already today, with more undoubtedly to come. When he'd appeared in front of my door Mr. Balfour had seemed a distraction at best. With the announcement that he had killed a man, he became a definite liability. But it occurred to me it might not be advisable to tell a walking mountain range with a track record for homicide to go to hell.

"Is that right, Mr. Balfour?" I said. I tipped back in my desk chair with a casual disinterest that implied most of my clients had *at least* one homicide on their record and probably my pizza delivery boy did as well. "Tell me about it."

He shrugged. "Not much to tell. I was young, I was drunk. I was in a barroom brawl. A man hit me and I hit him. I got up. He didn't."

I waited for more, but that was it.

"How long ago was this?"

"Twenty-five years."

"What happened to the case?"

"I was arrested and charged with murder. My lawyer plea-bargained it down to manslaughter. I got three to five."

"What'd you serve?"

"One and a half."

"Uh-huh," I said. I couldn't help wondering what three to five meant, when time served was a year and a half. I shuddered to think how bad you'd have to behave to wind up serving five.

"So what's your problem?" I said.

"Well, I have a daughter."

"Uh-oh."

He looked at me sharply. "Why do you say that?"

"Well, if the two things are connected, that's trouble. I assume your wife and daughter don't know you have a record and someone's threatening to tell?"

He looked at me as if I were clairvoyant. "How'd you know that?"

"Just a lucky guess."

"So what can I do?"

"There's only one thing to do. You sit your wife and your daughter down, and you tell 'em just what you told me."

"I can't do that."

"I knew that too. Now, I'm gonna give you a little more advice, then I got an appointment in the Bronx. You say you can't do that, and I hear you, and I appreciate what you say. Now, what you need to do is step back and say, here's what happens if I *don't* do that. And then start listing all the things that happen in that event. When you get to the part where your wife and your daughter *find out* what you did, try to explain to yourself why that result is preferable to the one where you sat down and told them."

He looked as if his mind was whirling, trying to follow all that. When he caught up, or at least appeared to, he gulped and said, "That can't happen."

"I'm glad to hear it. When it does, I'm sure it will console you to know that happenstance defied the laws of physical possibility."

He scowled. "Stop talking cute. I need your help. I wanna hire you. Whaddya say?"

"I told you. I have a job."

"How much does it pay?"

"I beg your pardon?"

"I pay cash, and I don't file ten-ninety-nines, and what you tell the IRS is between you and them."

Mr. Balfour reached in his pocket and pulled out a fat wad of bills.

"Now, do you want this job or not?"

I wanted the job.

You gotta understand. I am not the type of private detective you see in movies and TV shows who says, "There, there, Citizen," straps on his gun, and goes out and deals with the bad guy. I am a poor son of a bitch working my ass off to support my wife and kid. In New York City, that's not easy. Particularly if, as in my case, you have a liberal arts degree, which to date has been useful in pleasing my mother and serving as a bookmark in one of our family photo albums. In terms of a job, I am virtually unemployable. My skills are writing and acting. Oddly enough, it is not often that anyone wishes to hire me for either. Which is why I work the private detective shift. It is a permanent job-job. I do it for the money. And the money's not that good.

Mr. Balfour's money looked good.

I didn't grab for it, however. I leaned back in my desk chair, distancing myself from the cash, and said, "What is it you want?"

"I told you. To keep this from my wife and kid."

"And how would I go about doing this?"

"I don't know."

"That's less than helpful."

"I'm sorry. I'm flustered. Here. Take a look at this."

Mr. Balfour's briefcase was on the floor next to him. He put it in his lap and popped it open. He took out a piece of paper, folded in thirds like a letter, and passed it over. "This was sent to me at my office."

I unfolded the paper.

There was no date, no salutation, no signature. Just a typed message: *I know who you are. And I know what you did. Be at the Purple Onion Thursday night at 6:30. Wear a red rose in your left lapel. Don't fail me.*

"This came in the mail?"

"Yes."

"Where's the envelope?"

"I threw it away."

I paused just long enough to let him know what I thought about that, then said, "When did you get this?"

He frowned. "Yesterday. Why?"

"Why'd you wait till now?"

"I was figuring out what to do."

"You figured me?"

"You're near my office."

I considered, hopelessly conflicted. That pile of bills was awfully big.

I sighed. "Mr. Balfour, this is probably just a prank. Whoever sent this doesn't mention anything about a criminal record. My personal opinion is you don't need my help."

"Fine. That's very ethical of you. But I disagree, and I want to hire you. At least until I know what this is all about. The meeting is tonight at six-thirty. Can I count on your help?"

"You want me to hang out in the Purple Onion and keep an eye on you, and when this guy shows up, you want me to tail him?"

"No."

"No? Then what *do* you want?"

"I want you to *be* me."

Two

"MANSLAUGHTER," RICHARD ROSENBERG SAID. HE LEANED BACK IN HIS desk chair, steepled his fingers. "What an interesting word."

"It interested the blackmailer," I said.

Richard frowned, waved it away. "No, no, no," he said, dismissing my comment, the way he would dismiss the arguments of opposing counsel in court. Richard Rosenberg was one of New York City's leading negligence lawyers. That *one of* is hedging a bet. I could think of none better, and neither could he. A little man with big aspirations, Richard had boundless confidence in his own abilities, and this opinion was infectious. Opposing counsel had been known to settle the minute they heard Richard was on the case. In a way, giving in was the only way to thwart him, as he loved nothing better than beating an opponent down. Richard was prone to argue with any adversary, even me.

"What do you mean, no, no, no?" I inquired. From long experience I knew the best way to handle Richard was to ask for an explanation. He always had one, and the ensuing lecture gave me time to catch my breath.

"I mean, the word itself," Richard said. "Manslaughter. When you hear it, you think it's made up of the words *man* and *slaughter*. But if you look closely, it's also made up of the words *man's* and *laughter*. *Manslaughter* equals *man's laughter*. And why is the man laughing? He's laughing because he got off with manslaughter and beat a murder rap."

5

"*Man's* would be *apostrophe 's,'*" I pointed out.

Richard looked offended. "You're gonna fault me on a punctuation mark? I am wounded. I am cut to the quick."

"You'll live. So what do you think I should do?"

Richard steepled his fingers again. "You paid blackmail before. As I recall, that didn't work out too well."

"This is different."

"How so?"

"It's not blackmail. All I gotta do is show up and meet the guy. There's no evidence. No incriminating photos. No bone of contention. Nothing I am responsible for."

"If it's that simple, why bring it to me?"

"Oh."

Richard grinned. "Ah. Hadn't thought that one up, had you? You can't want advice, you've already agreed to do it. And you don't need to be told *how* to do it, since it's a piece of cake. Which means you came to me merely for approval. I am touched. I am moved. I am overcome."

"Actually, Richard, I came to tell you I've accepted this employment, so I may have to turn down a few of your cases."

"Oh, yeah, sure. Like that's really an issue. No, you wanted my blessing. I think that's rather sweet."

I muttered something that could barely be considered sweet.

Richard frowned. "Did you just invite me to go fuck myself?"

"I'm sure I would never do such a thing."

"See that you don't." Richard sighed. "Okay, you better give me the background on this blackmail."

"I thought you agreed it was a piece of cake."

"With your track record, nothing is a piece of cake. If I have to come bail you out of the hoosegow, it would help to know why you're there."

I gave Richard a rundown of Joe Balfour's problem.

"Twenty-five years?" Richard said. "That's a rather long time."

"Yes, but there's no statute of limitations on murder."

"Huh?"

"Murder never outlaws. If it could be shown he murdered the gentleman in question, he could still be prosecuted on the charge."

"No, he couldn't," Richard said impatiently. "He's been found guilty of manslaughter. That conviction would be a bar to further prosecution."

"Are you sure about that? Seems to me it's a fine line."

"Yes, and do you know why? Because you have the most devious mind I've ever encountered. Composed almost entirely of murder plots from Erle Stanley Gardner, Agatha Christie, Rex Stout, and Ellery Queen."

"I also watch *The Practice*."

"I'm thrilled. But that's not the case here. All you have is a twenty-five-year-old manslaughter conviction the blackmailer's threatening to make public."

"I have a twenty-five-year-old manslaughter conviction my client *supposes* the blackmailer's threatening to make public."

"Worse and worse. It's the most nebulous case I ever heard."

"The money was real."

Richard frowned. "And that's wrong too. Why should the guy pay you up front. Nobody pays up front. Who says you're gonna be successful? What's so special about you?"

"Hey, hey!"

"Not to run down your abilities, such as they are. But Jesus Christ, you got a situation here that screams to high heaven, where the odds of success are very small. You have to stop a man from revealing something he hasn't threatened to reveal yet. If he has no intention of revealing it, you can succeed by doing nothing. However, if he *does* intend to reveal it, nothing you can do will stop him. Short of paying him the hush money he hasn't demanded."

"Could you point out any other drawbacks in my situation? It'll keep me from getting overconfident."

"Then there's the part about pretending to be him. As long as he's not a cop, you're okay. There's no law against impersonating a person. The most they could get you with is wearing a flower with intent to deceive. If that were illegal they'd have to arrest every prom date in America."

"You're in rare form this morning, Richard."

"Well, whaddya want from me? You come in here, you bring me this outrageous story. You pretend you're asking for time off to handle it, but closer examination reveals it's happening tonight after work. Further examination reveals you haven't the faintest idea what you're doing besides making a pile of money."

"Because my client doesn't know. He's meeting someone, he'll find out more then."

"*You'll* find out more then if you agree to do this."

"I already agreed."

"My point exactly. What do you want from me?"

"I would like some assurance what I'm doing isn't illegal."

"I'm sure you would. Unfortunately, I'm not the one to ask."

"Who is?"

"Try a cop."

Three

SERGEANT MACAULLIF SCOWLED. "I HATE HYPOTHETICAL QUESTIONS."

"No, no, no. You *love* hypothetical questions. Hypothetical questions are great. They allow you to talk about things without getting in trouble."

"Getting in trouble? I'm a *cop*. Why would *I* get in trouble?"

"You wouldn't, of course. And that's where the hypothetical question comes in."

"Wrong," MacAullif said. "I wouldn't in any case. I am *not* in trouble. And you can't *get* me in trouble. You can get *yourself* in trouble. You have an *amazing* knack for that. A hypothetical question lets you skirt the edge of trouble. The worst part of it is, it allows you to talk to me. Whereas, without it you couldn't talk to me at all."

"That's rather rude."

"Tough shit. You come in here to ruin my day with a hypothetical question, fine, that's par for the course. You wanna pretend it's wonderful for me, go fuck yourself. I'm too busy for that kind of crap."

"All right, hypothetically, suppose this hypothetical weren't hypothetical."

MacAullif's mouth dropped open. "God save me." He jerked his desk drawer open, fumbled inside.

I thought he'd come out with a cigar. His physician had made him give up cigars, but he played with them from time to time, usually when I was driving him nuts.

This time he came out with several plastic pill bottles. He squinted at them, dumped two pills out, chewed them up.

"For my stomach," he said. "I got acid reflux, whatever the fuck that is. Apparently new and fashionable. Never heard of it all my life, suddenly everyone's got it. According to my doctor, it's either caused by stress or the other pills he's giving me." MacAullif shook his head. "You know the ads on TV for all these drugs: May cause drowsiness, liver damage, flatulence, and pissing in your pants."

"I believe that's exactly how they phrased it."

"And you ask yourself, is all that shit worth low cholesterol? I mean, compared to that, maybe high cholesterol ain't all that bad."

"It'll kill you."

"That's what the doc said. So he's got me on this one for high cholesterol, this one for high blood pressure, this one for clogged arteries, this one for sinus condition, this one clogged lungs, this one for heartworm—"

"Heartworm?"

"That's the dog's pills. I gotta remember to take it home."

"You got a dog?"

"I got a backyard. My wife got a dog."

"How's your wife?"

"Same as ever. There ain't no pill for that. How's yours?"

"Not bad. Last summer I took her for vacation to a bed-and-breakfast in New Hampshire."

"How'd that go?"

"Someone got killed."

"That sort of puts a damper on the trip."

"And she got sick."

"Acid reflux?"

"I don't recall. I think it was just a cold."

"Uh-huh. Well, it was really nice of you to drop in, catch up on old times."

"Fine. Be that way. I *won't* tell you about meeting someone in a bar with a flower in my lapel."

"A flower."

"Yeah. A rose."

"This is for identification?"

"Well, it ain't for looks."

"Who you meeting? Man or woman?"

"I have no idea."

"And they don't know you?"

"They don't know my client. At least, I hope they don't."

"Your client's meeting someone in the bar?"

"Hypothetically."

"Don't start that again."

"Okay, my client's *not* meeting someone in the bar. If my client *were* meeting someone in the bar—"

"I said don't start that."

"It's not a hypothetical. I told you. *I'm* wearing the flower. My client was asked to be somewhere wearing a flower. He's not going. I'm going instead. Now then, am I in trouble?"

"You're always in trouble. If it weren't for me getting you out of trouble, you'd probably be in jail. That's assuming you weren't dead."

"I thank you for that egocentric, self-aggrandizing assessment. Do you think you could apply your finely tuned police mind to the current situation? If I were to follow the steps as I have outlined them to you, would I be in any legal trouble?"

"I would say the odds are very good."

"I'm not talking odds. I'm talking facts. I do like I said. You got any grounds to arrest me?"

"That would depend."

"On what?"

"On what happens next. A guy walks up to you, says, 'Hi, you Julius Gottsagoo?' You gonna say, 'Yes'?"

"If I don't the conversation's over."

"No, it's not. See, that's where you fall down. You're not devious enough. Your thinking is too logical, straightforward. But 'Are you Julius Gottsagoo' is not necessarily a yes-or-no question. You can always say something noncommittal, like tell him to go fuck himself."

I smiled. "That's a quote from W. C. Fields. Not from the movies, of course, not back then. But supposedly his reply on being told the producer wanted to know when he was going to stop drinking and get back to the set. I'm surprised you know it."

"I *don't* know it," MacAullif said, irritably. "I was suggesting what you could do."

"Thanks. I'll bear it in mind. Anyway, despite this clever deflection you suggested, it seems to me entirely likely the perpetrator will see through the subterfuge and know he's being had."

"In which case I would advise staying in the bar. He'll have a harder time shooting you there."

"That's encouraging."

"At any rate, I'd be very wary if the gentleman asks you to take a walk."

"Thanks for the advice."

MacAullif scowled, then reached in his drawer again. This time he came out with a cigar, and began drumming it on the desk. "This whole adventure strikes me as very high risk, low reward. I mean, what's the best result? The guy takes you for your client, levels with you, tells you what he wants. It's something absolutely simple, and your client handles it and the problem goes away. I would say the odds of that happening are at best a hundred to one.

"Scenario two: The guy realizes you're not your client, gets pissed off, and spills the beans to his wife and daughter. The chance of that happening: excellent, probably an even-money bet.

"Scenario three: Guy could care less whether you're you or your client, demands hush money to fade from the scene. Also an even-money chance.

"Scenario four: Guy does not want money but has other demands. Requires that your client do things with or without knowing why they are being done. Odds of that, maybe one in four."

"You're already over a hundred percent."

"Huh?"

"Your odds don't add up."

"Give me a break. I'm trying to help you here."

"Good. Cause I need your help. Only not in fixing odds."

"No? What did you have in mind?"

"First off, I agree with you right down the line. This is a high-risk, low-reward game, and I think it's entirely likely no matter how this is played that the perpetrator doesn't tip his hand, even to the extent of letting us know who he really is."

"A-ha," MacAullif said. "Your plan is to tail him after the meeting to see if you can get a line on him. Only problem is he'll have met you. He'll know who you are. If this deal is as unkosher as it sounds, he'll be watching his tail to make sure you're not tagging along behind."

"You happen to be free at six-thirty?"

MacAullif rolled his cigar between his hands as if it were Play-doh. "You certainly took a long time to get around to it. My part in this whole wretched enterprise finally becomes clear. You want me to hang out in the bar, pick up the perpetrator when he contacts you, and tail him when he leaves."

"Not at all."

MacAullif frowned. "You don't want me to tail the guy? So what the hell do you want me to do?"

"I want you to wear the rose."

Four

MACAULLIF LOOKED EMBARRASSED AS HELL SITTING ON THE BAR STOOL with a flower in his lapel. And for good reason. The Purple Onion wasn't exactly a gay bar, but it wasn't exactly a straight bar, either. In the half hour he'd been there, two guys had hit on him already. Growling at the second one had earned him a momentary respite, while others weighed the risk of coming over.

I, on the other hand, had only been hit on once, and I hadn't growled at anybody. I wondered if I should take it personally.

I also wondered, belatedly, if the guy MacAullif had growled at could be our man. Wouldn't that be a kick in the head? But surely a black-mailer would be somewhat more persistent.

Anyway, I sat at the end of the bar, sipping a three-dollar Diet Coke, which I was damn well getting a receipt for and billing to Mr. Balfour.

Yeah, I know. A TV detective would have worn the rose, made the contact, bluffed it through. But that works on TV because the script *needs* it to work, and the star has to have the big part. I'm not on TV, and I don't have to have diddly if I don't feel like it. Besides, MacAullif was big and beefy, and looked like he could have killed someone with a punch. Indeed, at the moment, he looked very much like he might do it again.

At any rate, if our man didn't know what Balfour looked like, MacAullif ought to be able to make the sale.

I glanced around. The bar was quite full, the customers enjoying happy hour, or whatever other come-on the joint had going. It was a trendy midtown bar, neither its high prices nor its purple walls having managed to drive the clientele away. Nor had the oil paintings hanging there, rather garish numbers depicting either French countrysides or rural America—my expertise in art extends only so far as being able to distinguish naked women from poker-playing dogs.

The room was long and narrow, boasting a street frontage of no more than fifteen feet. The bar itself ran from shortly inside the door to halfway back to the men's room. Per MacAullif's instructions, he was sitting at the back end of the bar, and I was seated at the end nearest the door so that when our man left I would have no trouble following him out. This was a fairly obvious tactic—I flattered myself even *I* would have thought of it.

It was a quarter to seven when she showed. I spotted her the moment she came in the door. But I take no credit for it. I would have spotted her anywhere. She was a living, breathing Barbie doll, dressed to thrill.

It was still quite warm for October, and she wasn't wearing much. But what she was wearing was choice. Her maroon dress probably clashed with the purple decor, but who could care? It was of a thin fabric that hung loosely from her bare shoulders by narrow straps, a one-piece outfit, cinched at the waist by a fanny pack, and stopping just below the hip. If she was wearing panties, they must have been of the thong variety, as she was flashing plenty of cheek. She was certainly wearing no bra, clearly depriving Victoria's Secret of a few C-cup sales. She was somewhere in that dangerous age between too-young-for-me and how-did-I-ever-get-to-be-so-old? Don't get me wrong—I'm a happily married man, basically a noncombatant. Still, a cat may look at a queen.

Anyway, there she was with her little ski-jump nose, her bright blue eyes, her medium-cut auburn hair bouncing along as if she hadn't a care in the world, striding into the Purple Onion with determination on her face, and a manila envelope in her hand.

It was like an old western movie when Black Bart entered the saloon. Conversation stopped. Heads turned. Even some of the gay guys gawked. Singles parted like the Red Sea as Barbie sashayed the length of the bar and straight up to MacAullif. She leaned in, smiled, and said something to him. MacAullif smiled and said something back.

And she hauled off and slapped him across the face with the quickest right this side of Madison Square Garden. It was open-handed, but it had some muscle behind it. It was as loud as the crack of a bullwhip.

I have never seen MacAullif quite so startled. Or quite so humiliated. His face was bright red where she had slapped him, and bright red where she hadn't slapped him as well. He was so surprised, she was halfway to the door before he even caught his breath. He turned, jerked the flower from his lapel.

That was our signal, but I didn't need it. My radar was locked on before she traveled the length of the bar.

Barbie came out the front door of the Purple Onion, headed for Fifth Avenue. I wondered what MacAullif had said to her. Of course, that made me no different than anyone else in the bar. I just had a little more to go on. Apparently, MacAullif's deflection had not been as successful as he'd hoped. I wondered if he'd told her something noncommittal, like to go fuck herself.

The girl crossed Fifth Avenue, headed for Sixth. I shouldn't say *girl*, I'll get trashed by feminists. She was a young woman. And how. She was turning heads and stopping traffic. I swear, a taxi driver almost drove into the back of a bus. Barbie took no notice, just smoothly strode along, creating havoc. She either didn't care if she was followed, or hadn't considered it, because she never looked back. Even so, I kept a good distance and stayed out of sight.

As she walked along, Barbie whipped a cell phone out of her fanny pack and made a call.

She didn't talk long. Yet another reason to like her. Some women walk along with a cell phone plastered to their ear. Not her. Barbie was all business. She was on the phone less than a minute.

Barbie kept walking west. At Broadway and Forty-fifth Street she went into the Virgin Megastore and headed for the side wall where the top fifty albums were arranged at listening stations. I ducked into the alphabetical rock-and-roll section and watched from a distance while she donned headphones to check out the latest popular music. While I watched she sampled the likes of *NSYNC, Destiny's Child, and Britney Spears. I wasn't sure if that was an indication of just how young she was, or just how old I am.

When they show surveillance on TV they always resort to a dissolve, or cut-to, or a fade-out fade-in. Real life is different. There's no time limit, no commercial interruptions. If a girl wants to listen to the whole CD rack, she can damn well do it. Luckily, Barbie hung up her earphone and turned to go.

Only, she didn't leave. Instead, she headed straight for me.

I did what any good private eye would do in a situation like that. I had a moment of panic. I jerked a CD from the rack in front of me and pretended to look it over. In point of fact, I couldn't even tell you the artist. I just wanted to put something between me and her. Here she comes right at me and what am I gonna do now?

Actually, I stood there like a statue while she went right by, fanning herself with the manila envelope and humming some tune or other, probably by Britney Spears. Out of the corner of my eye I watched her pass me and disappear down a row of CDs. I tried to peer over the rack, but it was too high. I could just barely see the top of her head. That was okay, as long as I could keep her in sight and not lose her until she left the store.

Assuming she ever left. The Virgin Megastore is indeed mega, boasting various levels, the bottom of which housed a multiplex movie theater. If she opted for a film, I hoped it was one I hadn't seen.

She took the escalator down to the lower level. I hurried to the railing, peered over just in time to see her head into the bookstore.

Excellent. As far as I was concerned, that was my first break of the day. I had been in that bookstore before. It had only one exit, right out the same way she went in. I popped into the DVD section, settled down to watch the door.

She was out five minutes later, sailed right by the cash register without buying anything, got on the escalator up. Good. At least she wasn't going to the movies. Maybe she'd leave the store and go home.

It sure looked that way. I hit the main floor just in time to see her going out the front door.

There she went with long, purposeful strides, turning heads again, her full breasts bouncing underneath the thin fabric, both arms swinging free as she—

Uh-oh!

Where the hell was the manila envelope? Had she lost the manila envelope? Had she forgotten she was carrying the manila envelope? Had she set it down and walked away without thinking? Could she really be that careless with the blackmail evidence?

What the hell did I do now? Go back inside the megastore, try to retrace her steps, see if it was still where she left it? That envelope was pretty damn important. Or I could follow her and see where she went. No choice there. I'd lost the envelope, an embarrassingly bad move. But there was no way to rectify it. I had to stay with the girl.

Yeah, I know I said *girl* again. I'm upset. I'm not going to apologize every time. I'll try to remember to call her Barbie. Though that's even worse.

I came out on Broadway into the crush of a million tourists moving through Times Square. Ah, Forty-second Street, once a hallowed haven for hookers, smut, and pornography, now transformed by Disney and Warner Brothers and *The Lion King* into a mecca of movie shops and multiplexes. I cannot walk through Times Square these days without a sense of loss.

I followed Barbie as she mingled her way downtown through the tourists. At Forty-third Street she hailed a cab. That might have been a good move, if there hadn't been another cab just two cars behind. I hopped in, and made the driver's day.

"The cab up there," I said. "Don't lose it."

The cabbie had a turban and a beard and a name with no vowels on his license. I was sure he was going to ask me for identification, but he just reached up and touched a button on his meter, lighting up the fare, a two-dollar base charge, plus the fifty-cent surcharge some cabs charge after dark—in twenty years in New York I still haven't figured out for what.

The light changed. I waited for the cab ahead of us to pull out.

It didn't.

Instead, the girl hopped out and disappeared into the crowd, heading up Broadway, back the way she came.

I tried to hop out of my cab, but it was no use. The driver, wily bastard that he was, hit autolock, a device designed to keep passengers from beating him out of his fare. It worked well. There was no way I was getting out of his cab without coming up with two dollars and fifty cents.

Cursing mightily, I dug in my pants pocket, fumbled for change. The fifty cents I had. The two bucks I didn't. I had to break a five. I handed it to him, said, "Give me three bucks back." He didn't look pleased, but I was damned if he was getting a tip.

Freed from the cab, I fought my way up Broadway, searching for Barbie. Naturally, she was nowhere to be found.

On a hunch I headed back to the megastore, in case her cab maneuver had not been to ditch me, but because she suddenly remembered she forgot her envelope. It was a good theory, it was just wrong. There was no envelope, no Barbie, no nothing.

In attempting to tail Barbie, I had done the worst possible job. What was I going to say to my client?

I had no idea. But that was the least of my worries.

What was I going to say to MacAullif?

Five

"YOU SON OF A BITCH!"

"MacAullif—"

"You hang me out to dry and then you lose the girl?"

"I didn't hang you out to dry."

"I suppose you didn't lose the girl, either?"

"Actually, the word *girl* isn't politically correct."

"Hey, a girl smacks me in the face for no reason at all, I'll call her whatever I want."

"What did you say?"

"I didn't say a goddamned thing. Girl walks up to me, says, 'Who are you?' I say, 'Well, aren't you a sight for sore eyes,' and she gives me the mitten."

"Probably tired of cliche pickup lines."

"I wasn't trying to pick her up and she knew it. I was the guy with the flower."

"You were the *wrong* guy with the flower."

"No shit. *You* should have been the guy with the flower, and I should have been the guy on her tail. Then we wouldn't be having this discussion."

"Think you wouldn't have lost her?"

"That piece of work? Please. Take ninety-nine out of hundred PIs, put 'em in Times Square, and if they wound up followin' someone, it would be her."

"Yeah, MacAullif. But if she wanted to ditch you, she would."

"She wanted to ditch *you* and she *did*."

"Yeah, and why did she want to ditch me?"

"What do you mean?"

"How did she know she was being tailed?"

"Are you kidding me? The way you work? You might as well hang a neon sign around your neck: PI ON SURVEILLANCE."

"I bought you coffee for this?"

MacAullif and I were rendezvousing in a joint on Sixth Avenue where we'd agreed to hook up at nine P.M. if all else failed. As all else had failed, I was sitting there not having a particularly good time of it.

MacAullif sipped his coffee, grimaced as if he'd been poisoned. "Jesus Christ, this stuff is bad. I'm gonna have to take some more pills."

"Be my guest."

"Thanks. I just was. It got me slapped in the face and wasted my evening for no purpose whatsoever."

"That's not true, MacAullif. We learned a lot."

"Such as?"

"For one thing, the girl knows my client. She took one look at you and knew you weren't him."

"This is not big news. Blackmailers usually know who they're black-mailing. There's no reason to assume otherwise just because *you* wouldn't."

"I'm not a blackmailer."

"Thank god. You'd give the profession a bad name."

"Any time you're through having fun at my expense."

"How can I help it? You just came out with the remarkable deduction the girl knew her victim. I'm overwhelmed. I'm floored by your logic."

"Yeah, but it doesn't add up. The blackmailer may know Balfour, but Balfour doesn't know the blackmailer. Why would she want to reveal herself now?"

"Reveal herself is a good way to put it. Did you see that dress?"

"She looked good."

"I'll say. A real show-stopper. Every eye in the place was on her when she pasted me one."

"Could we stick to the topic?"

"Sorry. I keep forgetting my getting slugged is entirely coincidental."

"Come on! I mean, suppose you'd been Balfour. How does that make sense?"

"How the hell should I know? Suppose the girl knows him but he doesn't know her. Suppose the girl's working for someone. So she doesn't *care* if he knows her."

"In which case she wouldn't know him."

"Right. That's the reason for the flower."

"Yeah, but if she doesn't know him, how does she know you're *not* him?"

"We're going around again."

"We sure are, because your theories keep going around. Come up with a theory that doesn't."

"Okay," MacAullif said. "The girl doesn't know him. She's a hired functionary. She's been told to meet the man with the flower. She's also been given a picture to make sure the man with the flower *is* the man with the flower."

"That's better," I said. "Not great, but better. And why did this hired functionary take such offense at you?"

"I don't know. Maybe she gets paid on completion of the job. Your client not showing up negates that possibility."

"You're sure you didn't compliment her tits?"

"Swear to god."

"Okay, then what's the manila envelope?"

"The blackmail evidence."

"What blackmail evidence? Normally there's a bunch of dirty pictures that could be made to go away. The guy has a criminal record. He served time in jail. Evidence of that criminal record can be reproduced again, and again, and again."

"Having a copy of it is proof she knows."

"So is calling him an ex-con. This guy doesn't want the news leaking to his wife and daughter."

"True, but producing a rap sheet is a good move. It has just the right psychological effect. If the guy wasn't ready to pay before, that should ice it."

"Pay what? He hasn't been asked to bring any money."

"Exactly. And he won't be asked until he sees the rap sheet. 'Here's what I got, here's what I want you to pay me to go away.'" MacAullif's stomach growled ominously. "Oh, this is not good. I should not be doing this. I should be home, digesting a bland but hearty meal in front of the TV."

"Your wife okay with that bland but hearty assessment?"

MacAullif's face darkened. "Hey, one blackmail per night. You don't even know my wife. No way you could pass that along. Anyway, I meant it as a compliment."

"I'm sure you did. So what am I gonna tell my client?"

"Tell him you fucked up."

"That's not exactly helpful."

"Yes. That will probably be his opinion."

"Listen, MacAullif. I'm in trouble here. Can you think of anything to get me off the hook?"

"No." MacAullif shook his head. "You lost the girl, you lost the envelope. You haven't the faintest idea who the girl was or who she represents. All you know is whoever it is, they're not pleased. Instead of *lessening* the chances of this information leaking to the wife and kid, you've *increased* them. Not only that, you screwed up the only means the guy had of contacting this blackmailer. Now he couldn't buy him off if he wanted to. There's no two ways about it. Taking everything into consideration, you've done the worst job you possibly could."

Six

"YOU DID FINE."

God save me. I knew she'd say that. My wife is so predictably unpredictable. After years of trying to figure her out, I have thrown in the towel. All I know is, whatever I think is wrong.

Which should be enough. Which should save me. I should be able to say to myself, "I expect Alice to react this way, therefore she won't, so I know she will do the opposite." Only, such doublethink only comes back to haunt me. I find my original, utterly logical assessment to be absolutely true. It is my abandoning of it that is my undoing.

Sorry. I'm talking in abstracts. I know that's not helpful. I just lose all reason when dealing with my wife.

In this instance, Alice had pulled a simple reversal. There being no reason on god's green earth to assume I had done anything other than kick my client's case to hell and back, I had been in such a funk about it that I had overlooked the obvious. The obvious being a totally supportive Alice, blithely interpreting every bummer as a groove. But here she was, radiant as ever, a smile lighting up her perky face, reassuring me everything was all right.

I wasn't buying it. "Fine? How can you say I did fine? I screwed up the contact, lost the evidence, let the girl give me the slip. Can you point out a single thing I did right?"

"You had MacAullif be the contact. He's the one compromised, not you. So what's the bottom line? You learned a ringer isn't going to work. Which is good, because that was your client's idea, not yours. *His* idea failed, so if he wants you to try again, he's got to cough up more money and either give you more leeway or suggest another tack. If he suggests another tack, that's good, because if it doesn't work, *he's* blown it again."

"I suppose."

Alice and I were in bed watching the eleven o'clock news. Alice was looking good in her blue-and-white flannel pajamas. She always looked good, but pajamas tended to enhance the effect, suggesting, not without reason, that she wasn't wearing much underneath. Of which, I must say, I approved.

Unhappily, as was more often the case, this availeth me naught. Alice and I are getting on in years, which I find only tends to emphasize the difference in our genders. Alice is basically a sensitive, mature, intelligent, perceptive, discerning woman.

I am basically a sex maniac.

Even in normal times this is enough to create a somewhat strained relationship. With Alice on the brink of menopause, the situation is almost more than I can bear. And quite unfair, if you ask me. Men don't go through womenopause. At least, I don't. Quite the opposite, actually. And when I pointed out to Alice that she wasn't going through menopause *yet,* she stopped me dead in my tracks with something called *perimenopause,* which I'd never heard of before, but which suddenly was all the rage. Sort of like acid reflux. A lot like it, apparently.

"So," Alice said, pressing her advantage. "That puts you in an awfully good position. You've been paid for your services—you *have* been paid, haven't you?"

"Yes, of course."

"There's no 'of course' about it. You're such a softie. A client with a good story can talk you into anything. Though that's usually women clients."

"You were saying something about my wonderful position," I reminded her. "Speaking of which . . ."

"Don't even think it. Tommie's still awake."

"Well, that's not right. He has school."

"It's good to hear you being a responsible parent."

"Was that sarcasm?"

"Not at all. Why don't you tell him to go to bed?"

I found Tommie dispatching Nazis on his computer, told him to cease and desist. He did so with the usual ritual grumbling. Tommie's a good kid, but he is a teenager. He pled some level or other he had to reach, and we struck a deal. Minutes later, Alice and I heard him crashing around in the bathroom.

"So," Alice said, resuming her lecture as if there had been no interruption. How she does this is beyond me. I can barely remember the *topic* of a conversation. Alice can pick up in the middle of a sentence, even after a thirty-minute phone call. "Since you've been paid up front, there's nothing much your client can do. Even if he's unhappy with your services."

"Why should he be unhappy? I did fine."

"Was that sarcasm?"

"It strikes me as a legitimate question. If my client's displeased, that's not good."

"Well, you can't please everyone."

"That's for sure. Luckily, I pleased you."

"What makes you think so?"

"Alice. You said I did fine."

"You *did*, but that doesn't mean I'm *pleased*. You expect me to be *pleased* every time you do okay?"

"Just *okay*? I thought I did *fine*."

"Let's not quibble over words. You did fine. You have nothing to be ashamed of. I hope you'll pardon me if I don't give you a medal for it."

"Alice. How did we get so far off the track?"

"What track?"

I had no idea. As usual in my discussions with Alice, I had no clue what we were talking about. All I knew was I had gotten Tommie to go to bed, and I wanted our conversation to reach a satisfactory conclusion so that I could move on to more important topics, if you catch my drift.

"You're looking awful good," I said, a daring, blunt, abrupt change of subject.

Alice looked at me as if I'd just thrown a hail-Mary pass. "The point is," she said, refusing to dignify my desperately unsubtle compliment with comment, "you have done no harm. That is the important thing to remember. Not that you did anything good. Just that you didn't do anything bad. This blackmailer—assuming that is what this guy is—isn't going to run to the guy's wife and say, 'Nhay, nhay, your husband's a convicted killer.' What good does that do him? If you ask me, this is a case where the blackmailer's in a no-win situation. If you don't play ball with him, he's screwed. If he releases the information, he immediately ceases to be a threat. Only withholding it empowers him. Since last night was a total washout, the poor guy's back to square one. You haven't hurt a thing."

"Except my client has no means to contact the guy."

"So what? He doesn't *want* to. The other guy wants to. If he doesn't, the problem is solved. If he does, the problem of how to get in touch with him is solved."

"Are those new pajamas?"

"See what I mean?"

"Yes. I think Tommie's gone to bed."

"Zelda has to go out."

On cue, Zelda, curled up in front of the television, wagged her tail. Zelda is a Portugese Water Dog, which are very fashionable these days. We didn't know she was fashionable when we got her—we just wanted a dog who wouldn't shed.

"I already walked her," I said. I'd run Zelda down to Riverside Drive the minute I got home, as I often do. It's convenient. I hold the elevator door, whistle for her, and she comes running out, wagging her whole rear end like Chubby Checker. Zelda is black with white markings on her nose and paws, and I generally have a good time walking her. I just didn't want to walk her right now.

"Fine," Alice said. "You set the alarm?"

"Yes, I did."

"Good. I'm beat."

"Come on."

"What do you mean, *come on*? Do you know what time it is?"

"Earlier Tommie was awake."

"Yes, and you were at me then too."

I blinked. Surely there was some place in the conversation I could score if not a winning point, at least a moral victory. A small moral victory. Even an immoral victory. I mean, damn it, was I going to let Alice argue both sides of every issue?

The phone rang.

Alice and I looked at each other. Phone calls after eleven o'clock are not good. People don't call after eleven o'clock. Phone calls after eleven o'clock are either wrong numbers or emergencies.

Alice reached for the phone. I sucked in my breath, prayed for a wrong number.

"Hello?" Alice listened a minute, then said, "It's for you."

I took the phone with some trepidation and was relieved to hear MacAullif's voice. "Sorry to call so late. Just thought you'd wanna know."

"Know what?"

"I stopped by One Police Plaza on the way home. 'Cause I hate bein' slapped in the kisser and taken for a ride."

"What are you talking about?"

"I ran a check on your client. Which I should have done before if this whole thing hadn't seemed like such a piece of cake."

"And?"

"Joe Balfour never took a fall for manslaughter. As a matter of fact, there's no record of any Joseph Balfour ever being convicted of anything."

Seven

"YOU BLEW IT."

"That's one way to look at it."

"Well, perhaps you could suggest another."

I bit my lip, stifled several angry retorts. I wouldn't have been too cheerfully disposed toward my client just then, even if I *hadn't* known he was faking. In light of that little tidbit, I wasn't taking guff from him for long. I leaned back in my desk chair, cocked my head. "Actually, if anyone blew it, you did."

That brought him up short. He stopped pacing and scowled at me, utterly bewildered. "How do you figure that?"

"I just did what you told me. It's not my fault if it didn't work."

"But you *didn't* do what I told you."

"Sure, I did. *You* were told to be in the bar. *You* decided to run in a ringer. The blackmailer didn't like it, and that's where things went wrong."

"Absolutely not," Balfour said. "You PIs, the way you distort the truth, it's unbelievable."

"Excuse me? And just what is distorted about that?"

"Practically everything. *I* ran in a ringer? No. *You* ran in a ringer. I asked you to be in the bar wearing a flower to make the contact. You didn't do that. You got some stooge to do it for you. *You* ran in a ringer, and *that's* where things went wrong."

"Bullshit. The girl came into the bar, and saw the guy with the flower wasn't you. It didn't matter who was wearing the flower. All that mattered was the fact that you weren't."

Balfour wrung his hands, invited the gods to witness his tribulations in dealing with mere mortals, and stupid ones at that. "Jesus Christ, if I'd known what a moron you were, I wouldn't have hired you! What do you mean, it makes no difference? It makes all the difference in the world. You may be a dip-shit, but you're a respectable-looking dip-shit. Amiable, pleasant-looking, certainly no threat. A person might talk to you just to know what the score was." He grimaced. "On the other hand, you take a big, beefy cop who looks like a big, beefy cop, a guy who might as well have the word *cop* tattooed on his forehead, for Christ's sake. A person looks at him and says, 'Uh-oh, let me out of here.'"

"So she slaps him in the face?" I said skeptically.

"A guy might just keep walking. A girl who's turned every head in the place and who's not that quick a thinker doesn't know what to do. So she falls back on old faithful. Slap the guy and walk out. Odds are he won't try to stop her. Even if he did, odds are some macho jerk would come to her rescue."

"Is that what you did?"

"Huh?"

"Your barroom brawl. Is that how it happened?"

"Don't change the subject. The fact is, you fucked up running in this cop, and now I'm in trouble and it's all your fault."

I took a breath, made a note to pass that assessment of the situation along to Alice at the first opportunity. "So, what was in the envelope?" I asked.

"Since you lost it, we'll never know."

"A record of your jail time, perhaps?"

"Perhaps."

"You don't sound sold."

"Well, what would be the point? The blackmailer doesn't have to prove his case, just make the claim."

"Interesting," I said.

"Why is that interesting?"

"It's interesting that you refer to the blackmailer as *he*, when it's the girl who made the approach."

"So? I assume she's working for someone."

"Who might that be?"

"Once again, thanks to you, we'll never know."

"Not at all. If the blackmailer's serious, he'll contact you again. If not, you have no problem." Before he could retort, I said, "What about the girl? Who might she be?"

"I have no idea."

"You know anyone who fits that description?"

"Not at all. My friends are all my age. They're not twenty-year-old *Playboy* Playmates."

"Well, she obviously knew you."

"There's nothing obvious about it. She just knew the guy was a cop."

"That would probably make her a pro."

"What's wrong with that?"

"I find it hard to imagine our guy letting a hooker in on the deal."

He frowned. "There's no reason to assume she's a hooker."

"What did you think I meant by a pro?"

He took a breath. "I don't have time to argue with you. I paid you money to do a job and you didn't do it. I figure you owe me something. If this guy tries again, you'll be hearing from me."

"Have your wallet ready."

He blinked. "What?"

"You paid me for one job. You want another, you can pay me again."

"You didn't *do* the job."

"Yes, I did. You may not like the result, but the job is done."

"I could hire someone else."

"Be my guest."

He scowled again. "I don't want everyone and his brother in on this. You're incompetent, but you're honest. You must be, to tell me the story you did. Most guys would have gone out of their way to make themselves sound the least bit intelligent. The story you told must be true, or why would you make yourself sound like such a jerk?"

"Thanks a lot."

"So next time you're hip. No ringer cops. No deviating from instructions. No figuring you're smarter than me. Is that clear?"

I shrugged. "You bring me another offer of employment, we'll talk."

Balfour shook his head. "You're a piece of work."

He scooped up his briefcase and went out the door.

Eight

My office is on West Forty-seventh Street, just off Broadway, in the heart of the diamond district. My father-in-law, the noted plastic bag manufacturer, still carried it on his company books, otherwise I could never have afforded it, midtown office space being only slightly more precious than gold. At any rate, it's in a six-story prewar building boasting both an elevator and stairs.

Joe Balfour took the elevator.

I took the stairs, two or three at a time, jumping on the landings, thundering like a herd of buffalo, and managed to reach the lobby just as Balfour was heading out the front door.

When it comes to clandestine surveillance, there is none better. Except, of course, when it comes to tailing nubile nymphettes without underclothing. But a businessman with a briefcase is dead meat. Or so I told myself as I followed Joe Balfour down Seventh Avenue.

A few blocks down the street he turned into the Virgin Megastore. This presented a small problem. It wouldn't do for him to see me there. Feigning a sudden need for mood music wasn't going to fly. And that time of day, there was almost no one in the store.

I hung way back, kept Joe Balfour in sight, watched to see what he would do. He went down to the third level, disappeared into the bookstore. Well, at least I knew the drill. I also knew if he came out clutching a manila envelope, I was really going to lose it.

He didn't. Balfour was out minutes later, headed for the escalator. Of course the manila envelope could have been in his briefcase. But there was no reason to assume so. Unless it had been in the store all along and I had somehow missed it. That seemed a little much, even for one as insecure as I. I tried to resist such paranoid thoughts, followed my quarry outside.

Balfour went down Seventh Avenue, crossed Forty-second Street, hung a left on Forty-first. Halfway down the block he went into a large office building. I hung back, watched through the door as he headed for the elevators. There were two banks, one for the 1 through 10 elevators, and one for 10 through 21s. Most of the people waiting in the lobby were gathered around the 1s through 10s. In front of the 10 through 21s was a little blonde number holding a Starbucks coffee that probably cost as much as my watch. Granted, it's just a cheap Casio digital; still, it keeps the time. Anyway, the elevator bell dinged and Balfour and the Starbucks lady got on.

I hurried into the lobby to watch the show. According to the electronic readout, the elevator stopped at 12, 14, and 15. For two people, that seemed excessive. Maybe Balfour and the coffee lady were careless with their buttons, or someone got on at 12 or 14.

The elevator next to me dinged. I got on, discovered I'd been joined by a middle-aged woman in a business suit, an Asian delivery boy with a cardboard tray of coffee and doughnuts, and a man with a mustache who must have hated his job. The delivery boy pushed 17, the woman pushed 18, and the sourpuss pushed 21.

I pushed 12. The elevator zoomed straight up to the twelfth floor, where the doors opened to reveal the lobby of Fabrics Inc., clearly a textile manufacturing company. Pictures of sheets and towels adorned the walls. The lobby was empty except for a receptionist, seated at her desk.

I stayed on the elevator, waited for the doors to close, and pushed 14. Behind me, the businesswoman cleared her throat. I could imagine her exchanging glances with Sourpuss.

The fourteenth floor proved to be a suite of doctors' offices. I stayed on the elevator and pushed 15. This time it was Sourpuss who snorted.

I'm not big on being hated. I decided I'd get off on 15, no matter what, and catch the next elevator down.

The fifteenth floor proved to be Allied Associates. An efficient-looking black receptionist sat at a computer terminal. Standing in front of her desk was my client, holding a bunch of memos.

Oops.

Now I couldn't get off at 15 either. I shrunk back away from the door, trying not to be seen.

"Are there any floors you like?" Sourpuss grunted.

His voice seemed loud enough to fill Yankee Stadium. And the elevator had dinged when the door opened. And no one had gotten off.

Wouldn't Balfour notice? Wouldn't he turn around and see me?

"You getting off or not?" the businesswoman said.

"Wrong floor," I said, as the elevator doors closed.

"We can't stop on every floor."

"I'll go back to the lobby and verify the address."

"What company are you looking for?"

I had a moment of absolute panic. I had not even considered what fictional company I might in fact be looking for, and the question caught me completely off guard. Suddenly, here I was, about to blow my cover just riding up in the elevator.

All right, so maybe I'm *not* the best in the world at clandestine surveillance. It happens to be damn hard.

"Warner," I said. "I'm looking for Warner Books. Isn't that here?"

"Not that I know of."

"Time-Life Building," the Asian messenger said. "Fiftieth Street and Sixth Avenue."

The woman and the cranky businessman fixed him with a malevolent stare. I wasn't sure who was in deeper shit—me for being in the wrong building, or the delivery boy for knowing more than them.

Anyway, I got off when he did, caught the next elevator down, and was relieved when it didn't stop on 15. Minutes later I was out of the building.

So, that was that. Barring the possibility that he happened to have a nine o'clock appointment at the company, it would appear that Joe Balfour worked for Allied Associates. The memos in his hands seemed to cement that theory, though, god knows, I've been fooled by circumstantial evidence before. However, judging from the suit, the briefcase, and the time of arrival, everything seemed to indicate that Mr. Balfour was a businessman who worked nine to five.

That was good, because I'm a working man too. I went back to the office, checked my assignments, grabbed my briefcase, got the car out of the municipal lot, and headed for Harlem.

Nine

TIFFANY WEBER LIVED IN A FOURTH-FLOOR WALK-UP OF A CRACK HOUSE next to a methadone clinic, which made her one of my least favorite clients. She was a perfectly nice woman, but getting there was half the fun. It required sucking in my gut, squaring my shoulders, and bulling my way through the gaggle of junkies hanging out on the steps. All I can say is, god bless dope. Straight men might have discerned the anxious, middle-aged man that I am. These guys just saw a cop. They got out of my way.

Tiffany Weber was a young black woman with three preschool kids, no husband, no job, and a broken leg. All of which would please Richard immensely if it turned out she had a case. Tiffany had tripped on a crack in the street and wanted to sue the city of New York. Actually, she just wanted money. Where it came from didn't concern her.

Tiffany had answered Richard's TV ads: "Free consultation. No fee unless recovery. We will come to your home." He wouldn't, of course. He'd send me.

"Hi, I'm from the lawyer's office," I said. As usual, she took me for a lawyer, and I didn't do anything to disillusion her. Please understand, I never *say* I'm a lawyer, I just never say I'm not, and I always deflect such misassumptions by saying something like, "I'm not your lawyer. Your lawyer is Richard Rosenberg, the senior partner of Rosenberg and Stone. I'm just doing the preliminary work for him."

Anyway, I filled out Tiffany's fact sheet, taking down the details of her accident and her hospital stay, had her sign forms for us to get the police report and her medical records, and, last but not least, a retainer of Richard Rosenberg as her attorney. Which is my real job. Getting the client to sign. Which they are under no obligation to do. And which I manage to accomplish ninety-nine percent of the time. I might feel bad about it if it didn't cost the client absolutely nothing.

After she signed, I took photographs of Tiffany's broken leg. That was one of the first things I learned on the job. You always take the photos last. If they don't sign the retainer, there's no reason to waste the film.

When we were done, Tiffany took me outside and showed me the scene of the accident, a horrendous-looking crack in the pavement of the crosswalk at the corner of One Hundred and Thirty-Eighth. I photographed it from all angles, hoping it was registered with the city of New York. Since the pothole law, only defects that had been reported and not repaired were liable. When the law first went into effect, negligence lawyers employed paralegals to run around the city, registering every pothole they could find. Others merely looked for reported defects and attributed accidents to them.

I was sure Richard Rosenberg had never done anything of the kind.

When I was done I bid a fond farewell to Tiffany Weber, and headed out to Queens, where an elderly man had fallen on a city bus.

I was just cruising over the Triboro Bridge when my beeper went off. I have a cell phone now—I finally caved in—but I don't let the switchboard girls call me on it. If they want me, they can beep me, and I'll call them. I do that because I don't want to be in the position of having to answer the phone while driving. I got the cell phone just as a convenience, to keep me from going nuts searching the South Bronx for a working pay phone. When the office beeps me, I stop the car at the first opportunity and call in.

That resolve lasted about a week. After all, the cell phone has an autodial. All I have to do is press a button. I pressed it now, held the phone to my ear as I tooled over the Triboro Bridge.

"Rosenberg and Stone," said Wendy/Janet.

Richard Rosenberg employs two switchboard girls who have identical voices. I can never tell 'em apart. On the cell phone it's even worse.

"Hi, it's Stanley," I said. I found that preferable to a gambling, "Hi, Wendy," or "Hi, Janet," a fifty-fifty proposition I would invariably lose, and, "Who is it?" tended to piss her/her off.

"Stanley," Wendy/Janet said. "A Mr. Balfour's trying to reach you. Do you know who that is?"

"Yes, I do. What's he want?"

"He wanted your phone number. I wouldn't give it to him."

"Good girl."

"Thank you."

Ah. That identified her as Wendy. Janet would have taken exception to the word *girl*.

"Did he leave a message?" I asked. I was nearing the end of the Triboro Bridge, and cars were jockeying for position.

"He wants you to call him. His phone number's—"

"Hold on, hold on. I don't have a pen."

"You don't have a pen?"

"Hang on. Let me get off the road here."

"You're driving? I thought we couldn't call you when you're driving."

Damn. Between them Wendy and Janet had the brains of a turnip, but Wendy also had a mind like a steel trap. Hammer an idea in there, and you'd never get it out.

"Ah, here's a pen," I bluffed. Instead I jerked out of my pocket the microcassette recorder Alice had given me to help me with my writing career. Alice figured if I thought of something while driving around, I couldn't write it down, but I could click the thing on and make a note to remember it. That way I wouldn't lose any of my brilliant ideas.

I was still waiting for the first one.

I clicked *record*. "Okay, what's the number?" I was now holding the recorder in one hand and the phone in the other, and steering with my elbows. Don't try this at home. Only the most reckless, devil-may-care private eyes ever attempt such a feat.

Actually, recording the number was easy. Playing it back and dialing it was hard. I got a pizza parlor, a gas station, and a company switchboard. Luckily, it was the right company. Minutes later I heard Joe Balfour's voice.

"It's Stanley Hastings. What's up?"

"They called."

"Who called?"

"Who do you think? The blackmailer."

"Man or woman?"

There was a pause.

"You thinking it over?"

"All right, they didn't call."

"Oh. That's different."

There was another pause. I could imagine steam rising from his head.

"There was a message," he said.

"A phone message?" I asked. I remembered all the message slips in his hand.

"No. A letter. In this morning's mail. Postmarked today. Obviously mailed last night."

"What did it say?"

"'Naughty, naughty.'"

"Not exactly high praise."

"You're being rather wise-ass."

"I have work to do. You call me up with some nutty message, what do you expect me to do about it?"

"Nutty message, hell. Obviously this is a result of what you did last night. In which case I want you to do something about it."

"Was there a return address?"

"Of course not."

"Then what do you expect me to do? We have no idea who's involved or what they want."

"Of course not. This is just preliminary. Obviously they're going to contact me again."

"When they do, you'll know."

"When they do, I wanna call you. What's your number?"

"You can reach me through Rosenberg and Stone."

"I don't wanna call Rosenberg and Stone. I wanna call you on your cell phone."

"Yeah," I said. "But there's a problem."

"What's that?"

"I don't *want* to you to call me on my cell phone," I said, and hung up.

I could imagine Balfour steaming. I switched off my cell phone just in case it occurred to the son of a bitch to dial Star 69.

Ten

I DROVE OUT TO QUEENS, SIGNED UP ANGELIO FELICIO, WHO'D FALLEN on a city bus, then headed for Patterson, New Jersey, to interview a guy who'd been hit by a car. The Patterson, New Jersey, case was lucky. Not for the guy—he had a broken arm, a broken hip, and multiple lacerations—but the fact the case was in New Jersey meant a lot of time and mileage.

I got back to Manhattan at a quarter to five, which answered the burning question, should I keep my car or ditch it? There wasn't time to ditch it. I'd just have to make do.

I drove to Forty-first Street, turned onto the block of Balfour's office, and settled down to wait. That in itself was tricky. In midtown, cars are discouraged in no uncertain terms. There's no parking, no standing, no driving by. In fact, I think you can get arrested just for *owning* a car. Plus, the trucks loading and unloading make even illegal parking spaces a premium. I double-parked and proceeded to back up and pull forward, never returning to the same spot, and just generally giving my impression of a man who was *not* parked, a man who was still in motion.

Balfour was out the door at ten after five, by which time I had an incredible stiff neck from all the backing up. I would have been glad to see him, except he headed for Sixth Avenue, and of course Forty-first Street runs west, toward Seventh.

I was not to be denied. I threw the car into reverse and began backing toward Sixth, trying to ignore the taxi honking indignantly. I found my neck hurt less when I was backing up. Either that or the rather excellent prospect of wrecking my car pushed the pain from my mind. At any rate, I reached Sixth Avenue and hung what would have been a right had I been going forward. In other words, I backed out onto Sixth, heading uptown.

If Joe Balfour had also turned right, I would have been a very unhappy camper. Backing down Sixth Avenue at rush hour is not high on my list of things to do. Balfour turned left. I heaved a sigh of relief, followed him up Sixth Avenue to a parking garage. I hung back, watched him go in.

I played a little game with myself to guess what kind of car Balfour would drive. I had it narrowed down to a Lexus or a BMW when the guy drove out in a Jaguar. I made a mental note to readjust my fees.

I fell in line, tailed Balfour down the street. So far I was batting a thousand. He could have commuted by subway. Then I'd be dorked. Or he could have gone home early. Then I'd be dorked. Or he could have decided to work late. In which case I would be dorked. But, no, things were working out.

I didn't like it. Life usually dorked me. Why were things going right?

I know, I know, that's really bad double thinking, obsessively applying a negative to a positive. MacAullif says I'm an analyst's dream. Maybe I am. Even so, I distrust anything that's too easy.

I followed Balfour to the West Side Highway, north under the George Washington Bridge, and onto the Henry Hudson Parkway.

At the toll bridge leaving Manhattan, Balfour got into the EZ-Pass lane, and so did I. EZ-Pass is one of those things I had to fight out with Richard. My expense accounts are supposed to include receipts. With EZ-Pass, you don't get one. But EZ-Pass is so popular now, at the bridge there are five EZ-Pass lanes and one or two very long cash-only lanes. So my question for Richard was, would he rather pay me for signing up a client, or waiting in a line? Richard, prince of men, came up with a compromise. I could photocopy my monthly EZ-Pass bills and circle the appropriate charges.

I tried not to be too effusive in my thanks.

I followed Balfour up the Henry Hudson to where it turned into the Saw Mill River Parkway. That used to be a toll booth too, but it's long gone. If my understanding is correct, what happened was the toll booth finally collected enough money to pay for the road, so they took it down.

The mind boggles.

Balfour kept going, took the Cross County Parkway east to the Hutchinson north, and got off in White Plains. He cruised around a few blocks of mid- to upper-scale suburbia, and turned into the driveway of an ultramodern two-story monstrosity that might have served as a term project for some architectural student. One with a gentleman's *C*.

A Nissan Sentra and Ford station wagon were parked side by side in front of what appeared to be a garage—it was hard to tell, as the wall pattern was carefully designed so as to belie the presence of any discernable door. Balfour pulled in behind the Nissan.

A young girl erupted from the front door of the house. She was wearing a sweater and blue jeans, the sweater rather baggy, the jeans rather tight. Her hair was cut in an irregular pageboy, the bangs straight, the rest of the hair casually haphazard. A young, fresh look, as if she had taken no care whatever with her hair. A look, it occurred to me cynically, that probably took hours to perfect. Her schoolgirl face was bright, her eyes were flashing, and her white teeth gleamed as she opened her mouth in protest. Without hearing a word, I could read her lips perfectly.

"No, no, no, Daddy," she cried, waving her arms.

The message was clear. She was going out, and she didn't want her father blocking her car.

Balfour gave in with good grace, backed up, and parked behind the station wagon.

His daughter got in the Nissan Sentra, backed down the driveway, and pulled out.

I gave her a two-block head start, then fell in behind.

I must say I felt rather smug.

Alice is always ragging me about how unobservant I am, and what a terribly memory I have, and how I couldn't even recognize Madonna, for instance, if she changed her hairstyle.

Well, Balfour's daughter may have had a different hairstyle, but I recognized her all right.

She was Barbie from the bar.

Eleven

I FOLLOWED BARBIE BACK THE WAY WE CAME, DOWN THE HUTCHINSON, across the Cross County, down the Saw Mill River Parkway through the toll that wasn't there, down the Henry Hudson through the toll that was, under the George Washington Bridge and down the West Side Highway.

She got off at Ninety-sixth Street, took Broadway to Eighty-sixth, and went through Central Park. She came out at Eighty-fourth Street. That's the benefit of the Eighty-sixth Street eastbound crosstown—you gain two blocks. At least you do if you're going downtown. If you're going uptown you lose two, but nobody takes it uptown.

Barbie went down Fifth Avenue, across Seventy-ninth, and down Lexington. She slowed as she hit the Fifties and pulled into a parking garage.

Here's a hint for wannabe PIs: If you're tailing someone and they go into a garage, don't. Not unless it's a huge multilevel affair attached to a shopping mall where you park it yourself. But if it's the type of thing where you have to surrender your car to someone, that's bad news. You either wind up standing face-to-face with the person you're tailing while you wait for your car, or alone like a schmuck while the person you're tailing drives off. Neither is a good result.

Anyway, there were parking meters on the street. I took one of them. The fact Barbie hadn't indicated she might be staying awhile.

Barbie hopped out of her car and accepted the claim ticket from the parking attendant. She jammed it in the back pocket of her jeans and headed down the street.

I followed at a discreet distance. After all, the girl had ditched me once.

She walked down Lexington and turned into a door with the sign in front, MIDNIGHT LACE. The sign was simple, understated. No neon lights, no photos, pictures, or even silhouettes. Just a simple, hand-painted sign.

Well, if she could, I could. I gave her a minute or two, then followed her in.

It was an upscale topless bar. Very upscale. The clientele for the most part wore suits and ties, gave the impression they had just stopped in on the way home from work. There were even some women—not hookers or shills, but actual women—sitting at the tables chatting with the men, just as if it were a perfectly natural thing to do. Unless they *were* hookers or shills. In which case they were wonderful actresses, superbly cast.

So were the dancers who paraded on the catwalk between the tables. There were no over-the-hill strippers with too much makeup, who only got by by virtue of the tons of silicone pumped into their chests, and the fact no one ever looked at their faces much anyway. The girls were reasonably young, reasonably attractive. They didn't strip naked and twist their bodies like pretzels into a series of revealing poses. Instead they kept their G-strings on, paraded the catwalk like fashion models. This added to the upscale image, allowed the patrons to pretend they were doing something they were not. Or rather, to pretend they were not doing something that they were, i.e., gaping at female flesh. The entertainment at Midnight Lace was discreet, artistic, high class.

It was also boring as hell. Don't get me wrong. I never met a breast I didn't like. Gazing at them is one of my favorite pastimes. But I have nothing against vaginas either. And if you're going to spend your time gaping at naked women, it seems to me you ought to admit that's what you're doing and go the whole hog.

Please don't write in. I'm aware that was a sexist comment. I'm a guy. I like naked women. I understand in certain circles that makes me socially unacceptable. On the other hand, saying I *didn't* like naked women would be hypocritical. Is there a safe middle ground? I doubt it. So when you start putting together your list of sexist pigs, count me in.

A waitress in a plaid skirt and a black leotard came by my table. She was attractive, but her outfit implied if I tried to touch her there'd be trouble. There was a large gentleman seated at the bar who seemed to be watching the customers more than the girls.

"Can I get you something?" the young lady said. Her tone implied if I said no, the large gentleman might escort me to the door.

I ordered a Diet Coke, was impressed by the speed with which she got it to my table. And by the fact it cost seven fifty. I gave her a ten. She seemed surprised I expected change, reluctantly counted it out. I threw a dollar back on her tray. She looked at me as if I were the last piker on earth and hurried off in quest of fresh game.

I whipped out my cell phone and called Alice. "Hi, I'm in a titty bar."

"What?"

"I'm going to be home late. I'm in a topless bar."

"Talk louder. I can't hear you."

"I can't talk louder. I'm in a titty bar."

"Stanley, have you lost your mind?"

"Oh? You heard me that time?"

"Stanley, what are you talking about?"

"You remember the girl I lost?"

"Yeah."

"Well, I found her. I just called to say I'm gonna be late."

"Stanley—"

"Here she comes. Gotta go."

Barbie came down the runway like a queen, head back, chin high, eyes bright.

Breasts out.

I tell ya, there's nothing like familiarity. Barbie was certainly a beautiful girl, but no more so than some of the others who had preceded her. But having seen her slap MacAullif in the bar, having seen her saunter down Broadway and give me the slip, having seen those breasts bob under that skimpy outfit and wanting like hell to see them. There they were. Same breasts. Instant wish fulfillment. Ultimate gratification.

Balfour's daughter?

Damn.

My adolescent fantasies came to a screeching halt. This was my client's daughter. Those were my client's daughter's nubile young breasts.

Bummer.

It was a relief to know she'd keep her G-string on.

Boy. Talk about approach/avoidance. Or whatever the hell the word is. Ambivalence?

Barbie left the bar at ten-fifteen, after a good three hours of work, during which time I had nursed thirty dollars worth of Diet Coke. It would have been less. Believe me, I was drinking those suckers slow, but every time I had to run out and put quarters in the parking meter, the waitress would clear my glass, then appear like clockwork upon my return to inquire what I was having.

What I was having was a very bad time.

The dancers were all the same. Literally. Some old ones left, some new ones came on—after a while it was all a blur. But Barbie went on a half a dozen times, and I'm sure her playmates did too. The only thing that turned over was the crowd.

Except for me.

Long about the end I noticed the waitress eyeing me with more than her usual disdain. And the bouncer at the bar was eyeing me with downright suspicion. Which was only natural. No one, except an obsessive stalker, sits at places like the Midnight Lace drinking Diet Coke and gawking at the girls for three hours straight. I had a feeling the next time I returned from my car I was going to get stopped and patted down.

It occurred to me long about then that since my car was parked with a clear view of the front door, I could just as well sit in it waiting for Barbie to show. That would thwart the waitress and save on my Diet Coke bill.

I pondered that proposition as I headed back into the bar.

Anyway, Barbie appeared in her street clothes a little after ten. A guy with greasy black hair and a shiny suit and tie, the only man in the place besides me and the bouncer to have been in the bar all night, rung up *no sale* on the cash register and began pulling out bills. Even from where I sat I could see him lift the cash tray and fumble underneath where the hundreds and fifties were kept. Evidently topless dancers made more than PIs. I found that somewhat depressing.

Barbie accepted the money from Greaseball without a hint of thanks. Her body language gave the impression the son of a bitch had hit on her and she had put him in his place, not the most difficult of deductions.

Barbie folded the money, jammed it in her pocket, sailed out the door.

I got up from my table, found my way blocked by the bouncer. Kicked myself in the head for not waiting in my car. The guy had indeed taken me for a stalker and wasn't about to let me follow one of the girls out.

I quickly converted my frown at seeing two hundred and fifty pounds of malevolent roadblock into a slightly anxious inquiring glance. "Where's the men's room?"

His face relaxed. He pointed.

Of course, it couldn't have been near the front door. And now I had to go. In more ways than one.

I picked my way across the floor, went through a beaded curtain where there was a sign, REST ROOM. I pushed open the door, found a single toilet and sink. I availed myself of them, went out, peeked through the beaded curtain, a needless precaution. Since I had asked for the men's room, I would no longer be of interest to the bouncer.

Wrong again.

He was sitting at the bar, watching for me to come out. Right between me and the front door.

While Barbie made her getaway.

I walked over to the bar, jerked a dollar bill out of my pocket, said, "Excuse me, can I get change for the parking meter?"

I could feel the bouncer next to me relax. Greaseball was close enough to hear me too. If I could just get change, I was home free.

I waited impatiently while the bartender drew two drafts. I looked at my watch to give the impression my anxiety was not from the girl escaping, but from my parking meter running out. I accepted the quarters, headed for the door. No one tried to stop me. I went on out to my car.

Next to the meter a street sign proclaimed, ONE HOUR PARKING, 8:00 A.M. TO 10:00 P.M. As I got in my car, it occurred to me that metered parking in this neighborhood stopped at ten o'clock, after which one could park for free.

There was no need to put money in the meter.

Down the street, Barbie stood in front of the garage, waiting for her car.

In my rearview mirror, I could see the bouncer and the sleazy manager come out the door. They didn't look happy.

The bouncer's eyes locked on my car.

I fired the engine, pulled out of the space. Or at least tried to. A Cadillac had boxed me in. I maneuvered forward, back, forward, back. Did I remember to lock my doors? Would it matter? Would his hand come right through the glass? Even if it didn't, what was going to happen when I got out of my spot? Was I going to roar off and leave Barbie to her own devices? Would they connect me to her? Would they stop her and grill her? And what would she say? Had she seen me in the bar? Had she tipped the guy a wink, ratted me out to the Greaseball? Was that why they were on me now? Were they all in collusion? Was she just standing there pretending to get her car to hang me out to dry?

I lurched free of my parking space just as Man Mountain collided with the back of my car. Under other circumstances I might have considered suing for whiplash. After all, I know a good negligence lawyer. As things were, I was merely happy to be alive. I gunned the motor, screeched down the street.

Ahead of me, Barbie pulled out of the parking garage. So she wasn't in collusion with the others. She caught the light at the corner, drove down Lex. I sped up as the yellow changed to red, and gave chase.

Behind me, Greaseball and the Incredible Hulk stood in the street, glaring after me helplessly in impotent rage.

Some days you get lucky.

Twelve

BARBIE DROVE UP THIRD AVENUE, STOPPED AT A FIREPLUG ON EAST Eighty-first. I'd already turned onto the street, so I had no choice but to double-park or drive on by. I pulled to the side, put my flashers on, popped the trunk release. I hopped out of the car, keeping my head averted, raised the trunk, and peered around it to see if Barbie had noticed.

She hadn't. Barbie was out of her car and heading away from me down the sidewalk. She suddenly froze like a deer in the headlights, then shrunk back into the shadows behind the front steps of a brownstone.

Two doors down a woman was coming out of a town house. It was hard to tell at that distance, but she seemed well dressed, attractive, in a matching red skirt and jacket that neither hid nor revealed her figure but appeared quite stylish. Her hair was short, her features delicate.

She turned left at the bottom, heading straight for Barbie, who crept further back into the shadows, and me, who stifled an impulse to climb into the trunk.

The woman breezed on by. Though attractive, she was older than she had looked at a distance, probably in her forties. Her face was drawn, her chin set, her lips determined.

Her eyes hard.

Seeing her expression, I couldn't fault Barbie for wanting to keep out of her way. I continued playing with my tire iron as she sailed on down the street and disappeared around the corner on Third Avenue.

Barbie emerged from her hiding place and hurried down the street to the town house. She went up the front steps and went in.

With her car at a hydrant Barbie didn't figure to be long.

She was long enough. A cop car came down the street and pulled up behind the Nissan. The cop got out, looked at the plate. He jerked a fat ticket notebook out of his pocket, flipped it open, took out a pen.

Barbie came out the front door of the town house, spotted the cop. Her face drained of color. Then she came pelting down the front steps, yelling and waving her hands. As a New Yorker, I understood the motivation. A parking ticket is upward of fifty bucks, and once a cop puts pen to paper you're sunk. There's no way he's voiding it, tearing it up, going through the paperwork and making the explanation that would entail. If the guy's started writing, you're dead meat.

The cop hadn't started writing. And Barbie was one attractive girl. Feminists, take note. You want true equality, accept the parking tickets *I'd* be dorked with if it were *my* car. Don't flirt your way out of them.

Barbie did. She gave him the *Aw shucks, aren't I stupid* routine, the *Hey, big boy, give me a break* routine, and the *Oh, you big handsome man, can't you help out poor little old me* routine. I suppose you can't expect a topless dancer to be a true feminist; even so, it burned me up knowing it was going to work.

It did. The cop folded his ticket notebook, put it away, then stood there grinning like a dope while Barbie hopped into her car, practically blowing him a kiss good-bye. The officer watched her drive off, then turned and looked down the street.

Uh-oh.

I could imagine his mind going. Having failed to tag the car at the plug, how about one double-parked? That wouldn't do. I am frankly rather poor at flirting my way out of parking tickets.

I hopped in my car, fired the motor, switched off the hazard lights, and pulled out. I did my best not to look guilty as I drove past the cop.

I could feel his eyes burning into me, looking for an excuse to pull me over. Alice would say I'm being paranoid. But Alice could flirt her way out of a ticket too.

It's a no-win situation.

The light at the corner was red, so I had no problem catching up with Barbie. I followed her up Madison to Eighty-fifth, went into the park, and came out at Eighty-sixth. That's the benefit of the Eighty-sixth Street crosstown west. If you're going uptown, you gain a block.

Barbie was. She took Amsterdam to Ninety-sixth and got on the West Side Highway.

I figured she was heading home, but I tailed her awhile just to make sure. I told myself that going through the toll booth would clinch it. She did, but then I had to go through the toll booth too. Once I'd done that, I figured I might as well make sure she got on the Cross County Parkway. When she did, there was no way to turn around, so I had to get on too.

I followed her as far as Route 100 in Yonkers, which runs parallel to the turnpike, so there are a zillion cloverleafs. I took the exit for Route 100 north, which spiraled me around and spat me out just in time to catch an exit that spiraled me around and spat me out on the Cross County Parkway west. I was now heading back the way I came, having executed the equivalent of a U-turn as performed by a confused or drunken driver.

Just before I reached the Saw Mill River Parkway, a Jaguar whizzed by in the other direction on the Cross County. I couldn't really tell at that speed, but the driver sure looked like my client. I briefly considered going through another series of cloverleaf turns and giving chase.

Very briefly.

I drove home in a rotten mood. I was only slightly mollified to find a parking space right in front of my apartment building.

Alice was still up. I had to admire her forbearance. On the one hand, she hadn't called me on my cell phone.

On the other hand, she was still up.

"All right," Alice said. "What's this about a topless bar?"

Thirteen

RICHARD ROSENBERG LEANED BACK IN HIS DESK CHAIR. "WHAT'S YOUR problem?"

"Ethically, how am I bound?"

"Ethically, schmethically. I'm not even sure what you're asking. What do you want to do?"

"I don't know."

"Exactly," Richard said. "That's your whole problem. Ethics have nothing to do with it. You just don't know what you want."

"I want to do the right thing."

"Then you're in the wrong business. You wanna do good deeds, join the Boy Scouts. You wanna work as a PI, sometimes it won't be nice."

"That's the problem. Was I really working?"

"What do you mean?"

"Balfour didn't ask me to tail his daughter. And he sure didn't ask me to tail him."

"Ah. You wanna charge him for your time. Now, there's a matter worth consideration."

"I don't wanna charge him for my time."

"Why not?"

"Because he didn't ask me to do this."

"Yes, he did. He hired you to find out who sent the blackmail note. Your efforts in that direction have been invaluable."

"But they're not what he wanted."

"What, you think PI work comes with guarantees? If not satisfied, the investigator will refund your money and tear up your bill?"

"Of course not. But . . ."

"But what?"

"I tailed his daughter."

"Exactly. And that's your whole problem. You don't wanna charge the guy for looking at his daughter's tits."

"I don't even wanna tell him."

"Once again, you're in the wrong game. If you're a doctor, you're gonna have to tell patients they're gonna die. Comes with the territory. As a PI, you will sometimes be the bearer of bad news. This happens to be one of those times."

"Yeah, but there's bad and there's bad. 'I'm sorry, Mr. Balfour, but the blackmailer's your daughter the topless dancer.'"

"I think it's the topless bit that's hanging you up. The blackmail you could handle."

"Well, it's the guy's daughter, for Christ's sakes."

"So? He may not have the same prudish inhibitions as you."

"Suppose it was your daughter."

"I don't have a daughter."

"Suppose you did."

"You want me to assume a hypothetical daughter?"

"Richard—"

"More to the point, you want me to assume a hypothetical daughter's hypothetical tits?"

"I'm sorry I asked."

"You should be. You're a professional. At least, you *should* be a professional if you weren't still crazy after all these years. A client is a client and a case is a case, and you don't get involved. What's the first thing I taught you?"

"Make sure they sign the retainer."

Richard made a face. "Don't be silly. That goes without saying. I don't mean procedure. I mean how you approach your job."

"Richard, I don't know what you're getting at."

"Don't get involved."

"I'm not getting involved, I'm just getting confused."

"No, that's the answer. Don't get involved with your clients."

"I know that."

"I know you know that. You get involved all the same. You do it all the time. You take a perfectly easy job that would be a piece of cake, and you torture it and twist it into knots, because you want things to come out nice for your client. Well, guess what? That's not always possible. Because clients aren't always nice. This particular one you're so concerned about, this Balfour, if I recall correctly, happens to have a manslaughter conviction."

"Not according to MacAullif."

"Oh, I'm sorry. Has *lied* about having a manslaughter conviction. Which makes him much more trustworthy. I would certainly advise taking a personal interest in his well-being. To the point of agonizing over whether or not to give him the information you've collected."

I heaved myself out of my chair.

"Going so soon?"

"I don't intend to stay here and be abused."

"Oh? Just where do you intend to go to be abused?"

"Great, Richard. That's one of those unanswerable questions, like 'Have you stopped beating your wife?'"

"I'm not married."

"Your hypothetical wife."

"Ah, yes. The mother of my hypothetical daughter. The one with the nice tits."

"Very funny. I'd love to stay and banter, but I happen to have a client."

Richard called after me, "Don't forget the first rule."

I stopped in the doorway. "Don't worry, Richard. I won't get involved."

"No, no." Richard waved it away. "Make sure he signs the retainer."

Fourteen

THE RECEPTIONIST AT ALLIED ASSOCIATES WASN'T EXACTLY welcoming. "You don't have an appointment?"

"No, I don't."

"Then it's unlikely Mr. Balfour will be able to see you. He sees people only by appointment."

"Then let's make one," I said. "It's nine-forty-five. Let's make an appointment for nine-forty-six. By the time we're done making it, it will probably be time for you to call him."

The receptionist was not amused. "You don't understand."

"Oh? It seems perfectly simple to me. Where did I go wrong?"

"I don't make Mr. Balfour's appointments."

"Who does?"

"Mr. Balfour."

"All right, let me talk to him."

"You can't talk to him."

"Why not?"

"You don't have an appointment."

"What is this, a *Saturday Night Live* sketch? Is there a hidden camera?"

"No, sir. Company policy. Employees inform me of their meetings, and I don't let anyone else in."

"And you're doing a fine job of it. When I see your superiors, I will be sure to commend you. In the meantime, could you get Mr. Balfour on the phone?"

"I'm not supposed to ring through."

"You did when I called yesterday."

"That was a phone call. That's entirely different."

"I see." I whipped my cell phone out of my pocket, punched in the number on the switchboard phone. It rang. She picked it up.

"Allied Associates."

"Mr. Balfour, please."

"Who's calling, please?"

"Stanley Hastings."

"One moment, please. Mr. Balfour, I have Mr. Hastings on the line."

His voice came on a moment later. "What's up?"

"We need to talk."

"Okay, talk."

"Not on the phone."

"So get over here."

"I *am* over here."

"Huh?"

"I'm at the switchboard. They won't let me in without an appointment."

"So make an appointment."

"I can't make appointments. You have to."

"Okay, let me talk to her."

I handed her the cell phone. "It's for you."

Minutes later, Joe Balfour was ushering me into his inner office. "This better be good," he said. "I'm pressed for time."

"Fine. Then I'll be brief. The blackmailer is your daughter. She's the one who showed up in the bar looking like millions and slapped the cop with the flower."

Balfour's mouth fell open. "That can't be."

"Why not?"

"It just can't."

"Well, maybe I'm wrong. When you went home last night after work, who was the girl who climbed into the Nissan and drove off?"

"You followed me?"

"Was that your daughter? 'Cause I would hate to go on a misassumption here. If you have a teenage mistress who hangs out at home, now would be the time to speak up."

"I don't believe this."

"I find it hard to believe myself. But facts are facts. The girl in your house is the girl in the bar. Now, would that be your daughter?"

"You followed me home?"

I shook my head. "You're getting repetitive. From that I conclude you're stalling for time. Don't bother. I'm a very minor person in your life. What I think of you doesn't mean much in the general scheme of things. Failing in my eyes is not the worst thing that could happen. Why don't you just bite the bullet and come clean?"

Balfour, after sputtering a few moments, picked up steam. "Who the hell are you to talk to me like that? I hired you. You fucked up. Muffed the job. Then you start poking around in my personal life. I would think I have a cause of action here."

I nodded. "I would think so too. It will be interesting airing these stories in court."

Balfour blanched. "What the hell do you want?"

"I might ask you the same thing. I just told you your daughter's the blackmailer. But you don't want to hear about that. You just want to gripe about how I got the information. From which I would assume you already knew."

"And now you're trying to trick me into talking. My god, you're the lowest of the low."

The door banged open and a cop walked in. He was big and beefy like MacAullif, with a little more of a potbelly and a little less of a chin. He was in plain clothes, so he didn't have to be a cop, but I knew him.

In all my dealings with the New York Police Department, I've found the officers to be capable, intelligent men. Oh sure, there's an occasional rotten apple, but even the bad cops are good at what they do. In particular, any cop who had risen to the rank of sergeant was not likely to have done so unless he was proficient in his job.

With one exception.

"Well, Sergeant Thurman," I said. "What brings you here?"

Sergeant Thurman stopped, took in the scene, registered my presence. I'm not sure he appreciated the significance beyond the fact he didn't like it. "What the hell are you doing here?" he demanded.

"Just conferring with my client," I said. "Mr. Balfour, allow me to present Sergeant Thurman of the NYPD. Are you still with Homicide, Sergeant?"

Thurman's face darkened. "Okay, get the hell out of here."

"I'm afraid our business isn't over, Sergeant. But don't let us hold you up. What did you want?"

"You heard me. Get out."

"Well, no, I don't have to do that," I said. "Unless you're placing Mr. Balfour under arrest. You're not doing that, are you Sergeant?"

Thurman turned to Balfour. "Where were you last night between the hours of eight o'clock and midnight?"

"That's rather broad," I said.

"Shut up, Hastings. Where were you?"

Balfour hesitated.

"Find out why he's asking before you answer the question," I suggested.

Thurman glared at me as if he might punch me out. He'd actually done that, once. I wasn't angling for it again.

Balfour, who'd seemed awed by the presence of a policeman in his office, rallied enough to take the hint. "Why do you wanna know?" he asked. "What's going on?"

"We're investigating an accident that took place last night. There's a possibility you might be a witness. If you tell us where you were, maybe we can cross you off the list."

"Since when did Homicide investigate traffic accidents?" I asked.

"I didn't say it was a traffic accident."

"What kind of an accident was it, Sergeant?"

"I'm not talking to you." Thurman kept his eyes on Balfour. "So, can you tell me where you were?"

"I didn't see any accident. I'm afraid I can't be of help."

"I'll be the judge of that. Where were you last night?"

"See, he's not going to take your word for it," I said. "You're better off saying nothing."

Thurman wheeled on me. "If I have to drag him downtown to get you to shut up, I will. Believe me, you're not doing the guy any favors."

"I can't go downtown now," Balfour said. "I have a client coming in."

"Don't be a sap," I told him. "Missing an appointment's the least of your worries. Focus in on the situation. Thurman's a Homicide sergeant. If he's here, someone's dead. So who is it, Sergeant?"

"It's gonna be you in a minute. Mr. Balfour, you claim you didn't see an accident last night on the corner of Third Avenue and Eighty-first Street?"

"Absolutely not."

"You were nowhere near that street corner from eight o'clock till midnight?"

"No, I wasn't."

Thurman fished a piece of paper out of his pocket. "Then perhaps you could explain how it happens your car was tagged for double-parking on East Eighty-first Street at ten-forty-five. That is your plate number, is it not? You do own a silver Jaguar?"

Balfour looked to me for help.

"Go ahead and tell him," I said.

Balfour blinked. "What?"

I shrugged. "He has reason to suspect you of a crime, and he hasn't advised you of your rights. Nothing you say can be used in evidence against you. Go ahead and tell him the whole thing."

Thurman grabbed my shirtfront and threw me up against the wall. The partition was not substantial. I had visions of flying through it, leaving a hole like a cartoon character. It merely rattled my teeth. What few I have left.

Thurman released me, whipped out a tattered card, and began reading. "'You're under arrest. You have the right to remain silent. . . .'" He droned through the rest of it, shoved the card back in his pocket. "There. You happy now?" He jerked his thumb at Balfour. "All right, asshole. Let's go."

"You're arresting me?" Balfour said incredulously.

"I sure am, and you can thank your friend here. We could have cleared this up with a few simple questions, but, no, he's gotta be a wise guy. So now we're going downtown and we can do this nice and legal. Just the way your buddy wants."

Thurman took Balfour by the shoulders, spun him around. A moment later came the click of handcuffs.

"Okay, you're comin' with me." Thurman stuck his finger in my face. "And *you're* not."

"But, but—" Balfour sputtered.

"Don't say a word," I advised. "Just demand to see a lawyer. Aside from that, don't give 'em the time of day."

Before Balfour could reply, Thurman jerked him out of the office.

Fifteen

RICHARD ROSENBERG WAS MADDER THAN A WET HEN. HE CAME
stomping out into the hallway of the Criminal Court Building, glared at
me as if it were all my fault. "Come on. Let's go."

"They wouldn't let you see him?" I said incredulously. I found it
hard to imagine that happenstance.

"Let's not talk in the corridor," Richard said tersely.

I realized the well-dressed young men and women who looked like
college students to me were probably assistant district attorneys. Yet
another reminder that I am slightly older than Haley Joel Osment.

I held my tongue until we got outside. But not without some difficulty.
There is nothing in the world Richard Rosenberg loves more than bopping
cops around. The thought of him giving up so quickly simply didn't compute. I expected him to be inside, biting some ADA. in the leg, whipping
another to a standstill through skillful cross-examination. Securing, at the
very least, a written apology from the police, and their assurance they would
never do it again. But, no, here he was, slinking away in abject defeat. I made
a mental note to circle this day on my calendar, for future reference. "*No,
Richard, you can't always push everyone around. Remember the Balfour case?*"

It was torture riding down in the elevator, but I managed to hold
it together until we got out the front door. "Richard," I said. "What
happened?"

He stuck a hand in my face, marched over to one of the hot dog vendors who lined the street. He bought a Coke, gulped it down, slammed the empty can back on the hot dog stand.

He turned on me. "Stanley, what made you think that man wanted a lawyer?"

My eyes widened in surprise. "You mean he didn't?"

"What made you think so?"

"He was being arrested, for Christ's sake."

"Yes, he was."

"I told him not to say a word, and to demand a lawyer."

"That's what he did."

"I beg your pardon."

"He called a lawyer. Gordon Millsap. From the firm of Millsap & Millsap. I believe he's the elder Millsap, though I'm not that well versed in Millsaps. Anyway, he's representing Mr. Balfour, and he did not take kindly to the idea I might be trying to steal his client. So it was rather embarrassing having to assure him I was not."

"Richard—"

"That's why I'm curious, you see, as to what made you think he wanted a lawyer in the first place."

"Richard—"

"I assume this was entirely your idea. If I might offer a suggestion. The next time you take it in your head to have someone hire me, I suggest you clear it with them first."

"Are you enjoying this, Richard?"

"Of course I am. I cancelled two appointments, lost a morning's work. Thank goodness I didn't have to be in court. It would be embarrassing explaining to the client and the judge just what emergency had required the continuance."

"So, what's the charge? Did they tell you?"

"No one told me a damn thing. Since it's none of my business. I assume it's murder, with Homicide involved."

"He might just be a material witness."

"Could be. Either way, it's an odds-on bet the corpse lived on East Eighty-first Street. But it's not my affair. If you're lucky, it won't be yours."

"What do you mean?"

"I can't imagine the guy hiring you, but you could wind up a witness. I would take pains to see that doesn't happen."

"What a nightmare."

"No shit, Sherlock. Thanks for letting me in on it."

"It's a murder case. I thought you'd be pleased."

"You thought wrong. Now, if you'll excuse me, I've gotta get back to work."

"Don't you want to know what happened?"

"Sure, but no one's gonna tell me, and I got no authority to ask." Richard cocked his head. "Don't *you* have work to do?"

"I have some appointments later on."

"I thought you had a sign-up at ten o'clock."

"I called, said I'd be late."

"Oh, you don't have one for noon?"

"I'll push it back."

"Sounds like a full day. Guess you better get going."

I sighed. "Yeah, I guess I'd better."

Sixteen

MACAULLIF WASN'T GLAD TO SEE ME. "WELL, AREN'T YOU THE KISS of death?"

"I beg your pardon."

MacAullif pointed to a paper on his desk. "Among the arrests this morning was one Joseph Balfour. Name ring a bell?"

"That's what I came to talk about."

He shook his head. "I should have known. I'm sayin' to myself, 'Joe Balfour,' 'Joseph Balfour,' it doesn't *have* to be the same guy. Could be just coincidence. I don't believe in coincidence, but that doesn't mean it couldn't happen."

MacAullif picked up the paper. "Attorney of record, Gordon Millsap, no clue there. So I'm minding my own business, looking for a break."

"Tell me about it."

MacAullif took out a cigar, began drumming on his desk. He was, for MacAullif, in a fairly good mood. "So I'm banking the odds this is our boy, and here you are with a confirmation. Not that I happen to give a rat's ass, just as long as it doesn't involve me."

"It doesn't involve you."

"How do you know?"

"You know anyone on East Eighty-first Street?"

"You mean like Philip T. Grackle?"

"Who?"

"The dead guy. Mr. Grackle. Which I gather is a type of bird. I'm not big on birds."

"What's Mr. Grackle's story?"

"He's dead."

"Before he died. Did he have any raison d'etre?"

"I'm not supposed to know what that means because I'm a dumb cop?"

"Pray enlighten me."

"I have no idea how the young man got raisons in his d'etre. 'Cause by the time I learned of his d'etre, he had ceased to d'etre."

"That's less than helpful."

"And more than required. Here's what I got. Grackle, age thirty-nine, killed last night in his apartment on East Eighty-first Street between the hours of eight and midnight. The murder weapon's a carving knife, stabbed directly into the heart. The knife matches a set in the kitchen, probably his, no prints on the knife." MacAullif looked up from the report.

"And that's it?"

"That's it."

"So what ties Joe Balfour to the crime?"

"A double-parking ticket issued outside the building at ten-forty-five."

"They arrested him on that?"

"It does seem an overreaction," MacAullif said. "But when the cops came around on a strictly routine follow-up of the parking ticket, they ran into a PI with an attitude, who practically hung a neon sign around the guy's neck, blinking *guilty*."

"Oh, for Christ's sake."

"So I'd like to commend you on your good work. I'm sure you were only copying what you read in some book. And I'm sure it worked real good for the PI there. Only problem is, in real life you run into cops who haven't read the book. So, instead of confounding them with your expertise, you merely get their backs up. In case you were thinking of dropping in on Balfour's lawyer, I would imagine the gentleman is not too kindly disposed toward you."

"Oh, hell."

"Hey, you fucked up. So what else is new? My advice to you is go home, lie down, pull the covers up over your head, and pretend none of this happened."

"Sounds like a plan."

I went out the door.

MacAullif called after me, "If anyone asks, you never heard of me."

Seventeen

IT WAS GREAT HAVING THURMAN, AND RICHARD, AND MACAULLIF ALL tell me to go to hell. I mean, one opinion you could dismiss. But when they all started lining up against me, and you added in the fact Balfour wasn't my Number One Fan, and his lawyer probably wasn't Number Two, it really told the tale. I spent the afternoon signing up clients for Richard Rosenberg, secure in the knowledge that as far as the Joseph Balfour case was concerned, it was none of my business.

"What, are you nuts?" Alice said. "Don't you want to know what happened?"

"It's not my place," I told her.

"Not your place? Weren't you employed by this guy?"

"Not anymore," I pointed out.

Alice steamrolled over it. "You were employed to find out who was blackmailing him. Well, here's a dead man, presumably the blackmailer. Wouldn't that warrant investigation?"

"If I were still working."

"When did you stop?

"Huh?"

"After you lost the girl, after you found the girl, after you tailed the girl to the murder site? A rather relevant detail, I would think."

"I suppose."

"You suppose. What did MacAullif say?"

"Oh."

Alice's eyes widened. "You didn't mention that to MacAullif?"

"It seemed like a touchy subject."

"So MacAullif doesn't know you were at the scene of the crime last night?"

"I wasn't at the scene of the crime."

"That's rather technical. You mean you didn't go in?"

"Of course I didn't go in. Don't you think I would have mentioned it if I'd found a dead body?"

"Well, you're not being very communicative. After all, you didn't tell MacAullif."

"I'm not married to MacAullif."

"You mean you'd tell me if you found a corpse? Stanley, I'm flattered. I don't know what to say."

"Alice, I've had a rather hard time of it. Everyone I know is beating up on me. You don't need to join the club."

Alice raised her eyebrows. "I wasn't aware I was beating up on you."

"Let's not get into it," I said irritably. "The point is, no, I didn't mention it to MacAullif. Because I don't want him to have a coronary. The guy's a walking pharmacy. Another drug would probably kill him."

"You're very considerate."

"Is that sarcasm?"

"Is your concern for MacAullif's health genuine?"

"Alice—"

"Or are you just afraid of what he'll do to you when he finds out?"

"Thank you for putting my darkest fears into words. Now I can confront my demons."

"Stanley, stop sparring. How bad is it?"

"That's the problem, Alice. I have no idea. Because I have no information. I know a guy named Grackle's dead, and that's it. He was stabbed with a kitchen knife sometime last night between eight and midnight. I have reason to believe the topless daughter called on the guy long about ten-thirty."

"Topless daughter?"

"Well, I don't know her name."

"Even so, that's rather curious shorthand."

"Yeah. I don't know what made me think of it."

"Stanley—"

"How's your stomach?"

"I feel terrible."

"You're looking awful good."

"Don't go there."

"I hate that expression."

"Damn it, Stanley. I'm concerned. How mixed up are you in this murder?"

"I have no idea."

Alice considered. "You should probably tell the police what you know."

"I can't do that. It would be violating a confidence."

"Whose confidence?"

"Balfour's."

"You didn't see Balfour. You saw his daughter. You're not working for her."

"That's no reason to throw her to the wolves."

"There's no reason to lose your license over her either."

"I'm not going to lose my license."

"I'm glad to hear it."

"Come on, Alice. Why would I lose my license?"

"You're withholding material evidence in a murder case. What do you think they're gonna do, give you a medal?"

"Alice, I don't know that I have any evidence at all."

Alice made a face. "Give me a break. You saw his daughter go into the building. That plays out one of two ways. One, she killed him, which gets Daddy off the hook. I think that would be a material point, exonerating one suspect and convicting another. Yeah, that would probably be worth mentioning."

Alice raised a finger, in full lecture mode. "Or, the guy was putting the bite on the topless daughter, giving Daddy the motivation to do him in."

"Topless daughter?"

"Don't change the subject. The point is, you have material evidence relating to this crime. When the police *find out* you have material evidence relating to this crime, and you *neglected to mention* you had material evidence relating to this crime, they are going to be less than pleased."

"Will they be less pleased than you?"

"I'm not joking, Stanley. I think you're in trouble here."

"So what do you want me to do? Go to the police and spill my guts?"

"Boy, talk about loading the question."

"Okay, you phrase it then."

"Stanley, the cop is Sergeant Thurman. That's not good. He found you in Balfour's office. You told Balfour not to talk."

"Under the mistaken impression I was working for him. Which I'm not."

"It doesn't matter. As far as Thurman's concerned, you're meddling in his case."

"I'm *not* meddling in his case."

"Yeah, but Thurman doesn't know that. You have to *show* him you're not meddling in his case."

"How do I do that?"

"By meddling in his case."

Eighteen

SO THERE I WAS, ONCE AGAIN, HEADING FOR MIDNIGHT LACE. WHY, you might ask? Well, that's a very good question. Barbie seemed unlikely to be working today, what with her father being arrested for murder and all. And what with her having presumably called on the man who wound up dead. Those seemed fairly good grounds for her not to be there. But I was going anyway, driven by one compelling reason I'm sure most husbands can relate to. When your wife sends you to a topless bar, you go.

There was one small problem. After my exit from the bar the night before, I was likely to be persona non grata. At the very least, the owner might want to have a little chat. Which was apt to prove embarrassing if not downright hazardous to my health.

So what could I do? A wig? False mustache? A *Mission Impossible* rubber face mask? I had a feeling outside of the movies a person would look like a fugitive from Halloween.

I still hadn't figured it out when I got to Midnight Lace. There was a parking spot right in front. I pulled in and surveyed my options. They seemed pretty much the same as they had when I'd been driving over.

I got out of the car, fed quarters into the parking meter.

She came out the front door just as I dropped in the last one.

I might have been surprised if it weren't for the quarters. It was the same theory by which you can get an important phone call just by hopping into the shower. Paying for the parking space invited the god of Dork to fly down and make sure I didn't need it.

I hopped in my car, started the engine. Prayed Greaseball and the Hulk wouldn't come out the front door and see me. I swerved out of the spot, backed up past the entrance to the parking garage. Pulled over to the curb to wait.

I wasn't sure what I was going to do next. All I knew was, I wasn't going to do it there. I had no particular location picked out. Just as far away from Midnight Lace as possible.

I was roused from my musing by a tap on the window. It was lovely Rita, meter maid, directing me to move on. Only in New York City.

I considered flashing my PI license, telling her I was on a case. That only would have made her laugh. Anything short of a police shield wasn't gonna cut it.

I smiled and pulled out.

I circled the block. Rita now was nowhere in sight. This time as I neared the garage I saw Barbie getting into her car. I passed by the garage, drove to the corner. I pulled in next to the fire hydrant there and settled down to wait.

Barbie wasn't long. She breezed by two light changes later without giving me a glance.

I pulled out and tagged along, giving her about a half a block head start, while making sure I made the light. She turned left, went over to Third Avenue, and headed uptown.

I was having a bad sense of déjà vu, and if she'd stopped at Eighty-first Street I was apt to freak out. However, she went right by, hung a left on Eighty-fifth, and went into the park.

Okay, I'd done that too, and I wasn't about to follow her home. By the time she came out of the park on Eighty-sixth, I was right on her tail. I pulled up next to her, hit the horn, and flashed my ID. I know it wasn't great, but I don't *have* a red light. Only one of my many failings.

Luckily, it worked. She pulled up in the bus stop. Evidently she was young and naive enough not to question why a guy in a Toyota might be pulling her over.

I parked alongside and wedged her in before she had time to change her mind. I walked up, banged on her window.

"All right. Get out of the car."

She opened the door and squeezed out. She was wearing a sweater and blue jeans, looked like a college kid. A frightened college kid.

I hadn't the slightest idea what I was going to say to her. That had been the small flaw in Alice's plan. But when I'd mentioned it to Alice, she had gotten on my case about how I was a moron who couldn't order a sandwich without rehearsing what I was going to say to the waitress. Which was hardly fair. I could have ordered a sandwich, no problem. I just wasn't sure what to say to Barbie.

So I was winging it. "Sweetheart, you're in a lot of trouble."

She grimaced. "Don't I know it."

"I don't think you do. You were followed last night."

Her mouth fell open. "How do you know that?"

"How do you think?"

"You followed me? Why? That makes no sense."

"I didn't say I followed you."

"Well, who then?"

I just smiled.

She scowled. "Come on. This isn't a game. I did everything you asked. Don't play with me."

I tried not to look surprised. "I'm not playing with you. I want to know what you're going to do now."

"What do you mean, now?"

It was like walking through a minefield. I had no idea who she thought I was, or why she was talking to me. "Now that Grackle's dead."

"I didn't do it."

"I never said you did."

She frowned. "That's funny." She pursed her lips. "Who's Headly?"

"What?"

"Who's Headly?"

"What are you talking about?"

She hauled off and slapped me full across the face, just like she slapped MacAullif.

She was good at it. It was loud and it stung.

It attracted the attention of a young couple strolling down the street. When I tried to follow Barbie, the guy stepped out and grabbed me by the arm. He was a jock type, with muscles and crew cut and attitude. "Young lady doesn't like you, Mister."

Great. All I needed was some macho stud trying to impress his girl. Never mind the fact the guy was younger, faster, stronger. Everyone seems younger, faster, stronger these days. The fact is, even if I'd been inclined to fight the gentleman, which believe me I was not, there wasn't a prayer of me escaping his clutches before Barbie got away.

"You know why she slapped me?" I said.

That caught him up short. "Huh?"

I whipped out my ID. "She's a material witness in a case I'm investigating. She needed a distraction to get away."

Studly might have had trouble processing all that, but his date tuned right in. Her mouth was open and her eyes were wide. You'd have thought I'd just admitted to being secretly James Bond.

"Help him, Jack," she said. "Come on. She's getting away!"

Actually, she'd *gotten* away. By the time I gave chase, Barbie was long gone. Of course, I knew where she was going. I could have just followed her home.

All right, I hate to be ignoble. But I am not a romantic hero. Not a knight in shining armor. Just a poor schmuck trying to make ends meet. Just your basic common man trying to get by. And if you live in the real world, at some point you gotta stop and say to yourself, "Hey, I'm not getting paid for this."

Particularly when you get slapped in the face.

I got in my car and drove home.

Nineteen

IT ONLY MADE PAGE 12 OF THE *POST*. AND A SMALL ARTICLE AT THAT. A Mr. Philip T. Grackle, of East Eighty-first Street, described as a businessman, had been murdered in his apartment. A Joseph Balfour, of White Plains, also described as a businessman, had been arrested for the crime. There were no details other than it was a stabbing. No picture accompanied the article. In a city where murders happen almost daily, it was no big deal.

Except, of course, to Mr. Balfour.

But he had dispensed with my services.

I finished my coffee and corn muffin, got in my car, and drove up to Harlem to see why Phyllis Miller, of West 149th St. had requested the services of Rosenberg and Stone.

It was—surprise, surprise—because she had broken her leg. There was no way to be coy about it. The cast gave it away. The woman had obviously fallen. The only question was where?

That was difficult, because there were so many excellent choices. She could have tripped on the concrete rubble that passed for sidewalk in front of her tenement building. She could have trusted the broken handrail and fallen on the rotting stoop. Or she could have stumbled over one of the passed out winos or drug addicts who littered the front hall.

In point of fact, none of these had happened. The young woman had aimed a foot at the groin of her philandering boyfriend and lost her balance. Just who that made the defendant wasn't quite clear, but that was Richard's problem, not mine. I signed the errant place kicker to a fresh new retainer, and headed off to Brooklyn to sign up Kenneth Rex.

No suspense there. The assignment listed him as having fallen in a supermarket. The only question was which one?

I was not to find out. My beeper went off as I sailed over the Brooklyn Bridge, and when I checked in with the office, Wendy/Janet told me to call MacAullif.

"Get in here," MacAullif growled, and hung up the phone.

He didn't sound pleased.

I called Wendy/Janet back, told her I was wanted by the police. She didn't ask questions. That was sort of depressing. I've been at Rosenberg and Stone long enough for being wanted by the police to have become a matter of course.

I drove to One Police Plaza, hurried to MacAullif's office.

"Close the door," he said.

He was alone and he was calm.

Remarkably calm.

With his high blood pressure he was supposed to be calm. But even so, MacAullif this calm couldn't be good.

I flopped into a chair, said casually, "What's up?"

I could practically hear his teeth grinding to a halt. See the lines on his forehead attempting to relax. See his lips give a try at a smile.

I wondered how bad it was.

"The Grackle case," MacAullif said. "The police made an arrest in the Grackle case."

"Yesterday's news, MacAullif. I was in here yesterday. We went over that."

"Yes, we did, didn't we?" MacAullif's left eye looked like it was about to twitch, like Peter Sellers's boss in the Pink Panther movies.

"So what's up? Did Balfour make a statement?"

"No."

"You wanna tell me, or should we play guessing games?"

"The police made another arrest."

"Oh?"

"Also by the name of Balfour. Jenny Balfour. Daughter of Joseph Balfour. How's that for a kick in the head? Not twenty-four hours after arresting Daddy, they turn around and arrest his daughter for the crime."

"Daughter?" I said innocently.

"Yes. The man has a daughter. College-age kid. On the hook for the murder."

"I don't understand. What evidence did they arrest her on?"

"She was involved with the decedent. Exactly how, I don't know."

"Then how do you know she was?"

"Well, here's the funny thing." MacAullif didn't sound as if he thought it was funny. "The cop who tagged her father with the parking ticket. Name of Sammy Dawson. He's a good cop, leaves nothing to chance."

"I'm glad to hear it."

"I thought you would be. Anyway, he's got a habit. Anytime he stops a car, before he gets out to talk to the driver, he scribbles the license number on a pad of paper. Just in case the driver bolts."

"Good habit."

"I thought you'd approve. On the night in question, just before he tags Mr. Balfour, he rousts a car at a hydrant in approximately the same spot. Only, the driver returns before he writes the ticket, and talks him out of it."

"Am I supposed to guess who the driver is?"

"The car's registered to one Jenny Balfour. Daughter of the afore-mentioned Joseph Balfour. Officer Dawson, his memory refreshed by his notepad, recalls the young lady who drove off in that car. Recalls her quite well. Picked her out of a lineup, no less."

"I'm not sure I follow the police theory here. Are they arbitrarily charging anyone illegally parked near the place?"

"Seems that way, doesn't it? Anyway, news of this new arrest is no skin off my nose, what with Balfour having given you the pink slip. Only, I have a little chat with Dawson, just in case. Guess what he recalls? Another car double-parked in the street right about the same time. A silver Toyota Camry."

"It's in his report?"

"No, it's not. Because he didn't roust it like he did the girl. Just saw it double-parked there. But the driver was in it. Before he made a move on it, it drove off."

"Sounds like nothing."

"Sure does. He didn't even write it down."

"Amazing he'd even remember."

"He didn't till I questioned him. And, like I say, he's a good cop. He didn't write down the license number, but when prompted, he remembered seeing it. He didn't get the whole thing, but the first three letters stuck in his mind. *UNC* ."

"Is that right?"

"So I ran it through the computer, and guess what I came up with? For Toyotas with license plate *UNC* ?"

"MacAullif . . ."

"I find one registered to a Mr. Stanley Hastings. Now, this could be coincidence, but I don't believe in coincidence. I ask myself, could that double-parked car possibly be Stanley Hastings? Of course not. He was fired from the job. Surely even *he* is not stupid enough to continue to work on a job from which he's been fired."

I said nothing.

MacAullif's eyes bored into mine. "Did you follow Joseph Balfour last night?"

"The night before last, MacAullif."

"Whenever the hell it was. Did you follow him?"

"Yes, I did."

MacAullif exhaled with the force of an atom bomb. He controlled himself with an enormous effort, said, "Why in the world would you do that?"

"I wasn't happy with the situation."

MacAullif snorted. "I'm not happy with *most* of my cases. I still only work when required."

I said nothing, prayed MacAullif wouldn't ask any more questions.

He did. "Did you see Balfour go into that apartment?"

"It's a town house, MacAullif. You can't tell what apartment someone goes to."

"Did you see Balfour enter the town house?"

"You're talking about Joseph Balfour, my client?"

"Your former client. Anyway, you have no professional privilege. They can call you as a witness."

"To testify against Joseph Balfour? I thought they'd arrested his daughter for the crime."

MacAullif frowned.

"Even if I *had* seen Joseph Balfour enter that town house, MacAullif—and I'm not admitting I did—but if I *had* seen him, wouldn't that be totally irrelevant to the case? Particularly in light of the police theory he entered it well after the alleged perpetrator?"

"Not if he and that perpetrator were acting in collusion."

"Is that the police theory of the case?"

"I don't know the police theory of the case."

"Then there's no reason to suspect collusion."

"Damn it," MacAullif said. "I am trying to be calm. Let me spell it out for you. It is bad news for a policeman to be involved in a murder. One he is not investigating, I mean. Somewhat against my better judgment, I allowed you to rope me into your little sting. Immediately your client goes and gets arrested for murder. That's not good, because it puts me in the very uncomfortable position of possibly being a witness.

"Miracle of miracles, the police decide he didn't do it. Instead, they arrest his daughter for the crime. I am saved. I am off the hook. If his daughter killed the guy, it is too damn bad, but at least it doesn't concern me."

MacAullif took a breath. His eyes gleamed. He exhaled slowly. I could practically see steam coming out his ears. "Except for one thing. The outside event. A totally illogical, irrational happening, such as a sane man should not have to guard against. You, for reasons best known to yourself, decide to follow Mr. Balfour. The double-parked car is inconclusive. However, he's right back in the soup if someone saw him go in. If you saw him go in, you're a witness. As a witness, you might be asked how you happen to know Mr. Balfour. I would hate it a great deal if that explanation happened to involve me."

"Why would it?"

"It could, because the defense attorney's gonna ask any damn question he can think of."

"Or she?"

"Huh?"

"Some attorneys are women."

"Save the PC shit for someone who gives a damn. Right now I would like to know if that male or female attorney happened to get you on the stand, would you be testifying to seeing Mr. Balfour go into that town house on the night of the murder, yes or no?"

I took a breath. "No, I would not."

MacAullif stopped in midmoderate, low key, low blood pressure, underplayed, scathingly sarcastic remark. "You would not?"

"That's right."

"You mean you would *say* you didn't see him go in, or you *didn't* see him go in?"

"Both."

MacAullif blinked. Digested that information. For the first time since I'd entered his office his calm appeared genuine. "Well," MacAullif said. "That's the best news I've had all day."

"Glad to help. Now, if you don't mind, I have an appointment in Brooklyn."

"Go, go," MacAullif said. "God forbid you should be delayed in helping someone sue the city of New York."

MacAullif was in a good mood by the time I left his office.

I wasn't.

I had been perfectly candid in answering MacAullif's questions. I hadn't misrepresented a thing.

I'd just left a few small facts out.

Like Balfour's daughter being Barbie, and tailing her instead of him.

Twenty

RICHARD ROSENBERG WASN'T PLEASED. "YOU BLEW OFF MY CLIENT TO bring me this?"

"I rescheduled the sign-up."

"Suppose the guy goes somewhere else. You know how many negligence lawyers there are in New York City?"

"I thought the case would interest you."

Richard rolled his eyes. "Oh, it utterly fascinates me. I suppose I should count myself lucky you didn't trick me into posing as her lawyer."

"She has a lawyer. What's-his-face. The one representing her dad."

"Isn't that a conflict of interest?"

"You would think so. He evidently doesn't."

"Of course not. One of those shysters who will take a retainer from anyone."

I couldn't recall Richard ever turning down a retainer, but it seemed a bad time to bring it up. "Come on, Richard. I'm in a stew here. How do I get out?"

"You ever think of minding your own business? If you hadn't tagged along after this girl, you wouldn't know who she was or where she went."

"Right. But I did, so I do, so whadda I do now?"

Richard shrugged. "No one seems to want you to do anything."

"Yes. Because no one has all the facts. As soon as they do, I'm toast."

"That's when you would like me to step in as your lawyer and keep you out of jail?"

"Among other things."

"Uh-huh. Well, as far as not being candid with MacAullif, I don't really have anything to offer. Why don't you just tell him the truth?"

"I thought he knew the truth. By the time I realized he didn't, it was a little late to volunteer any information on the subject."

"You chickened out?"

"Guilty as charged."

Richard shook his head. "This makes little sense. You got a girl with a habit of slapping guys in the face accused of stabbing one with a knife. Is she in custody, by the way?"

"I think her mouthpiece got her out."

"I'll pretend I didn't hear that pejorative term. So, she's out of the pokey. It'll be interesting to see if she shows up at the topless bar."

"You thinking of dropping in after work?"

"Stanley, I'm a bachelor. If I wanna go to a strip joint, I don't need an excuse. But *you* might drop by."

"You're advising me to talk to the girl?"

"Certainly not. That would be infringing on another attorney's turf. I would never advise you to do such a thing."

"Oh."

"Should you choose to do so *without* my advice, let me know what she says."

"It's a deal. Now then, with regard to my status as a witness. . . ."

"What about it?"

"What is my responsibility to come forward?"

"As a conscientious citizen, it's your duty to come forward."

"If I'm not a conscientious citizen, am I liable for criminal prosecution?"

"For what? For failing to confirm what the police already know. The traffic officer who got flirted out of a citation puts her on the spot."

"Yeah, but not in the apartment."

"*You* don't put her in the apartment."

"I put her in the town house."

"Big deal. The cops put her in the apartment. How, I don't know, but they do. Which means you're not as important as you think you are."

"So I'm in the clear?"

"Not at all. If the cops can prove you tailed the girl there and didn't report it, they'll come down on you like a ton of bricks."

"So I should report it?"

"Not unless you have a death wish. You've *already* withheld the information. All that's at stake now is how *long* you withhold it. I doubt if that matters much. At least not in terms of your guilt."

"Richard, you're not cheering me up."

"Did you expect me to? You leave a client in the lurch to come in here and whine about what a spot you're in. You're gonna fault me for agreeing with you?"

"I guess not. Tell me, do you see any upside to this?"

"That would be a stretch. I guess you're lucky this cop didn't get your whole license plate number, or you'd be under interrogation right now. Of course, it's just a matter of time. He see you in the car?"

"I don't think so."

Richard shook his head. "No matter. By the time the cops make the connection that the PI Balfour hired is the guy double-parked there, whaddya wanna bet he makes the ID?"

"You're saying he'd lie?"

"Heaven forbid. Cops don't lie. They just make their stories a little better. It's not like he's gonna say you were out there when you weren't out there. After all, you were out there."

"He didn't see me."

"Oh, yeah? Try and prove it. He'll be lying, and so will you if you say you weren't out there. Only, his lie will be true."

"What can I do about it?"

Richard considered. Shrugged. "Nothing I wanna know about."

Twenty-one

I PULLED MY TIE DOWN A FEW INCHES, UNBUTTONED THE TOP BUTTON of my shirt, and mussed my hair. I descended on the young cop climbing out of his police car, flipped open a pad of paper, took out a pen.

"Officer Dawson. Officer Dawson. Could I ask you a few questions, please?"

"About what?"

"About the Grackle case."

Dawson seemed an amiable sort. He smiled good-naturedly and shook his head. "I'm not supposed to talk about it."

"Of course, of course," I said, tipping him a wink. "And I certainly wouldn't wanna quote you on it. Just between you and me, is there a story there?"

"Sorry. I can't tell you anything."

I put up my hand. "Never mind. Don't tell me. I'll tell you. The suspect. This Jenny Balfour. The one you saw in front of the apartment house. That would be a converted town house, would it not?"

"I really can't say."

"You don't have to. I have all this from other sources. She was parked at a fireplug when you started to write up a ticket. She batted her eyes and talked you out of it."

His face darkened. "You write that, we got trouble."

"So what's your version?"

He merely smiled.

"Okay," I said. "I gotta go with what I got."

"Nice try, buddy. I have no comment. You wanna print crap, you learn it somewhere else, I can't stop you."

I shrugged. "Okay. Just wanna check with you first. Word is you tagged Papa, let the girl go. That's certainly gonna look like favoritism influenced you."

The young officer seemed considerably less amiable. "What part of 'no comment' don't you understand?"

"Excellent," I said. "Great quote. Thank you very much."

He flushed, clamped his lips together, stared me down.

I let him. After all, I'm a nice guy. I didn't wanna push anything.

I rushed out to Brooklyn, quick like a bunny, and signed up Lester Phillips, a twelve-year-old boy who'd thought it was pretty clever to empty the fire extinguishers in his school hallway, and had subsequently slipped on the wet floor. I made quick work of the greedy juvenile delinquent, or rather, the juvenile delinquent's greedy parents, and shot back to Manhattan trying to figure out what else I could do to get off the hook.

I was juggling a time bomb, and I knew it. I just didn't know when it was set for. There was no way to defuse it. I just had to protect myself before it went off.

I called information, asked for Millsap & Millsap. It was, as I'd feared, a midtown address. I drove there, put the car in a midtown garage. Wished like hell Richard had a midtown client to charge it to. Midtown garages don't come cheap.

Millsap & Millsap had offices in a ritzy building on Madison Avenue. The elevator spewed me out into a hallway with a directory. That was encouraging. At least the Millsaps didn't have the whole floor. I followed the directions to suite 403, pushed open the door, and found myself in a modest reception area, where a gum-chewing redhead manned a kidney-shaped desk.

"Yes?" she inquired.

"I'd like to see Mr. Millsap."

"Which one?"

"Balfour's attorney."

"Which one?"

I blinked. Took a second to digest that. "Jenny Balfour," I said.

"That would be David Millsap. Do you have an appointment?"

"What do *you* think?"

She frowned. "Huh?"

"From the fact I didn't know what Millsap I wanted, what are the odds I have an appointment?"

She smiled the way only redheads can. I'm not sure what way that is, it just sounds like what a private eye would say. "If you don't have an appointment, he probably won't see you."

"I'll risk it. Give him a ring. See if he wants to see me."

"Your name?"

"Stanley Hastings."

She rang on the phone. "Hello? Mr. Millsap. A Mr. Stanley Hastings here to see you." She listened, covered the phone, said, "What is this with regard to?"

"I'm a private investigator hired by Jenny Balfour's father. I thought Mr. Millsap might like to debrief me."

He did. Moments later he ushered me into his private office.

David Millsap was young, though everyone looks young to me these days. Still, the man was probably younger than Richard Rosenberg. He had red hair too, and freckles. He was thin, trim. Didn't wear glasses, his handshake was vigorous.

He seemed glad to see me. "Come in, come in, Mr.? . . . "

"Hastings. Stanley Hastings."

"Mr. Hastings. I'm David Millsap, attorney for Jenny Balfour, who's been charged in the death of Philip T. Grackle. Please sit down."

He gestured to a chair. I sat in it. He sat opposite. A pad of legal paper was in front of him on the desk. "Now then, Mr. Hastings, what can I do for you?"

"For starters, is this conversation being recorded?"

He drew back, frowned. "Why do you ask?"

"The way you got me to state my name, pretending you didn't know it. When in point of fact the receptionist gave it to you and it's written on that pad. But you didn't answer my question. Is this meeting being recorded?"

Millsap took a breath. "It's company policy. We often record meetings. So we have a point of reference."

I nodded. "I'm pleased to hear it. And you *still* haven't answered my question. Is *this* conversation being recorded?"

"Why do you want to know?"

"I hate being sued. My wife gets on my case. Wonders why I wasn't more careful. So I try to be more careful. I'm trying now."

"I see."

"Since I've asked you three times without getting an answer whether this conversation's being recorded, I'm going to assume it is, and act accordingly. That, of course, will curtail free speech."

Millsap frowned, pulled open his right-hand desk drawer, reached inside, pushed the button. "Okay, the recorder's off. What do you want to say?"

"I just wanted to point out why I'm probably a liability to your case."

"And why would you want to do that?"

"Frankly, to make sure you don't throw me to the wolves."

"And why would *I* want to do *that*?"

"I take it you're not Joe Balfour's attorney?"

"No. My father is."

"He's the other Millsap? Of Millsap & Millsap?"

"That's right."

"Isn't that a conflict of interest?"

"Only within the family. Dad'll be cranky if he loses."

"Yes, but he doesn't plan to, does he? And neither do you. It looks like a conflict of interest, but actually it's great. You'll dump it all on Joe Balfour, and your father will dump it all on the kid. That's why you're not worried about me. I'm the old man's PI. You figure anything I know incriminates your father's client."

His eyes narrowed. "What are you saying?"

"That doesn't happen to be the case. Now then, as Jenny Balfour's attorney, you're not about to go rushing to the police with anything that connects her to the crime. It's not the sort of thing that would be good for business."

His mouth fell open. "Are you blackmailing me?"

"What a nasty word," I said. "I'm certainly glad you didn't record that nasty word. Of course I'm not blackmailing you. I'm not that kind of guy. I'd just like some assurance before I spill my guts that you won't go running to the cops."

"You have evidence that implicates my client?"

I sighed. "Oh, dear. Here we go with the hypothetical again. I would certainly not want to put a reputable attorney such as yourself in the position of withholding material evidence from the police." I caught my breath. "God, that's a mouthful. So, let's say the situation was this: Suppose I happened to see your client go into the town house on the night of the murder."

"That's impossible."

"I'm glad to hear it. That'll certainly make my life easier. But the officer who rousted your client ID'd a car that looked like mine right about the same time. The saving grace is he doesn't *remember* it's about the same time; he just knows it's in between the time she drove off and the time he tagged Dad. Suppose, just for the sake of argument, that happened to be me. Suppose I was there *exactly* the same time as your client, and happened to see what she did. The cop can only put her on the street. 'Cause he didn't see her first, he saw her car. All he knows is she came running up and stopped him. Suppose I saw her come out of the town house. Suppose, just for the sake of argument, I even saw her go *in*."

"Are you saying you did?"

"I wouldn't want to embarrass you with that information."

"Then how would I know it's true?"

"You can't, of course. But I'm gonna assume your client's confided in you, it bein' a murder case and all. So I'm gonna assume she's told you the truth. That she drove there directly from Midnight Lace, where she'd been working all night as a stripper."

David Millsap's freckles were much more noticeable against his ashen face. He said nothing, just gawked at me.

"Anyway," I continued, "if I were planning my defense, I would almost certainly put me on the list of witnesses I would least like to trot out."

"How do you know all this?"

"Hey, her old man hired me. You think I'm not gonna earn my money? Speaking of which, your client out on bail?"

"Why?"

"I don't know how bad she needs the money, but it's probably not a good time to be working at Midnight Lace."

A man stuck his head in the door. I'm not good at faces, still the guy was a dead ringer for an older version of David Millsap. His hair was whiter, and his freckles looked more like liver spots. He stopped and said, "Oh, sorry. Didn't know you had a meeting."

The look on David Millsap's face was priceless. He wanted to say, "Dad," but not in front of me. Aside from that, he wasn't sure what he wanted to say. He certainly didn't want to introduce me to his father, and he couldn't think of a deflection that wouldn't arouse the old man's interest.

I smiled and said, "Hi, you must be David's father. I'm afraid this is a little awkward for him. I'm here asking him if I should go to the police with information that implicates your client, Joe Balfour. You are representing Mr. Balfour, aren't you?"

The older Millsap's eyes narrowed. "And just who are you?"

"I'm the private eye your client hired. And then fired. Which looks bad on my resume. I was hoping to straighten things out."

His face was hard as nails. "What do you mean?"

"As an investigator, I try to give service. Just 'cause your client dumped me doesn't mean I stop working. In point of fact, I followed him to find out the score."

"Followed him when?"

"Good point. Excellent point. And just the one I was bringing up with your son. The cop who tagged your client makes a car that looks like mine in between his client and yours. When I say *looks like mine*, it's because the cops have only a partial license plate and haven't made the connection yet. When they do, it's gonna be rather embarrassing for all concerned. At the present time the cops believe the daughter did it. Under the circumstances, the parking tag is just that, a parking tag. Nothing directly ties it up. On the other hand, if an eyewitness *saw* your client go into that town house. . . ."

"Are you saying that's the case?"

"I'm very carefully *not* saying that's the case. I'm merely pointing out that under the circumstances, keeping me away from the police is probably to everyone's advantage. Since I happen to have the dirt on both daughter and daddy. Have you had a talk with Sergeant Thurman?"

"That's the arresting officer?"

"That's right."

"I didn't see the arresting officer. I dealt with an ADA."

"I'll bet you did. ADAs keep Sergeant Thurman as far away from the general public as possible. The man has the brains of a turnip. If he thinks your client's guilty, the fact someone else has been charged with the crime isn't going to faze him much. Unless he arrested the daughter. You happen to know if he did?"

"Doesn't ring a bell," the younger Millsap said.

"If it was Thurman, it would. Thurman rings bells."

The older Millsap looked as if he was getting a severe migraine. He held up a hand to his forehead, said, "Please, please. What is that, some type of tough PI lingo? You'll pardon me, young man, but you're having too much fun."

I loved him. Right then and there I decided if there was any way to help the senior Millsap, I would. Granted, the guy looked about a hundred and five. Still, he was the first person in years to call me "young man."

"Sorry," I said. "Sergeant Thurman is a bullheaded moron. I've dealt with him before. And he's dealt with me before. Frankly, it's two strikes against your client that I'm on the case. So it's really to your client's advantage to keep me out of it. Now, if your client's made a full disclosure to you, you know that to be true. So you know it, and I know it. I'm here trying to make sure your son knows it. Because right now, the only way I get dragged into this case is if he brings me in. I don't know if he listens to you, and it probably wouldn't be ethical anyway for me to ask you to intervene. The point is, I was on the verge of talking him out of throwing me to the cops when you came in. So why don't you butt out and let me finish the job?"

The elder Millsap stared at me a few moments, then turned, stalked out, and slammed the door.

David Millsap watched him go. A smile creased his freckled face. "Say," he said. "Nicely done."

I thought so.

Twenty-two

SOME DAYS YOU GET LUCKY. TODAY IT WAS MORE LIKE AN ANSWERED prayer. My beeper was silent. The office didn't want me. I had no pending job.

Except trying to save my ass.

So far, things were going well. The traffic cop couldn't ID me, and neither attorney would give me up to the police.

That left Sergeant Thurman.

Thurman would nail me if he could. Nothing would please him better. Thurman would turn me in at the drop of a hat.

That was a risk I couldn't afford to take.

I caught up with Sergeant Thurman at a greasy spoon near the Criminal Court Building, offered to buy him lunch.

Antennas went up. A radar screen of suspicion flashed between the cauliflower ears and on the flattened nose. Tiny blips registered on the eyes.

"Whaddya want?" Thurman grunted.

"I thought we might chat a bit."

I signaled the waitress. "Diet Coke and a cheeseburger for me. What'll you have, Sergeant?"

Thurman ordered a turkey club. I had visions of the waitress bringing a huge wooden club in the shape of a turkey, and Thurman beating me to death with it.

As the waitress retreated with the order, Thurman said, "Whaddya want?"

"What makes you think I want something?"

"Oh, sure. You just stopped in for lunch."

"I hear they make a good burger."

"Look, I don't want you messing in my case."

"Is it your case anymore?"

"Huh?"

"You arrested the father. Turns out he didn't do it. Doesn't that let you off the hook?"

"What, are you nuts? Are you stupid or something? Homicide's a homicide. You think it matters who the hell did it? You're on the case, you're on the case."

"So you're on the case?"

"Brilliant! What brain power! You must be a member of that whatchamacallit, that bright club, sounds like a woman's thing. You know, when you gotta buy tampons."

I tried to decode his twisted logic. "Mensa?"

"That's it. You must be one of them."

"Just a hint, Sergeant. If you're ever asked to speak at a women's club, decline."

He frowned. "What are you talking about?"

"You're on the case. That's the main point. You're on the Grackle case."

"Yeah. So?"

"I thought maybe you'd like to discuss it."

"Are you out of your mind?"

"No. I was Joe Balfour's investigator before he gave me the boot."

"You're off the case?"

"I'm afraid so."

"Then what the hell are you doing poking your nose in?"

"I'm not happy with the situation. I'd like to know what's going on."

"Oh, you would, would you?"

"What's wrong with that?"

"I'll tell you what's wrong with that. You're a wise-ass punk son of a bitch thinks he's smarter than the cops. You wanna solve this case for me? Is that what you'd like?"

"Of course not."

"I believe that. Just like I believe every perp says he didn't do it."

"Come on, Thurman. I'm curious, is all. It's unusual to arrest two members of the same family for the same crime within twenty-four hours. I'd like to know how it plays out."

"Buy a paper."

"Come on, don't be like that. I haven't seen the crime scene, I haven't seen the victim. I don't know what evidence you got."

"Yeah, well I'm sure it's not for lack of trying."

The waitress shoved the burger and club sandwich on the table in front of us.

"One check, and give it to him," Thurman told her. As she withdrew, he said, "I'll let you buy me lunch in return for some free advice. Stay the hell away from this case. I don't wanna *see, hear,* or *smell* you. You're not *involved* in this case. You're not *hired* in this case. You got no *business* in this case. There's no reason for you to *be* in this case. The old man hired you at one time: . . . big . . . fucking deal. It was way before the crime, and he's not the perp. So I *don't* wanna talk to you about this, now, then, or ever. Butt the hell out. This crime is no business of yours. Is that clear?"

Yes, it was.

Twenty-three

SO FAR I WAS BATTING A THOUSAND. GOD BLESS REVERSE PSYCHOLOGY, and a cop as simple as Sergeant Thurman to fall for it. If I'd tried to avoid him, he'd have run me in. By going to him I was safe. All I had to do now was butt out.

Unfortunately, I couldn't do that.

Not with the time bomb still ticking.

I got in my car and drove out to White Plains.

I had learned one thing from my meeting with the Millsaps. Jenny Balfour was out on bail.

I had no problem finding the house. It was the only one on the street that looked like it. I suppose it was Art Deco, or some other recognizable style— my expertise in architecture ranges from houses with stairs to houses without stairs. On the other hand, maybe it was just weird. Anyway, I got there.

Jenny's Nissan was parked in the driveway. I parked in the street, went up the front walk, and rang the bell.

The door was opened not by Jenny Balfour, but by an attractive older woman in a sweater and slacks. By older, I mean older than Jenny Balfour—I'm sure she was younger than me. A fact I have to keep reminding myself of when I meet women these days.

That wasn't the first thing that occurred to me.

This woman was a looker. Her auburn hair had clearly spent time in the beauty parlor, and it had worked. Her face, though lined, was attractive and a hint of what it must appear in less trying times. Her figure was trim and youthful. Her sweater showed it to good advantage. Even for one who had recently spent a good deal of time in a topless bar, she held allure.

But that wasn't what I noticed either.

She was clearly Jenny Balfour's mother. The family resemblance was uncanny. No, I'm not talking about her sweater. I mean the fullness of her lips, the tilt of her nose, the fire in her eyes. The resemblance was so close it was hard not to flinch for fear she might slap me in the face.

But that wasn't it, either.

The resemblance was clear up close, but it hadn't been from a distance. Even so, I'd had a good enough look to make the ID. She was the woman I'd seen leaving Philip T. Grackle's town house just before Jenny Balfour went in.

Great. That was all I needed. Assuming Jenny hadn't talked, I was the only one on god's green earth who knew she'd been there.

"Yes?" Jenny's mother demanded, making no move to let me in. I should point out that all my observations about her were made through a partially opened door. Not a big deal, perhaps, but one takes note when one's triumphs are so few.

"I'd like to see Jenny Balfour."

"She's not talking with the press."

"I'm not a reporter. I'm the guy she slapped in the face."

"What?"

"Not on a date, or anything. I'm a private eye, I have some information to share."

"Jenny isn't here."

"Oh?"

"What do you mean, 'oh?' You don't like that answer? You want an explanation? What makes you think you got one coming?"

"I don't, of course," I said. "No matter. If Jenny's not here, I'll talk to you."

"I don't think so."

She started to close the door.

I put my foot in it. A common move. One you read about in book after book after book. I tell you something. The guys who do it must have hard shoes. My soft leather jobbie crumpled like an accordion. The pain in my foot was excruciating.

I flung myself against the door.

Mrs. Balfour bounced back, tripped over a pair of boots in the foyer, and fell flat on her ass.

I lurched forward on one foot, howling like a hound of Satan, and collapsed on the prostrate woman like some demented rapist.

Scowling with rage, Mrs. Balfour pushed upward, managed to get her foot in my crotch, and kicked with all her might. Luckily, from that angle and purchase, all her might wasn't much. Instead of pain, it was like being fondled by an aggressive foot fetishist. It didn't feel bad.

I discovered I was holding her left breast. I released it, rolled off her, and sat up. "Sorry," I said. "I think we got off on the wrong foot." I looked ruefully at mine, which still throbbed. "I got some stuff you need to know. And vice versa."

I helped her to her feet, making sure I wasn't in a position where she could push me out the door.

"I've got nothing to say to you," she said defiantly.

"In that case, your answer is 'No comment.' It's too bad, but I'll ask the question anyway."

"What question?"

"The sixty-four-thousand-dollar question. Or it used to be. Now that's just one step on the way to a million. On that Regis Philbin show."

"Damn it, will you please make sense?"

"Fine. I'll ask you one question, then you can throw me out."

"What's the question?"

"Was Grackle alive when you left his apartment?"

Her face froze. I don't think she breathed. Her heart might have stopped beating. Then she started moving again, as if a freeze-frame had been released. "I don't know what you're talking about."

I shook my head. "Nah. No good. If you did it without the dramatic pause, like you'd just been brained with a sledgehammer, you might get away with it. You probably can if you know it's coming. Let's try it again. Was Grackle alive when you left his apartment?"

She pointed to the door. "Get out of here."

"No, no. Bad move. Let me explain why. Everything I've observed leads me to the conclusion you and your daughter have been somewhat less than communicative. If I can't talk to you, I'll have to talk to her. Would you like to know what I'm gonna say?"

"Leave her alone."

"I'm afraid I can't do that. I'm a witness in the case. At least, a potential witness. I'm doing everything in my power to *get out of* being a witness, but it still could happen. If it does, your daughter needs to know which way to jump. That's gonna be hard, with you holding out on her."

"I'm not holding out on her."

"Well, you're not speaking up, either. I don't see you rushing to the police and taking the blame."

"What good would that do?"

"I suppose it would depend on your story. Can you make a good case for wanting to kill the guy?"

A trace of an ironic smile played around the corners of her mouth.

I shook my head. "See, that's the problem. There's only two possibilities. Grackle was alive when you left. Or Grackle was dead when you left. If he was alive when you left, it puts your daughter right in the soup, because Daddy's gonna say he was dead. That's pretty ironic, isn't it. Here she is, sandwiched between two parents, both of whose stories will fry her. That's assuming the cops get a line on you."

"Are you threatening me?"

"Absolutely not. I'm here to help you. Only, I could do it better if I had the facts. What did Grackle have on you?"

"What makes you think he had anything on me?"

"If you were there for a social visit, that's interesting too. How'd you know Grackle socially?"

"Fuck you! You smug, condescending . . ."

"You flatter me. So why would you see a guy like Grackle? I assume you're locally prominent. A community leader of some sort. Are you active in the PTA? No, Jenny's too old for that. You running for city council?"

She blinked.

"Oh, no wonder you won't come forward. The thing is, this probably kills your chances anyway, it being your daughter and all."

"Get out!"

"You keep saying that. But you haven't answered my question. Was Grackle alive when you left?"

"You get the hell out of here."

"Or what? You can't call the cops, can you? You gonna throw me out physically? I'd be interested to see that. Give me an idea of how well you'd fare against Grackle."

She glared at me in helpless frustration. Then, abruptly, her face seemed to dissolve. Before I knew it, the woman was weeping on my shoulder.

I held her, tried to console her. Fat chance of that. The only thing I could think of to say was, "There, there." Somewhat inadequate, under the circumstances. I said it anyway. Patted her on the shoulder. Felt like hell.

The next thing I knew I was flying backward, arms and legs flapping in the breeze like a rag doll, and landing in a heap on the front stoop.

Dazed and confused, I staggered to my feet, just in time for Mrs. Balfour to slam the door in my face.

It occurred to me I don't do well with women.

Twenty-four

I PARKED AROUND THE CORNER FROM THE BALFOUR HOUSE AND settled down to wait.

I figured I had a fifty-fifty chance. The Balfour house was in the middle of the block. Jenny Balfour had to pass the east corner or the west corner. If she was coming from the Hutchinson Parkway, she'd naturally pass the east. That upped my chances to better than fifty-fifty.

My notorious luck with women knocked 'em down again.

But the fact I'd had such bad luck with the mother raised 'em up. After all, odds are averages. So the fact I'd just struck out surely increased the chances I'd score.

Or did it?

I seem to recall in the play *Rosencrantz and Guildenstern Are Dead* them flipping coins that kept landing heads, and they talked about how the phenomenon might be a dramatic vindication of the theory the tosses were totally independent of each other, and no matter what previous tosses had occurred, each individual coin was as likely to come down on its tail as its head.

I wondered if I was remembering it correctly.

The reason for such idle speculation was that I was sitting in my car with nothing to do but idly speculate. Mrs. Balfour had hinted her daughter would be home soon. Since Mommy hadn't invited me to stay and wait, I was doing the next best thing, attempting to head her daughter off at the pass.

I hoped like hell some enterprising news crew wouldn't get the same idea.

So far, so good. At least so far as I knew. Of course, she might have driven home from the west, parked in the driveway, and been upstairs taking a shower by now. But what the hell, at least she hadn't come from the east.

Confession of incompetence number 364. It was long about then that it occurred to me I wasn't going to see Jenny Balfour's Nissan flash by the corner, because Jenny Balfour's Nissan was parked in the driveway. So Jenny had to be out in the Jaguar or the station wagon. The Jaguar I'd probably notice, but Papa was likely to be out in that. The station wagon was another matter. I wasn't sure whether it was a Ford or a Chevy, assuming it was either. I wondered whether I could spot Jenny Balfour driving it. Assuming she *was* driving it. Assuming she wasn't holed up with her lawyer, who was advising her in no uncertain terms to stay the hell away from the private eye who was fucking things up.

Jenny showed up fifteen minutes later, tooling along in the station wagon as if she hadn't a care in the world.

I pulled out into the intersection, cut her off.

She screeched to a stop, looking just as indignant as she had every right to be.

I was out of my car before she had a chance to back up. I raised my voice to be heard through her rolled-up window. "The last time I stopped you, you slapped my face. That was before you got arrested for murder. I got some things you ought to hear. If you keep going, you won't hear 'em, 'cause your mama don't like me. She just threw me out on my ass. I'll follow you home if I have to, or I'll buy you a cup of coffee. Your call."

She thought that over. I could tell she didn't like it. She jerked her thumb back in the direction she'd just come. I got in my car, hoped I wouldn't have to chase her.

I didn't. She drove to a nearby diner and parked in the lot. It was fairly decent diner, not fancy, but clean. It was about half full. We slid into one of the booths.

I could see people pointing and whispering. If Jenny noticed, she didn't let on.

She ordered coffee and dry toast. I ordered coffee and a corn muffin.

"You want that grilled?" the waitress asked.

"What the hell," I told her.

She slid coffees in front of us. I dumped milk in mine. Jenny took hers black.

"All right," she said. "What's so all-fired important?"

"I had a talk with your lawyer. And your father's lawyer. You know, the Millsap twins. They agree it would be to the benefit of all concerned to keep me out of it."

"Then what are you doing here?"

"Making sure you feel the same."

"You got a lot of nerve."

"Hey, none of this is my idea. Your father hires me to make contact in a bar. The contact turns out to be you. You wanna tell me how that makes sense?"

"You wouldn't understand."

"Try me."

"It's none of your business."

"That's where you're wrong. That guy you slapped was a cop. He's a big boy, he can take it, but not when it's connected to a murder."

The waitress was back with our order. I noticed my muffin had been fried in butter to a tasty crisp. I wondered what that would do for my cholesterol. I wondered what this case would do for my blood pressure. I wondered if I'd wind up taking more pills than MacAullif.

"You were about to explain," I prompted, munching on a piece of muffin. "Your father's gonna meet someone who will recognize him from a flower. That someone is you. How the hell are you gonna pull that off? Granted, you look all grown up in your Barbie doll outfit; still, don't you think Daddy might have caught on?"

"I knew he was running a ringer."

"How?"

"Well, I didn't, really. But I knew he wouldn't be there."

"How did you know that?"

"He was taking Mom to dinner. Along with some friends. It was a long-standing engagement. No way he was gonna bail."

"So what were you doing in the bar?"

"Grackle sent me."

"Now we're getting someplace. What was Grackle after, and why were you working for him?"

"What do you think Grackle was after? Money, of course."

"He didn't ask for money."

"No, he never did. But somehow he always got it."

"Could you be a little less cryptic?"

"Not really. There's people trying to listen in."

There were indeed. Not everyone in the diner, but damn close.

"Drink your coffee, let's get out of here."

I paid the tab, left a tip, ushered her out the door.

"My car or yours?" Jenny said gamely.

I was beginning to like her. "Any place around here we could sit in one of them without attracting attention?"

"There's a minimall a few blocks up."

"Sounds like a plan."

I followed her to the mall, which consisted of an A&P, a Kmart, and a dozen small stores. We parked in the far corner of the lot.

Jenny climbed into my car and shut the door. She turned in her seat and looked at me. "Okay," she said. "Shoot."

Up close, Jenny had a small scar on her chin. A thin, diagonal line. It didn't detract from her beauty, however. If anything, it made her seem human, real, desirable.

"Actually," I said, "you were explaining to me about Grackle."

"Yeah, I was, wasn't I? I thought you started this off by saying you had something I should know."

"I do."

"So?"

"Tell me about Grackle."

"Tell me what I should know."

"You should know enough to keep me out of this. You should know enough to keep the cop you slapped out of this."

"Why?"

"Tell me about Grackle."

She looked at me as if she wasn't used to not getting her own way. I figured that was probably true. Except maybe where Grackle was concerned.

"Go on," I said. "Bite the bullet. Let me make it easier for you. Did you tell this to your lawyer?"

"No."

"I didn't think so. If you had, you wouldn't be having so much trouble telling me."

She bit her lip.

"What did you tell your lawyer?"

"I told him Grackle knew I worked as a stripper and was threatening to tell my folks."

"He buy that?"

"Why shouldn't he?"

"You tell him you found Grackle alive or dead?"

"Alive, of course."

"No *of course* about it. You could have walked in and found him dead. That would tie in with the fact you weren't there for long."

"The police don't know how long I was there."

"No, but they can estimate. The cop who ID'd your car didn't have time to write the ticket before you came out. Also, if you were gonna be long, you wouldn't have parked at the plug."

"Sure," she said sarcastically. "I knew he was dead, so I knew I wouldn't be long."

"Okay," I conceded. "Faulty logic. Anyway, you found him alive?"

"That's right."

"So what did you do?"

"I gave him the money."

"What money?"

"The money from dancing."

My eyes widened. "You're working as a stripper to pay off Grackle?"

She looked at me despairingly. "Even my lawyer knows that."

"That's what you told your lawyer?"

"Yeah. So?"

"So I guess he's gotta believe what he hears. *I'm* having trouble. You're working as a stripper to pay off Grackle. Grackle's blackmailing you for working as a stripper."

She made a face. "That does sound bad."

"Your lawyer didn't point that out?"

"It seemed a little over his head. The guy's pretty young."

"Why did you go to him?'

She grimaced. "*My* father brought me to *his* father. The old man saw a conflict of interest, palmed me off on the son."

"Interesting. And why were you paying Grackle? Not the reason you told Millsap junior. But the real one. What'd the guy have on you?"

"Nothing."

"You were just paying him out of the goodness of your heart?"

"No."

"What were you paying him for?"

"For my father."

As I grow older, the ability of my brain to take in information diminishes. Whether this is early Alzheimer's, or just normal deterioration, I have no idea. All I know is I find myself groping for words or phrases, having more and more senior moments, and just generally failing to process the simplest of information.

In this case, I think I could be forgiven. The facts in the case kept spiraling around and around and down and down in a whirlpool of Balfours, a genuine maelstrom that threatened to scuttle even the last vestiges of reason.

"He was blackmailing you for something your father did?"

"That's right."

"Would that be killing a man in a bar?"

"Exactly."

I sighed. "This gets worse. You're paying blackmail to cover up something your father did. Your father doesn't know you're paying it. Then the blackmailer starts to put the bite on your father. You turn around and help him do it."

"I didn't help him do it."

"Oh, no? You showed up in the bar with the envelope."

"So?"

"So what were you going to say to your father?"

"I told you. I wasn't going to meet my father. I knew he'd run in a ringer."

I put up my hand. "Let's not go 'round again. What did *Grackle* think you were going to tell your father?"

"To pay up."

"And why did Grackle think you would do that?"

"Because I told him I would."

I sighed. "Jenny, help me out here. Could you be just a *trifle* more forthcoming? Explain to me what was happening with regard to your father and Mr. Grackle."

"Just what I said. Grackle was a blackmailer. He was putting the bite on me. He decided to put the bite on my father. He made a preliminary pass at him to scare him, then set up a meeting. I found out, I asked him to let me handle it. Told him I'd get the money."

"You were going to shake down your father?"

"Of course not."

"So what were you going to do?"

"Stall things along."

"How?"

"I knew my father was running in a ringer. I didn't want that to work."

"How were you going to stop it?"

"Just how I did. Slap him in the face and walk out."

"How did that help you?"

"It bought time. It made nothing happen. Anyone else but me goes into that bar, they see a guy with a red flower and they take a tumble. They tell the guy what Grackle wants."

"Which was?"

"Ten grand."

"Oh, yeah?"

"Yeah. First bite, of course. If my father runs in a ringer, the ringer reports back, *Pay up ten grand, or else*. Then my father's in a bind. But I've got the advantage of knowing my father won't keep the appointment, see? So I tell Grackle I can convince my father to pay up. I ask for a chance to do that to keep things from getting ugly."

"And Grackle agreed?"

"Sure. He liked the idea. The guy had a perverse sense of humor. He wanted to see the look on my father's face when I came walking in."

"He was there?"

"Sure he was there, watching the play. If I deviated from the script, he'd have known. That's why I played it straight. At least so far as he was concerned. I walked into the bar, saw that the guy wearing the flower wasn't my father, I slapped his face and beat it."

"Uh-huh," I said. "So, what was in the envelope?"

"Envelope?"

"The big manila envelope you had. What was that, your father's police record?"

She flinched. Recovered. "Yeah. That's what it was."

"So what happened to it?"

"What do you mean?"

"You took it in the megastore. You came out without it."

"So you *were* following me. Boy, am I good."

"You saw me?"

"I sensed you."

I fought back the involuntary thrill that statement produced. *She sensed me.* It was impossible not to remember what she looked like as Barbie.

What she looked like at Midnight Lace.

"Yeah, good for you," I said bruskly. "What about the envelope?"

"Oh. I was stuck with it. I didn't want to take it to work, so I called Grackle on his cell phone, asked him what to do with it."

"Your father was supposed to take it?"

"Of course."

"So what happened to it?"

"Grackle said to leave it in the bookstore."

"In the Virgin Megastore?"

"Sure. He told me to leave the envelope on the top row of books in the sci-fi section. So he could pick it up."

"Why not just give it to him?"

"I was being followed. At least he thought so. He said to go into the Virgin Megastore and listen to a song or two while he made sure. If he didn't come up and tap me on the shoulder, after three songs I was to leave the envelope, go outside, and take evasive action."

"Oh," I said. "So what did you do next? After ditching me, I mean?"

"So that was you. Did you like how I did it?"

"Loved it. What did Grackle do with your father?"

"I don't know. He took me out of the loop. As if the whole bar fiasco was my fault."

"Wasn't it?"

"Yeah, but he didn't know that. Anyway, I argued bloody murder, but it was no use. Grackle said he'd handle my father himself."

"You warn him then?"

"No."

"Why not?"

Her eyes faltered. "I wish I had."

"Why?"

She said nothing.

"You think your father killed Grackle, don't you? You must, if you left him alive."

Jenny set her lips in a firm line.

"You told your story to the police?"

"No."

"You realize if you do you're putting your father's neck in the noose?"

"Well, duh. Thank you for that assessment, Mr. Brilliant PI. Are we done?"

"I have a few more questions."

"I don't know why I'm talking to you in the first place."

"I do. You can't talk to your lawyer. You can't talk to your father. You must be goin' nuts for someone to talk to."

"What are you, a shrink?"

"Not so you could notice."

"Well, you're dead wrong. I thought you had something that could help me. That's what you said. Turns out that was just a ploy to get me talking."

"Not at all. Truth is, I'd like to help you if I had all the facts."

"That's the same old song. I'm outta here."

She opened the car door.

"Just one more question."

"What would that be?"

"You wanna close the door?"

"That's your question?"

"You wanna close the door before I ask it?"

"No. Go on. Shoot. What's your question?"

"What was your mother doing in Grackle's apartment?"

Twenty-five

JENNY BALFOUR'S FACE WAS AS WHITE AS A SHEET.

That expression has always confused me. I mean, there's off-white sheets, pale blue sheets, patterned sheets. Kids' sheets with toy boats and superheroes. Anyway, if we're talking the pure white type, the hospital variety, the army issue, well, that's the one she looked like.

She stopped, the car door open, one foot out in the parking lot, for all intents and purposes a young lady about to exit a car. "What?" she stammered.

"Was that too difficult a question? I hope not, since it's the only one you're letting me ask. I can rephrase it. Would that count as the same question? I wouldn't wanna overstep my bounds."

"Damn it."

Jenny pulled her foot inside, slammed the car door.

"Do you have an answer? That's not another question," I qualified, "just a prompt to answer the first one."

"Shut up, shut up," Jenny cried irritably. "You and your goddamned word games. What are you, some sort of frustrated writer?"

"Actually, I am. But that's not the issue here. Why'd your mother go to Grackle?"

"Who says she did?"

"*I* say she did. And *you* say she did. Well, you may not *say* she did, but you *know* she did. You saw her out there."

Her eyes widened. "What are you saying?"

"You're stalling for time and it's not gonna work. You know what I'm saying. You went out to Grackle's. You parked at a fire hydrant. You saw your mother coming down the street. You hid in the shadows till she went by."

"You followed me?"

"Of course I followed you. See why I'm an important person? See why it matters what I think?"

"Are you going to the police?"

"Not unless I have to."

She drew back.

"That's not a threat, that's a fact. I didn't go to the police, I came to you. Which isn't gonna please 'em much. I'd like to think I made the right choice."

"What do you mean?"

"What about your mother?"

"I don't know what she was doing there."

"Try again."

"I assume it was the same thing."

"What do you mean?"

"Paying Grackle off."

"What for?"

"The same thing."

"The same thing as what? What you told your lawyer, or what you told me?"

She bit her lip.

"See, the problem with lying so much is it gets hard to keep your stories straight. I don't know if you've told me a word of truth, but frankly I'm not inclined to believe anything I can't check. And if you think I can't check, consider this. I know about your mom, I know about your pop, and I know about you. So tell me about your mom unless you want me to go ask her."

"I thought you tried to ask her and she threw you out."

"She threw me out alone. If I go back with you it could be fun."

Jenny thought that over. "That's the same threat you used before."

"Yeah. As I recall, it worked. Tell me about your mom."

"I have no idea what she was doing there."

"You haven't asked her?"

"I haven't let on I know."

"Now, *that* I believe. Go on."

"What do you mean, go on? That's all I know."

"No, it isn't. Did your mom know Grackle before? Has your mom had anything to do with Grackle? Were you shocked as hell to see her there?"

"Of course I was."

"Ah. You answered one out of three questions. Not a bad average. Should I ask three more?"

"Are you having fun?"

"Not at all. Tell me about your mom."

"I don't know anything about my mom."

"Do you suspect anything?"

"Don't be dumb."

"Tell me why you think she went out there."

"I told you. To pay him off."

"For which transgression?"

"My dad's."

"How does that make sense?"

"Grackle was an equal opportunity blackmailer. He hit my dad, he hit me, he hit mom."

"How did he contact her?"

"How should I know."

"I thought you might. You knowin' so much about Grackle and all."

"Well, I don't."

"And how did you know he was gonna hit your dad? He just happened to say, 'By the way, I think I'll hit your dad?'"

"I don't remember."

"Now, there's a sign of a witness in trouble. The good old, sorry-my-mind's-a-blank. A subject as important as blackmailing your father would usually be expected to make an impression."

"Are you always this sarcastic?"

"When I'm being lied to by a murder suspect, invariably. I've tried to cure myself of the habit, and I just can't. How did you find out Grackle was going to blackmail your father? How did you wind up in that bar?"

"He told me."

"Why?"

"He said I wasn't paying fast enough. He said I needed help."

"He tell you what he meant by that?"

"Sure. He laid it out. I begged him not to do it. When I couldn't talk him out of it, I asked to be the go-between."

I smiled. "That wasn't so hard, now, was it? Why did you think that was worth lying about?"

"I'm not lying," she said angrily.

"And your mom. He told you he was going to hit your mom?"

"No."

"He told you since the bar fucked up he was going to have to take matters into his own hands. He told you he was changing the target."

"No, he didn't. He said he was going to handle it himself, but he didn't say how."

"Or who?"

"Or who."

"And what about—"

Before I could finish my question, the driver's door was flung open, and I was unceremoniously jerked out of the car with such force that, had I been wearing my seat belt, I would have been sliced in half.

Twenty-six

"SON OF A BITCH!" MACAULLIF HOWLED. IF HE'D BEEN TAKING HIS blood pressure medicine, one wouldn't have known it. "Son of a fucking bitch!"

"MacAullif—"

"Don't you MacAullif me! Just stand there and shut up and take it till I'm done, and if you do a good job I might let you live!"

The sight of a big bruiser like MacAullif leaning on a relatively slim noncombatant like me was too much for Jenny Balfour. She exploded out of the car and said, "You leave him alone!"

"Butt out, bitch!" The vein in MacAullif's forehead looked ready to explode, like the alien in human form in some of the monster movies. "Keep your fucking yap shut! You wanna slap me and get away with it just 'cause you're cute? I don't care how nice and cute and perky you think you are, I'll rip your fuckin' tits off and kick your ass all the way back to Hoboken! I'll deal with you in a minute. Meanwhile, butt the fuck out!"

MacAullif wheeled on me. "Nice conversation we had in my office. Everything you told me was true. Let me ask you something I shouldn't have to ask you, you motherfucking son of a bitch. Did you happen to *leave anything out?*"

"MacAullif—"

"Did I ask you to talk? Don't you know a rhetorical question when you hear one? Or did you perhaps think I was being serious? Did you think perhaps I wasn't entirely *sure* if you might have left something out?"

I said to Jenny, "And you thought *I* was sarcastic." I probably shouldn't have. It was as likely a way as any to get the limbs torn from my body.

"Oh, yes," MacAullif said. "Play to the young lady. Get her good and worked up and then maybe she can pop me another one in the kisser. You two are quite a show."

Jenny opened her mouth to speak.

"Zip it!" MacAullif snapped. "So, you're down in my office reassuring me everything's gonna be fine. *Reassuring me*, you son of a bitch! That's nice to hear, because the department's not as close as one might think; for every good cop helpin' you out, there's another upwardly mobile asshole like, to climb up over your back. But, hey, I'm skatin' free on this one. 'Cause the bitch that slapped me in the bar is so peripheral to the case, it's unlikely to ever come up. Then it turns out Balfour's not even the perp; it's his daughter that's involved. There's one more degree of separation, makin' me the happiest cop in town.

"So I'm havin' a great day for myself. Only new homicide comes my way, whaddya know, I clear the sucker in a half hour flat. Not so tough, most homicides are pretty straightforward—this time it's a man/wife—but even so it's one chalked up in the plus column, job well done. And I'm leanin' back at my desk, enjoyin' a little quiet time, leafin' through the *New York Post*. And what do I see? A picture of the perp. A picture of Jenny Balfour, new suspect in the Grackle case. Granted it's a high school yearbook photo, made up, touched up, dumbed down to sweet-sixteen-prom-girl-moron-bitch sensibilities. But I'm a cop. I can make the ID. It's the same freewheeling spitfire gave me the mitten very publicly in a very public place. And I've suddenly zoomed from peripheral as all hell to right in the fucking middle. Which I could have known about earlier if anyone had bothered to tell me. Would you care to advance the theory that you just forgot?"

I said nothing. Just sat there and took it.

"Well?" MacAullif demanded.

"I'm sorry. I thought that was a rhetorical question."

MacAullif's lip quivered. I wondered if there was a drug in the world that might damp him down.

"Cyanide," I murmured.

"What's that?" MacAullif demanded.

"Nothing."

"The guy wasn't poisoned, he was stabbed. By Little Miss Muffett, here, according to the case file. I snuck a look at it before heading out."

"How'd you find us?" I ventured. It was a gamble. The type of question that could piss him off utterly, or ground him in reality. In this case, it was actually a little of both.

"How'd I find you? Easy. I got a police dog sniffs out backstabbing cocksuckers. Actually, I *couldn't* find you. Rosenberg's office had no idea. So I went about it the other way. Tried to find the girl. 'Cause what with you lying to me and all, if I found her, I'd find you."

"I didn't lie to you."

"Right, right. The sin of omission. You wanna skate by on that technicality? I don't think a jury's gonna buy it."

"A jury?"

"Compounding a felony. Withholding a witness. Conspiring to conceal a crime."

"I don't think you're really a witness."

"Not me, jerk. You. *You're* a witness. *You're* the one doin' the fancy footwork to get off the hook. Anyway, I found out slap-happy here'd been released. I called her house, got her mom, found out she'd gone off shoppin', should have been back long ago. On the off chance I ask if a dip-shit PI with the brains of a lemming happens to have been sniffing around."

"A lemming?"

"And whaddya think she said?"

"'Oh, *that* asshole?'"

"Practically a direct quote. So I figure you're together. All I had to do was canvass for cars."

"You make it sound easy."

"Shut up. I'm done with you for a minute. I wanna talk to Little Miss Perp. Sweetheart, you're young and pretty, and guys give you what you want. But that ain't gonna work no more, 'cause someone died. You can give the prosecutor a blow job, he's not gonna let you off."

"You're a class act, MacAullif."

"What? I'm not showin' proper respect for the slut murder suspect? I apologize, my dear young lady. And just what line of work do you happen to be in?"

"Is he really a cop?" Jenny said skeptically.

"What, you wouldn't have slapped a cop? I'm sorry, that's my fault. I should have been wearing my undercover police officer name tag."

"I don't have to talk to you," Jenny ventured.

"No, you don't," MacAullif agreed. "You have that constitutional right. But you have to listen. Nothing in the constitution about that. So shut the hell up and give ear."

"Give ear?"

"He's actually educated," I explained. "Sometimes he forgets he's a cop."

"I'm not talkin' to you." MacAullif didn't even turn his head. "Look here, you, your lawyer told you not to talk, right?"

"Right."

"That's good. That's very good. Your lawyer's a wise man, you keep it up. Now here's the thing. I don't wanna know anything about the crime. Anything your lawyer wouldn't want you to tell me. I just wanna know about the bar. Did you tell your lawyer you slapped me in the bar?"

"No."

"Of course you didn't. Because it has nothing to do with the crime. As long as it continues to have nothing to do with the crime, we have no problem. I, out of the goodness of my heart, will manage to overlook the fact I owe you a poke in the nose. Are we clear so far?"

"Now, look here—"

"No, no. There's nowhere to look. There's nothing to argue about. We're either clear or we're not. Actually, it doesn't matter whether *you're* clear. Because *I'm* perfectly clear. At least, on what I want. Why any of this happened is another thing entirely. You got any reasonable explanation for that?"

"My lawyer said not to talk."

"That's the stuff. Keep it up."

MacAullif managed to force a smile. I don't know how it looked to Jenny, but it was one of the most frightening things I've ever seen.

"Now, why don't you beat it on home? Your mother's worried about you."

Twenty-seven

I WATCHED JENNY DRIVE OFF WITH SOME TREPIDATION. IT LEFT ME alone with MacAullif. Not that I figured he'd stuff me in the trunk of his car, but still. It was enough to give one pause.

"Okay," MacAullif said. "How do we get out of this one?"

We sounded good. It was the best thing I'd heard all day.

"I don't know, MacAullif. I can't get a straight story. The father's lyin', the girl's lyin', the mother won't talk, and the lawyer don't know shit."

"An interesting assessment. Based on your track record, she and Dad are telling the truth, Mom's a blabbermouth, and the lawyer's omniscient."

"Any time you're through having fun."

"Fun? This is not fun. This is as bad as it gets. What's the girl's story? Do you know it?"

"I know what she told me. Whether I believe it or not is something else."

"A girl with tits like that you tend to believe. The fact you're dubious, her story must really suck."

"It's not good."

"Well, do I have to pry it out of you? What's the pitch?"

"Do you really wanna know?"

"Yes, I'd really like to know. Ignorance is not bliss. If I have to dodge a bullet, I would like to know where the bullet is."

I gave MacAullif a rundown of what Jenny told me. He wasn't pleased.

"You call that a story? That's not a story. That's a girl battin' her eyes, and pullin' the wool over yours. Where's the facts?"

"She doesn't know the facts."

"And if you believe that, I got this swampland in Florida you'll just love. The girl's involved with the corpse and don't know shit. Makes sense to me. I couldn't think of another question to ask."

"What part of *I-don't-know* would you like to dissect?"

"She came to pay the guy off?"

"Yes."

"And he was alive when she left?"

"That's what she says."

"So she gave him the money?"

"Of course."

"Which reduced the debt by how much?"

"I don't know."

"Well, how much did she give him?"

"I don't know."

"When she gave it to him, how'd he keep track of the balance? Subtract it from a sum? Did he mark it off in a book?"

"How the hell should I know?"

"Did you ask? Of course not. Because they weren't the questions that interested you."

"They were rather incidental to the crime."

"Is that so? They're rather central to whether or not she's telling the truth. The more details you can muster, the more likely she's not just blowing you off. Which she's probably doing. Good god, what a setup. Here's a girl with her whole family in her power. She hasn't told her story yet, and when she does, she can fry her mom or her dad."

"The cops don't know her mom was out there."

"They will if she says so. What if she says she found Grackle dead?"

"She said he was alive."

"That's what she told *you*. You wanna know how much that's worth? Last I checked, lyin' to *you* isn't perjury in this state. And if she hasn't told her lawyer. . . ." MacAullif shook his head. "That's a situation I don't wanna think about."

"You're sayin' we drop it?"

"I'm sayin' *I* drop it. Not that I was ever involved in the first place, wouldn't you agree?"

"Absolutely."

"Now there's the first right decision you've made this whole case. Good. I'm out of it. You, on the other hand, are right in the middle."

"How do you figure?"

"What, are you nuts? You're involved with the daughter. You're involved with the father. You've been around harassin' the mother. Not to mention the two lawyers. The only reason you're not involved in the case is 'cause Sergeant Numbnuts Thurman is. But it's just a matter of time. The minute that traffic cop with the partial plate manages to put two and two together and makes the ID, even a cop as obtuse as Thurman's gonna take a tumble."

My face betrayed me.

"Don't tell me," MacAullif groaned. "As if things weren't bad enough, you fucked with an ID witness?"

"What, I got no right to question the guy?"

"Save it for the judge." MacAullif shook his head. "This is bad news all around. You and I are teetering on the verge of extinction until this case is cleared up. With Thurman in charge, that could be years."

"So what do we do?"

"I told you, I don't do anything. But *you?* You gotta figure out what's what."

"And just how would I do that?"

MacAullif smacked himself on the forehead theatrically. "Oh, I forgot. No detective training. You didn't go to John Jay College of Criminal Justice? Why is it every time I got a case, you think you know more than me; every time someone else has a case, you need my help?"

"I didn't say I needed your help."

"Didn't you just ask me how to solve this sucker? Well, pardon me, I must have hearing problems too. I wonder if there's a pill for that."

"Fine. I'll do this on my own just to prove I can. The fact your reputation's at stake should have nothing to do with it."

MacAullif frowned. "You have a point. Leaving you to your own devices is not in my best interests. All right, let's start from the top. The girl is charged with killing the guy. Either she did or she didn't."

"That's helpful?"

"We need to wrap up the case. The point is, she's not your client, so we can wrap it up by proving her guilty just as well as proving her innocent. Better, actually, 'cause getting her off the hook may not clear the crime. So I'd look for things to fry her."

"Nice guy."

"Hey, if it does, it does. Girl's told a fairy tale that's most likely not true. If she gets hurt because of it, I'm not wastin' tears. So try to break down her story."

I found myself on the verge of saying "How?"

MacAullif rolled his eyes. "How do you think? You find discrepancies. That's why it would be nice to know how she paid the guy off."

"I can talk to her again."

"You'd like that, wouldn't you?"

"What are you implying?"

"I'm not implying anything. She's a nubile young thing with nice tits. I imagine you'd enjoy talking to her."

"What are we, in high school? You sound positively adolescent."

"I'm merely describing you. The girl seems to have triggered a second childhood. Of course, she hasn't slapped you yet."

Again, my face betrayed me.

MacAullif raised his eyebrows. "Oh, is that right?" His eyes twinkled devilishly. "Fresh."

"Damnit, MacAullif."

"No wonder you don't think she's guilty."

"Now, look here—"

"The white knight on the charger. One of your favorite parts, isn't it? Saving the damsel in distress? No wonder you're so callous about throwing an old friend to the wolves."

"She slapped me to facilitate an escape. So a couple of passersby would make the same mistake you're making."

"Uh-huh," MacAullif said. "So that's how come you're so set on provin' she didn't do it. Okay, assume she's innocent, and find facts to support her story."

"And just where am I going to find these facts?"

MacAullif cocked his head.

I put up my hand. "Never mind. I'll handle it myself." I considered. "Would you draw the line at facilitating things?"

MacAullif frowned irritably. "What?"

"Could you get me in the crime scene?"

"No, but thanks for asking."

"I suppose I could pose as someone looking to rent the apartment."

"You could if you want to wait awhile. The police haven't released it yet."

"You're not being very helpful. What about I forget the whole thing, go back to working negligence cases?"

"And leave a damsel in distress? You certainly could. And leave me hung out to dry? You could do that too. I happen to know you better than that. You wouldn't last twenty-four hours before you had a moral and ethical meltdown. You'd fund some shrink's Christmas vacation, and your self-esteem would need a twelve-step program. But if that's the way you wanna play it. . . ."

"Christ, MacAullif. I just asked if you can get me in the crime scene. You don't have to be so testy just because you can't cut the mustard."

"Hey, douche bag. I'm trying to keep my name out of the murder case. You wanna explain to me how showin' an interest in the crime scene would be a good move?"

"So how do you expect me to get in?"

MacAullif shrugged.

"That's your problem."

Twenty-eight

"I CAN'T DO IT."

That wasn't good. I hadn't even asked Leroy yet, and he'd already told me he couldn't do it.

I wondered why.

Leroy Stanhope Williams had seemed somewhat reserved as he'd opened the door of his Forest Hills home. True, I hadn't seen him in years, but even so. Leroy was one of the most aristocratic black men I've ever met. I suppose that's a racist statement. Everything is these days. What I mean is, Leroy looked and spoke as if he were a dignitary from some British commonwealth. He also dressed the part, discreetly, tastefully, but always elegantly in fashion. His hair was a little grayer than I remembered, his cheeks slightly more pinched. But everything in his character was right and proper. His greeting was perfectly cordial, Emily Post to a fault. Still I sensed a change.

Leroy's foyer was hung with oil paintings, as were all the rooms in his house. I don't know zip about art, but they looked good to me. As he ushered me into the living room, I caught words such as *Picasso* and *Degas*. Even to a cultural illiterate, that sounded good.

Leroy sat me on a moderately uncomfortable velvet-covered couch, which probably reflected the period of some painting or other, and which probably wasn't called a couch but a divan, or some such equally obscure name that I should feel uneducated for not knowing. He sat opposite me in an old throne of Louis Quatorze. It wasn't, of course, I just throw the name in because it's the only one I know.

Leroy offered me coffee and tea, which I declined, and inquired after the health of my wife and child. Friendly, polite, but still reserved.

And then suddenly, uncharacteristically, blurting out that he couldn't help me, when I hadn't even asked.

"Leroy!" I cried. "What's the matter?"

Leroy grimaced, and in that instant I had a premonition. I was about to hear something tremendous and life-altering. His sunken cheeks would be ascribed to some catastrophic illness, aggressive, fatal, and for which there was no cure.

I steeled myself.

Leroy sighed, glanced around. "You see the paintings on the wall?"

How could I help it? They were everywhere. Artistically displayed. The frames alone were probably worth more than the average collection.

"Yes, I see them," I said.

"Well, you probably haven't seen them before. It's been years since you've come to call."

"I guess it has."

"The Matisse I bought last year. Likewise the Van Gogh. The Renoir I've had slightly longer. And the minor De Vinci work, if you can call a De Vinci work minor. Even the sculptures are new."

The new sculpture to my left was of a naked torso, with one leg, no arms, no head, and no genitalia. I assumed, for reasons unknown to me, it was worth a good deal of money.

"Very nice," I said. Considering my talent for art appreciation, that was a rather bold comment.

Leroy registered this with only the slightest amused lift of an eyebrow. "Yes, it is rather nice, isn't it? I have on occasion even lent paintings to museums."

"Really? That's very nice."

"Yes, it is." Leroy paused, frowned. "Perhaps you're missing the big picture here. No, not the one on the south wall. I'm sure *Nude Bathing* struck your fancy. No, I mean the fact I loan my paintings. I am in fact on several boards of directors, and sit on various arts councils. Do you see what I mean?"

A lightbulb went on. My mouth fell open. "You're legitimate."

"Exactly," Leroy said. "These paintings are all mine. I have title to them. I have the right to own them, show them, lend them, exhibit them, sell them, auction them off. There is not one painting in this entire house that I dare not claim. Isn't that amazing?"

It certainly was.

Leroy Stanhope Williams was one of the first clients I signed for Richard Rosenberg. A cheerful black man with a cast on his leg, he had sat right in this very room, helping me fill out the fact sheet. And when I'd asked his occupation, Leroy had answered, "Thief."

That threw me somewhat. From a legal standpoint, the client's occupation was useful largely in attempting to recover lost wages. I was not sure how Richard would relate to that.

I also wasn't sure if it was a joke.

It turned out it wasn't. For Leroy Stanhope Williams was the modern equivalent of the gentleman jewel thief. And all of the art objects in his house belonged to someone else.

The idea these might be his was indeed astonishing.

"How'd you do it?" I asked.

Leroy leaned back in his chair. "Believe me, it wasn't easy. The opportunities to sell a painting without proper provenance at anywhere near its market value are indeed rare. Oh, there's the occasional collector who just wants to own it, and doesn't mind the fact he won't be able to show it—but for the most part, I was selling at twenty to thirty percent of what I was buying. So it's taken me a long time. But I've been legitimate for years now."

"Oh."

Leroy smiled. "I sense your disappointment. That and the fact I haven't seen you in years, leads me to believe you have the need for talents I no longer possess."

"Possess?"

"Practice, if you will. The point is, whatever you need done, I can't do it. I'm a respectable citizen now. I can't jeopardize that."

"I understand," I said.

"Thanks," Leroy said. He raised his eyebrows. "What is your problem?"

"No reason to burden you if you can't help."

"Perhaps I could offer advice."

I gave Leroy a thumbnail sketch of the situation. I omitted details such as MacAullif, Jenny's mother, and my stupidity, stressing instead the young lady's attributes and plight.

"It's a shame," Leroy said. "I'm sorry I can't help her."

I was too. I'd been laying on the damsel-in-distress business pretty thick, trying to play on his guilt. When he seemed to soften, I popped open my briefcase, took out the *New York Post*, and flipped it open to the picture of Jenny Balfour, the one that had sent MacAullif on my case. I got up, walked over, and showed it to Leroy.

I could see him waver. I knew why. Jenny's yearbook photo made her look young, innocent, virginal. Since I had neglected to mention her present occupation, Leroy had no reason not to believe it.

"Who's this?" Leroy asked.

I looked over his shoulder.

The picture next to Jenny Balfour was of the late Mr. Grackle, a thin-faced, sharp-nosed, squinty-eyed, dark-haired young man, with a stubby mustache and virtually no chin. Not the sort of chap to inspire confidence. Even in the photo his eyes looked shifty. He gave the impression that swindling girls like Jenny was his primary occupation.

Grackle was alive in the photo, standing in what was presumably the living room of his apartment. Behind him were a couch, a bookcase, and a framed picture on the wall.

"That's the dead man," I said. "Mr. Grackle. He was killed in his apartment. That's the crime scene I need to search."

Leroy might not have heard me. He was squinting closely at the painting that hung over Grackle's couch in the newspaper photo.

"Is that a Vermeer?"

Twenty-nine

GRACKLE'S VERMEER WAS A CHEAP PRINT. LEROY COULD TELL THE minute he got in the door. For my money, he could have told from the picture in the paper. Leroy was legit now. Why would he want to steal a painting, even from a dead man? Nah, I think he just wanted to help me out.

Anyway, even if he was legit, Leroy's skills hadn't atrophied. The downstairs door had taken him a good five seconds, the upstairs no more than ten.

Appraising the painting took less than that. Leroy pronounced it fake, wished me good luck, and split.

Okay, I was in the crime scene. Now what?

Philip T. Grackle's apartment was modest. He had half of the third floor, which allowed for the living room in the photograph, a small bedroom, a kitchen, and bath. In terms of searching, that was good and bad. It was good in that there were fewer places to search, and bad in that there were fewer places to search.

The police inspection seemed to have centered on the living room, where a chalk outline marked the last position Philip T. Grackle had occupied in his apartment, and the kitchen, where a knife rack on the wall featured an empty slot and a police tag. The knife rack had been dusted for prints, as had various other objects in the apartment. For instance, if after dispatching his victim the killer had stopped to call

149

777-FILM before leaving the premises, the cops would have had him dead to rights.

But aside from dusting for prints and tagging the alleged source of the murder weapon, what had the police done?

I had no idea.

I asked myself, *if I were the police, what would I do?* Unfortunately, *arrest Jenny Balfour* came instantly to mind.

I checked out the living room. Besides the couch and bookcase in the newspaper photo, Mr. Grackle had a TV, a desk, and a file cabinet. The desk had a computer on it, and the TV had a VCR attached. The file cabinet stood alone. I wondered if the police had searched it. If so, I wondered if they'd taken anything. More to the point, I wondered if there was anything to take.

Inside the file cabinet were files. I suppose that was to be expected. I examined them and discovered that Mr. Grackle had been a meticulous man. The file folders were all carefully labeled and dated. The dates ranged from April 1988, through March 1999. That seemed strange. Why would an orderly man such as Mr. Grackle suddenly stop labeling his files? Could it be that March of 1999 was when he fell in with bad company that led him to his eventual demise? Or had the police simply removed all the more recent files? No, the file cabinet was rather full. There didn't appear to be anything missing. So, had he run out of space and moved on to another file cabinet? There didn't seem to be one in the room. Perhaps in the closet, the bedroom, the—

It didn't take the ace detective too long to make the connection between the file cabinet and the computer that sat on the desk next to it. Aha! Mr. Grackle's more recent records would be computerized. Excellent. No fumbling through files. I had merely to bring them up on the screen.

Unfortunately, Mr. Grackle's computer was an Apple, and our computer is a non-Apple—I believe that's the correct technical term for it, though there may be another. Anyway, I am virtually a computer illiterate, even on a machine I know. On a machine I don't know, I am a menace. I can wipe out whole banks of data faster than you can say *Control, Alt, Delete*. I can freeze systems, crash programs, and destroy more gigabytes than most machines have.

When that happens to me at home, I go get Alice, and she does something magical to the computer and it works again. Alice is as versed in the computer as I am unversed. She speaks its language, including languages the layman never hears, reads, or even suspects are there. I swear, the screens she calls up on the computer don't exist in real life. They are some demonic concoction of her own, dreamed up for the sole purpose of bewildering me and making me feel like a schnook.

Alice is good at making me feel like a schnook. She is even more adept at wriggling out of the responsibility for making me feel like a schnook, and proving beyond a shadow of a doubt that it is I, myself, who is making me feel like a schnook.

Be that as it may, whenever I get in trouble on the computer, feeling like a schnook is the price I always pay for calling Alice. Or, as Alice so aptly points out, feeling like a schnook is how I feel *before* I call Alice.

Anyway, looking at Philip T. Grackle's Apple computer, I felt like a schnook.

I called Alice.

Thirty

"MY GOD, IT'S JUST LIKE IN THE MOVIES."

"Alice—"

"They really draw the outline on the floor."

"Did you think that was made up for TV?"

"And the fingerprint powder. Are the prints still there?"

"I think they lift them."

"Does that remove them entirely, or are the prints still in place?"

"I don't know."

"Some criminologist."

"They dust the prints with powder. The powder assumes the contours of the print. They cover the print with tape. The powder adheres to the tape. The impression of the print is lifted."

"And does the print itself remain?"

"I don't know."

This was not good. Alice was making me feel like a schnook, and we hadn't got to the computer yet.

"So where's the murder weapon?" Alice demanded.

"The police have it."

"Well, that's not very sporting, is it?"

I looked at Alice in exasperation. Her eyes were twinkling.

"I'm glad you're having a good time, Alice. I'm still on the hook for suppressing evidence and conspiring to conceal a crime."

"Oh, bullshit," Alice said. "You think Richard Rosenberg couldn't talk your way out of that? Hell, I could argue the case, and I'm not even a lawyer."

I was sure she could. The thought of Alice pitted against Richard was a scary prospect.

"Okay," I said. "How about a young girl's life is at stake?"

"Would this be the young girl with the nice tits?"

"What's your point?"

"Would you expend so much energy saving a flat-chested girl?"

"Alice, investigating this crime was your idea."

"Well, if you're going to hold me to everything I say."

I gulped at that and she said, "So, let's have a look at this computer."

Alice sat down at the desk, switched the sucker on. No sooner had it warmed up when she began clicking the mouse and typing in commands. Images flashed on and off the screen so quickly it was impossible to discern what they were. Within minutes she had settled on a screen that looked surprisingly like a word-processing directory, at which point she jammed a disk into the computer, highlighted the entire screen, and pressed some more buttons.

The machine made a series of buzzing, ringing, and clunking noises. Had we been in Vegas, coins would have spewed out. After a minute or so of this, the computer returned to relative calm. Alice popped out the disk, stuck it in her purse.

"There," she said. "The guy uses Microsoft Word. I downloaded all his files. You can study them at your leisure."

"We don't have an Apple."

"I'll rent you a PowerBook. Was there anything else?"

"I don't know. Was there anything else in the computer?"

"I can tell you the guy's favorite porn sites."

"Why, did he have 'em bookmarked?"

"No, but I can tell where he's been."

"You know what sites the computer visits?"

"Yeah. Why? You don't want me checking ours?"

"No. I'm just utterly amazed."

"I don't see why. Anyway, if that's all, I should be going. No sense both of us winding up in jail."

I didn't point out to Alice that not ten minutes ago she had been arguing that I *wasn't* going to jail. I just let her leave and turned my attention back to my task.

Okay, assuming what I wanted *wasn't* on the computer disk in Alice's purse, where was it? Since I didn't know what I was looking for, I had no idea.

I tried the bedroom. Philip T. Grackle had a king-sized bed, with nightstands on either side. The one on the right held a lamp, a clock radio, and a copy of *Penthouse*. It seemed unlikely the magazine held the key to the gentleman's death, but still, as a seasoned detective, I wasn't about to overlook anything, so I gave it a hasty perusal.

The other bedside table held a reading lamp, but nothing to read. I moved on to the bureau, which contained clothes. A promising-looking closet also contained clothes. Promising-looking shoe boxes turned out to contain shoes. A suitcase was empty, as was a briefcase. There was nothing under the mattress, nothing under the bed.

I went in the kitchen. From mystery novels, I knew flour and sugar canisters were prime hiding places. I searched them, found flour and sugar. Considered baking a cake. Rejected the idea. There was nothing in the cupboards, nothing in the oven, nothing under the sink. If there were diamonds frozen in the ice cubes in Mr. Grackle's ice cube tray, he could keep 'em. Enough was enough.

I went back in the living room and tried the file cabinet again. The files were old, but so what? Balfour's manslaughter conviction was old. Of course, it was also nonexistent.

I pawed through the files. They contained exactly what the labels said. The records of a small, independent investment business carried on by the late Mr. Grackle, apparently working out of his own apartment—there were no receipts for office space, and the expense for office space claimed on Mr. Balfour's meticulous tax returns appeared to be a percentage of his rent.

There was no record of a Mr. Balfour in any of Mr. Grackle's client folders, filed alphabetically, or in any of his business records, filed chronologically. As far as Mr. Grackle was concerned, unless he was on the computer disk Alice had, Mr. Balfour did not exist.

After a good half hour making sure every file was exactly what it said, that one labeled Trowbridge didn't turn out to be a code for some nefarious activity or other, I abandoned the file cabinet and moved on toward the desk. I did so with weary resignation. A quick perusal of the desk had shown one drawer to contain pencils, pens, paper clips, pushpins, page savers, paper, and various other stationery supplies not necessarily beginning with *P*. The other drawer contained instruction manuals for various equipment in the apartment. (If you're thinking I should have followed the one for the Apple computer instead of calling Alice, I would like to point out that it was two hundred and sixty four pages long, and probably had a prerequisite of at least two semesters of Introduction to Computer Manuals 101.)

Anyway, I leafed through the instruction manuals somewhat dispiritedly, having struck out everywhere. There was one for the VCR, one for the TV, one for the clock radio in the bedroom, one for the microwave, one for the toaster oven, one for the file cabinet—

The file cabinet?

Excuse me.

You open the drawer. You close the drawer. File folders hang from both sides. Granted, you have to buy the right size, but that was just a measurement. An instruction manual seemed like overkill.

Grackle's file, according to the instruction manual, was the RV925*. The meaning of the asterisk was not readily explained.

I opened the manual.

On page 1, under the heading OPENING THE SECURITY RECESS FILE, were the following instructions:

1. *Pull bottom drawer open until it will go no further.*
2. *Push front of bottom drawer down to tilt back of bottom drawer up, releasing catch.*
3. *Remove bottom drawer.*
4. *Grab spring rods on interior sides of file cabinet (see diagram A).*
5. *Pull rods, releasing catches.*
6. *Tilt hinged bottom up, revealing recessed compartment.*

I put the instruction manuals back in the drawer, being careful to leave the one for the file cabinet buried in the middle.

I knelt down, pulled the bottom drawer of the file cabinet out until it stopped, pushed down on the front, tipping the back up, removed the drawer from the cabinet, and set it on the floor. Right inside were the little spring bolts in the diagram. I reached in, pulled them, and raised the false bottom.

Inside was an accordion file folder. I took it out and put it on the floor.

There was something underneath. Something green and white. I reached in, pulled out a packet of bills. They were hundreds. I riffled through them. There appeared to be about fifty in the packet. A cool five grand.

The bottom of the cabinet was lined with packets. I pulled them out, stacked them on the floor.

All were hundreds.

All were in packets of fifty.

There were fifty-four packets.

A quick calculation showed the late Mr. Grackle had died in possession of two hundred and seventy grand.

I put the money back exactly where I'd found it, then turned my attention to the accordion file folder. I raised the flap, pulled it open.

Inside were several manila envelopes.

The one on top looked suspiciously like the one Jenny Balfour had been carrying when she pasted MacAullif.

It wasn't. Unless Jenny Balfour had been about to blackmail her father with Philip T. Grackle's latest tax return. According to the return, Philip T. Grackle was the self-employed, sole proprietor of Skyhook Investments, a small business apparently operating out of his apartment. The address was certainly the same.

The only difference was the name.

According to his tax records, Philip T. Grackle wasn't Philip T. Grackle, but a Mr. Paul Henry Starling.

I wondered if the police were aware of that.

I shoved the tax return back in the envelope, tried the next. I could tell just picking it up it contained papers of various sizes. I dumped them out on the floor.

It was quite an array. And it confirmed the fact that Philip T. Grackle was Paul Henry Starling, or at least pretended to be. There was a Social Security card, credit cards, and a driver's license, all in Starling's name. The picture on the license was of the same man whose picture was in the paper, the late Mr. Grackle.

There was also a birth certificate for Paul Henry Starling, and a marriage license taken out in Philadelphia, Pennsylvania, by Mr. Starling and a Miss Felicia Grant. The marriage license was ten years old. It had apparently been used, since divorce papers had also been filed by Miss Grant. There was no final decree.

That started a train of thought. I examined the file folders in the drawer on the floor beside me. Pulled out one for 1997, checked the letterhead. Sure enough, Skyhook Investors listed an address in Philadelphia. And the papers were signed by Mr. Starling.

I was on to something, but I wasn't sure what. Was it possible Mr. Grackle/Starling had been killed by a vindictive ex-wife?

I picked up the next envelope, undid the clasp, and pulled out the contents.

It was a number of eight-by-ten photos. They showed a woman in varying stages of undress. That is, varying from G-string and push-up bra to absolutely nothing. In some pictures the woman was spreading her legs, in others her posterior. In a couple of pictures, a naked man was present, doing the sort of things naked men tend to do in the presence of naked women.

I had never seen the naked man before in my life.

The naked woman was Jenny Balfour's mother.

Jackpot.

I was beginning to sweat. This was not what I was looking for. Or, rather, it was what I was looking for, but not what I'd been hoping to find. Not that I had any allegiance to Jenny Balfour's mother, but still. If ever there was a motive for murder, this was it. And Mrs. Balfour had been there that night, just before her daughter. Who had gone in and out of the apartment as if Mr. Grackle hadn't had much to say.

No wonder Mom was such a bundle of nerves.

No wonder she had thrown me out the front door.

No wonder she was still so limber.

Stop it.

Naughty.

I shoved the pictures back in the envelope and reached for the next one.

From outside the window came a squeal of brakes.

In New York City, that's no big deal. You hear brakes squeal, horns honk, sirens wail all the time, and it never has anything to do with you. As a New Yorker you get so used to it, you don't even hear it anymore.

This one I heard. Maybe because the magnitude of where I was and what I'd found had raised my paranoia level to the *nth* degree. Anyway, I tuned right in. That squeal of brakes was for me.

I jumped up, raced to the window.

The police car double-parked below was still rocking from having slammed to a sudden stop.

The burly figure of Sergeant Thurman was climbing out.

I raced to the desk, dug the instruction manual out of the drawer, and stuck it in the accordion file folder.

I raced into the bedroom, flung up the window, and hurled the file folder down into the side alley.

I raced back to the file cabinet, slammed the false bottom, and replaced the drawer.

I raced to the kitchen, snatched the phone off the wall and punched in the number.

"Rosenberg and Stone," Wendy/Janet said.

"It's an emergency! Get me Richard!"

She didn't argue, but she put me on hold, which was almost worse. Time was a paradox: It seemed an eternity before Richard came on the line, but those same seconds brought Thurman into the building like lightning.

Richard was at his peevish best. "Yes?"

"Take this down. Felicia Grant Starling, Philadelphia, Pennsylvania. She's the widow of Paul Henry Starling, alias Philip T. Grackle."

"Well, bully for her," Richard said. "Stanley, is there a point to this?"

I could hear Sergeant Thurman thundering down the hall.

"Felicia Grant Starling!" I cried desperately. "Got it, Richard?"

"I got it," Richard snarled ominously. "What about her?"

"She's your client," I said, and slammed down the receiver as Sergeant Thurman crashed through the door.

Thirty-one

THE ADA WAS HAVING NONE OF IT. BERT KINSEY, A NO-NONSENSE prosecutor, knew a blow job when he saw one. He just didn't know what to do about it. As a criminal prosecutor, he'd never had to deal with Richard Rosenberg before. But he'd probably heard stories. And he clearly wasn't happy.

"Mr. Rosenberg, your client was apprehended in the crime scene."

"*Apprehended?*" Richard said. "Now, there's a word. *Apprehended.* Is that how we wish away police brutality and false arrest?"

"Nothing false about it. Or perhaps your client failed to see the crime scene ribbon."

"Was I talking about that?" Richard said. "How can we have a discussion if you're gonna change the subject? I was talking about the *way* in which my client was apprehended. If you would like to inspect that crime scene, I believe you can find an indentation where he was slammed up against the wall."

"Here again, the words *crime scene*, which you concede we are talking about—"

"Concede? Whoa! I don't believe I made a concession."

"You referred to the crime scene."

"So did you. Was that a concession?"

"I'm referring to the fact your client was there."

161

"I'm referring to the fact my client was *physically abused* there. If that's a concession, I'll eat it."

"The point is, your client was at a crime scene where he had no right to be."

"Can we have a stenographer taking this down?"

"What?"

"If you're going to make statements of fact that are in error, I would like to have them taken down. Otherwise, how can I call you into account?"

"See," Thurman said. "He's going to squirm out of it. I told you he would."

Kinsey put up his hand to silence the officer. "Mr. Rosenberg, I understand you're very successful in civil court. This is a criminal matter. We do things somewhat differently."

"I hope you still do them according to law."

"Oh, we do. We just require that perpetrators do also."

"Are you referring to my client as a perpetrator?"

"Certainly not. I'm just stating a principle. Now I'm going to state some facts. Your client was apprehended at a crime scene. He is being charged with criminal trespass, obstruction of justice, and conspiring to conceal a crime. He has made no explanation whatsoever and demanded an attorney. He certainly has that right. And if you would like to accompany him while he is arraigned and arrange for his bail, you certainly have that right. But if you're here merely to make empty threats about police brutality and false arrest, I, for one, do not care to listen."

Richard clamped his lips together in a firm line. "Fine. Arraign him, then," he snapped.

I was taken downstairs to a holding cell. Richard didn't go with me. But then, neither did Sergeant Thurman. It was a private cell. I wasn't sure why I warranted one, whether it was my suit, my attorney, or the nature of the offense, but I was glad. Sergeant Thurman had once thrown me into the drunk tank with the great unwashed. It was an experience I will always remember.

About two hours later I was led, handcuffed, into court. Richard was there. So was ADA Kinsey. So were the judge, the bailiff, the court reporter, and a few dozen other people, most likely attorneys and clients.

The judge, identified by the bailiff as the Honorable Judge Hobbs, presiding, had a gray beard and thick eyeglasses. He looked at the arrest warrant and said, "What have we here?"

"This is Stanley Hastings, Your Honor. He was apprehended in the apartment in which Philip T. Grackle was murdered. He is charged with criminal trespass and obstruction of justice."

"Very well. Mr. Hastings, how do you plead?"

Richard was on his feet. "Richard Rosenberg, Your Honor. Attorney for the defendant. I would like to ask that all charges be dismissed and my client be released."

Judge Hobbs smiled. "I'm sure you would, Mr. Rosenberg. But this is an arraignment, not a probable cause hearing. All I'm interested in is how you plead."

Kinsey grinned broadly at seeing his rival rebuffed.

Richard whipped a paper from his briefcase. "Approach, Your Honor?"

Judge Hobbs frowned, motioned him up to the bench.

ADA Kinsey trotted up behind. "You're not going to let him argue."

Judge Hobbs raised one eyebrow. "Thank you for instructing me on what I'm going to do."

Kinsey flushed.

"Mr. Rosenberg," Judge Hobbs said, "think twice before wasting the court's time. The court would *particularly* not like to have technicalities argued. As it has already instructed you, this is not the time and place for such arguments. Should you persist in doing so, the court would feel that you were not listening to the court, that you were not heeding the words of the court, that you were, in fact, *in contempt* of court. Is that clear?"

"Perfectly, Your Honor."

"Then what could you possibly have to tell me?"

"I have a retainer here signed by Felicia Grant Starling, widow of Paul Henry Starling, empowering me to act as the conservator of her husband's estate, which she stands to inherit."

Judge Hobbs looked at Richard as if he just revealed himself to be an attorney from another planet. "I'm thrilled for you. Am I supposed to be impressed by the fact you have managed to find gainful employment?"

"No, Your Honor. You're supposed to take judicial cognizance of the fact Philip T. Grackle is an alias of the late Paul Henry Starling. Felicia Starling is his widow. She has employed me to conserve his estate. It is therefore not only my right, but my duty, to take charge of her husband's personal effects. Mr. Hastings is an investigator in my employ. He was in the process of inventorying Mrs. Starling's apartment when he was illegally prevented from doing so by the police."

"Mrs. Starling's apartment!" ADA Kinsey cried incredulously.

Judge Hobbs held up his hand. "I do not wish to get embroiled in a property title debate."

"But that's the whole point," Kinsey said. "It's not her apartment, and he knows it."

Judge Hobbs cut him off with a look. "One more comment and I'll have *you* up for contempt. Mr. Rosenberg, you claim the defendant was in the apartment legally?"

"Yes, of course."

"How did he get in."

"I don't know, Your Honor."

"You don't know?"

"I haven't had a chance to discuss the matter. I was called and advised that my client was in jail. I was astounded, of course. I rushed down here, to find myself confronted with hostility and suspicion. And, if I may say so, a rather bullying tone. My client, understandably, had declined to talk outside my presence. Once I arrived, no one wanted to hear anything outside of a complete confession. Naturally, they didn't get one. Instead, my client was dragged off, placed in a cell, and brought here. So I have no idea how he got in the apartment, because I didn't discuss it with him. However, my client, Mrs. Starling, was the wife of Mr. Starling, and undoubtedly retained her keys."

"How can you say that?" ADA Kinsey raged. "There's no evidence they ever lived in that apartment together."

"That will do," Judge Hobbs said. "I thought I made it clear I didn't want the case argued now. Mr. Prosecutor, may I point out that a dismissal is not a bar to future prosecution. But, for the time being, your grounds for proceeding against the defendant are very shaky, at best. The charges are dismissed, and the prisoner is free to go."

Thirty-two

Outside the Criminal Court Building, Richard said, "Dare I ask?"

"I'm not sure you want to."

"Yeah, but I better."

"How come?"

"You're going to be arrested again."

"You think?"

"I know. That ADA's pissed. Right now he's on the phone to Philadelphia, getting some cooperation from the so-called widow."

"You might wanna call her first."

"Thanks for the suggestion," Richard said. "I never would have thought of it. How *did* you get into that apartment?"

"You don't want to know."

Richard grimaced. "That bad."

"Worse."

"I'm your attorney. Anything you tell me is privileged."

"Even if I confess to a crime?"

"Are you about to confess to a crime?"

"Not at all. I'm carefully *not* confessing to a crime."

"Don't pull that shit. I'm the lawyer here."

"Glad to hear it. Suppose you can get a restraining order on the police stopping them from entering that apartment?"

"Sure. Right after I balance the national budget and institute world peace. You were discovered in the apartment, and we know Grackle's an alias and he's got an ex-wife. They're gonna search."

"I hope it's Thurman."

"Why."

"He won't search well."

"It doesn't matter."

"Why?"

"He'll search everything."

"Maybe. Anyway, do *we* have the right to go back in?"

"We have the right. Do we have the means?"

"You might ask the widow for a key."

"I did."

"And?"

"What do you think? Starling left her. My phone call was the first she knew of the place."

"Judge Hobbs isn't going to like that."

"No shit. Try and see he doesn't hear it."

"I'll do my best. Okay, Richard. Thanks for bailing me out."

Richard looked hurt. "You're keeping me in the dark."

"For the time being, it's the best place for you."

"Okay. Tell me this. Is what we want in that apartment?"

I grimaced.

"Yes and no."

Thirty-three

Mrs. Balfour was quite fetching in a blue scoop-neck sweater and short black skirt. Her hair bobbing loose on her neck gave her a girlish look.

"Going out?" I said.

She recognized me, but didn't try to slam the door.

"What's this I hear?" she demanded. "You were in court."

"How did you know that?"

"What difference does it make?"

"None. It's just rather interesting. My court appearance wasn't news. I wonder how it got around."

"My husband has connections."

"I bet he does, to get off the hook and leave his daughter on."

Her face flushed. "*Damn you.*"

"Why don't you ask me in and close the door. That way when you hurl me against it I'll still be inside."

"I have nothing to say to you."

"Actually, you do. I was in Grackle's apartment. The police wonder what I found. I bet you do too."

She glared at me defiantly a moment. Then her eyes faltered. "Come in."

I walked in, looked around. From the inside the house looked perfectly

normal. I don't know what I expected. An octagonal dining room, perhaps. A circular ramp.

"Let's go in and sit down," I said. "We have something to discuss,
and it's not going to be easy."

She faltered again and led me into a living room furnished with
a glass table, leather couch, and butterfly chairs, tremendously
uncomfortable-looking furnishings for one with money. I sat on the
couch, found it not as hard as I'd imagined. She continued to stand.

"Okay," she said. "What's your pitch?"

"I know you were there that night, and I know why. Paying Grackle
off, just like everybody else. What I want to know is, how much money
did you bring him, was he alive when you got there, was he alive when
you left, and did you pay him off?"

"That's all you wanna know?"

"Figure of speech. That's all I wanna know for starters."

She sat down in one of the butterfly chairs, crossed her legs. Seemed
to be considering the question. Her mouth opened slightly. She ran her
tongue around her lips.

I *hoped* she was considering the question. I shifted somewhat on the
couch.

Abruptly she reached a decision. "He was dead. Lying there in the
middle of the floor. I walked in and found him."

"The door was open?"

"The door was ajar. I knocked on it, got no answer. So I peeked in."

"Peeked in, or went in?"

"Peeked in, went in, what's the big deal? I pushed the door open,
took a few steps."

"That's when you saw him dead?"

"That's right."

"No chance he was alive?"

"Not at all. His eyes were open. Staring. It was horrible."

"I'm sure it was. How'd you get in the downstairs door?"

"Huh?"

"Don't you have to ring up and get buzzed in?"

"Yeah, but the buzzer was broken. So the door was left unlocked."

"All the time?"

"I don't know about all the time. But it was then."

"Had it ever been before?"

"No."

"So you'd been there before?"

"I don't wanna discuss it."

"How'd you know it was broken?"

"What do you mean?"

"Grackle was dead. You buzz the buzzer, get no answer. Of course not. The guy's dead. What made you think it wasn't working?"

"He said it wasn't."

"When?"

"What difference does that make?"

"Humor me. When'd he tell you? It wasn't when you were there before, because you say it was never broken before."

"What are you, a lawyer? What's with the questions?"

"Just trying to understand. You claim you never buzzed the doorbell, because you knew it wasn't working when you got there. You just pushed the door open and went upstairs?"

"Yeah. So?"

"How'd you know?"

She sighed in exasperation. "He called me, okay? Said the buzzer was broken, but the door would be unlocked."

"He called you here? When? That afternoon?"

"I don't wanna talk about it."

"Okay," I said. "So you walked in, saw Grackle on the floor. When you saw he was dead, you searched his files."

"Who says I did?"

"Don't be silly. You were paying blackmail. The blackmailer was dead. Of course you're gonna take the evidence. So did you find it?"

She said nothing, glared at me.

"You didn't, did you? That must have been frustrating. So you gave up. Good thing, or your daughter would have found you in there."

"Do you have a point, Mr.? . . . "

"Hastings. Yes, I do. The police found me searching the apartment. That's got them thinking. Odds are, they're searching the place right now. What do you think they'll find?"

"What did *you* find?"

"Evidence of blackmail."

"They caught you with it?"

"No."

"It's still there?"

"Unless they found it."

She took a breath, said, bitterly, "Why couldn't you leave things alone?"

"Why couldn't you talk to me the first time I came out here?"

"Why should I? What's so special about you?"

"You're talking to me now."

It was one of those remarks, the minute it slips out, you wanna kick yourself in the head.

Her eyes flashed. "Yeah. Because you said you found something. Well, maybe you did, maybe you didn't. So far, I haven't heard a thing to convince me one way or another."

"I found the evidence. I couldn't take it. It's still there."

"Oh, yeah," she challenged. "What evidence?"

"Nude pictures."

Her mouth fell open. She blinked, stammered, "Nude . . . nude pictures?"

"That's right."

"You mean . . . you mean? . . . " Her face twisted in horror. ". . . of Jenny?"

I frowned.

Time out.

Reality check.

Either Mrs. Balfour was one hell of an actress, or she really was afraid the pictures were of her daughter.

I shook my head. "No. Not Jenny. Pictures of you."

She stared at me a moment. Then her lips twisted in a grin. "Get out of here. No, I mean it. You get the hell out. Come in here, running a bluff. I thought you had something, but I guess you don't. I can't *believe* I let you pump me for information. What a dope I am. What a fool. You get out of here, or I'll call the cops."

"That's probably not a good idea," I warned. "It'll just get 'em interested in you."

She snorted. "You're a piece of work."

"So Grackle wasn't blackmailing you over dirty pictures?"

"What is this, Twenty Questions? Come on! Come on! Let's go." Mrs. Balfour was on her feet, trying to get me up from the couch.

I folded my arms. "What were you paying him for?"

"Go on! Get up!"

"If I can find the evidence, I'd like to get it out of there. It would help to know what it was."

"Yeah, sure. Like you're really gonna find something the police can't."

"You'd be surprised. What is it?"

Mrs. Balfour looked disgusted. "I knew you didn't know anything. I should have trusted my instincts. You had me going. You just seemed so sure."

"Now who's kidding who? Look here, Mrs. Balfour. I saw the pictures. Don't you wanna talk?"

"You don't give up, do you? Nice try, but it didn't work. I admire your persistence, but you're running a bad bluff."

That was annoying.

I wasn't bluffing. I'd *seen* the pictures. *She* was bluffing, pretending they didn't exist.

There was also the bit about finding Grackle dead.

According to Jenny, her mother left Grackle very much alive.

It occurred to me I was not having much luck with these Balfour women.

Thirty-four

MACAULLIF DROPPED TWO BICARBONATE OF SODA TABLETS IN A HUGE glass of water, stirred them around. He leaned back in his desk chair and regarded the frothy mixture with displeasure.

"You don't have to drink it," I said.

He cocked an eye. "You gonna tell me what you've done?"

"Yes."

"Then I gotta drink it."

"Pepto Bismol might be more soothing. That stuff just churns it up."

"Now you're a doctor?"

"Not at all."

"You're advising against Alka-Seltzer?"

"No. I'm just suggesting you take Pepto Bismol first. Then the Alka-Seltzer won't burn through your stomach lining."

MacAullif grimaced. "God save me."

"Advil might help that headache."

"You want a fat lip?"

"Just a suggestion."

MacAullif downed the Alka-Seltzer in a series of mighty gulps. One might have thought he was drinking poison. He put down the glass, belched tremendously, and groaned.

"Ever think of doing commercials?" I asked.

"There's a desperate tone to your joking," MacAullif said. "Like whatever this is is so bad it's blown every fuse in your nervous system. Come on, let's have it. What'd you do this time?"

"Thurman caught me at the crime scene."

I told MacAullif what had happened. His incredulity was comical, his sarcasm unsurpassed. I think the only thing that stopped him from leaping over his desk and strangling me was the fact it was so bad he couldn't really believe what he was hearing. Which was even more remarkable in that I left a lot of details out.

I left in a few I thought he'd like.

"Nude pictures of the *mother*?" MacAullif said. "What the hell does that mean?"

"I assume she took her clothes off and posed for a camera."

"Shithead. You know what this does to the case?"

"It complicates it somewhat."

"Now there's the understatement of the week. We got the mother going to the apartment before the daughter, and, by her own statement, leaving the guy dead. You throw in the blackmail photos, she's lookin' awful good. Even Thurman's gonna like her for this."

"Thurman doesn't know she was there."

"Yeah, but when he finds those blackmail photos. . . ."

"He won't."

MacAullif's eyes were wide as saucers. "Are you telling me you took those blackmail photos out of the apartment?"

"No, I'm very carefully *not* telling you I took those blackmail photos out of the apartment. You really should listen to what I say, MacAullif."

MacAullif took out his gun and shield, laid them on the desk. "I'll just resign. It's easier. Who needs a pension, anyway?"

"Right. And why wait to be prosecuted? I'll just check into the nearest jail."

"Safest place for you. How'd you get into that apartment?"

"Richard's representing Grackle's widow in conserving his estate."

"She had the keys?"

"She was married to the guy."

"She had the keys?"

"It stands to reason."

"Did you get into that apartment with her keys?"

"No one's asked me that yet."

"Why the hell not?"

"Richard wouldn't let them."

"I beg your pardon?"

"We were in court. Richard was manipulating things."

"You were in court?"

"Didn't I mention that?"

"There were gaps in your story."

"Well, they caught me in the apartment. What did you think they were gonna do, give me a medal?"

"What did they charge you with?"

"Breaking and entering, and compounding a felony. But Richard got it dismissed."

"How?"

"Widow's his client."

"Right. What are you gonna do when they find out she never had a key?"

"The case will be solved by then."

"Not at this rate. Now it looks like the mother did it, and the cops don't even know it."

I bit back a smile. I had MacAullif hooked good. There he was, saying *the cops* just like he wasn't one of them.

"Yeah, but she says she didn't do it."

"And you believe her?"

"Yes, I do."

"She look good in those pictures?"

"Not bad."

"Then she couldn't *possibly* have done it. Not with your storybook mentality. Beautiful naked women are never guilty."

"Ever read *I, the Jury?*"

"What?"

"Mickey Spillane. When I was a kid, I read the ending over and over."

"What are you talking about?"

"Your naked-woman theory. Anyway, you're missing the big picture, MacAullif."

"Am I? Well, I would be delighted to have it pointed out to me."

"The naked pictures don't faze Mommy at all. When I brought it up, she thought they must be pictures of her daughter."

MacAullif frowned. "That makes no sense."

"Tell me about it. The woman copped to bein' there, findin' the corpse, runnin' out. She also admits to searching for blackmail evidence, which she did not find. The naked photos fit in perfectly. Except, for some reason, they don't."

"In your estimation," MacAullif pointed out. "Which has never been wrong before."

"Granted," I admitted. "But I'm telling you, the pictures didn't bother her. In which case, she must have been paying him off for something else."

"Such as?"

"I don't know. But, whatever it was, the evidence must be in that apartment."

"*Be?* As in, *is there now?*"

"In a manner of speaking."

"I'm sure I don't wanna know what manner that is. I think that's a long shot, and I think you're wrong. If there are naked pictures, they have to be it." MacAullif peered at me quizzically. "Is that why you're here? To have me talk you out of this idiocy?"

"No. There's more. According to Mrs. Balfour, the downstairs door was unlocked, so she didn't have to buzz up."

"And that's important because? . . . "

"Come on, MacAullif. Just 'cause you're pissed, don't make me spoonfeed you. The guy's dead, he's not answering his bell. If she's telling the truth, the buzzer's out, the downstairs door is open, so she can go right up and find the body. If so, the killer must have done that deliberately."

"Why? Doorbells fail all the time."

"Yeah, but look at the timing. The buzzer breaks that very day. Grackle calls Mrs. Balfour, tells her the downstairs door will be open."

"Oh, now he arranged his own death?"

"Don't be dumb."

"Me? You're the one feeding me this shit. So, what about the girl? Did *she* know the buzzer was broken? Did *she* know the downstairs door was unlocked?"

"I haven't talked to her."

"You were playin' kissy-poo in the front seat with her."

"That was before I talked to the mother. I didn't know the buzzer was out."

"And, god forbid you should learn any details on your own. Okay, say the buzzer was out. So what?"

"It's an interesting detail that seems to have escaped Sergeant Thurman's attention. I'm hardly in the position to point it out to him now."

"You son of a bitch."

"It's a no-brainer, MacAullif. Tip off the ADA to check on the buzzer. If it doesn't work, he'll find out why."

"It's not my case."

"Yeah, but the investigating officer's Thurman. You can second-guess him with a wink and a nod."

MacAullif frowned. "Say the buzzer wire's cut. That just substantiates the mother's story, which no one's ever heard."

"It's also a point for the daughter. She's gotta explain how she got in."

"I thought she claims the guy was alive."

"She does. But she hasn't told her story yet. It may be subject to change."

"Wonderful." MacAullif grimaced, rubbed his stomach. "Any more work you want me to do for you?"

I looked at the empty glass on his desk.

"That's probably enough for one bicarbonate."

Thirty-five

MACAULLIF CALLED ME ON MY CELL PHONE ON MY WAY TO SIGN UP Jack Ham, the victim of a cruel city government that failed to adequately pave its streets, causing the gentleman to stumble on his appointed rounds, most likely selling crack.

I answered while driving. "Hello?"

"Something's up," MacAullif said. "Lid's on tight, and Sergeant Thurman's prancin' around like his wife just had a baby."

"Maybe his wife just had a baby," I suggested.

"I doubt if they'd clamp the lid on that. Odds are, he found something in the apartment, but I don't know what."

"Neither do I."

"Wouldn't be a bunch of naked photos, would it?"

"I sure hope not. You manage to plant the seed?"

"What?"

"About the downstairs door. Any word on that?"

"Give me a break," MacAullif said. "I'm not in the loop, nor do I wanna be. Thurman's all excited about some theory of the case. Be a hard time to sell him another."

"You're saying you didn't do it?"

I could imagine MacAullif turning bright purple, reaching for pills. "Sorry," I said. "I'm just touchy. So Thurman's back from the crime scene?"

"That's right."

"And you have no idea what he found?"

"You're two for two."

"I guess the only way to tell is go over there."

"Yeah, well I wouldn't do it."

"Why not?"

"You got a death wish? Even a moron like Thurman's gonna stake the place out."

"Yeah? And how many cops will that take?"

"One."

"He's gonna stake the place out with one cop?"

"Don't be stupid. He'll put him *in* the apartment."

"Really? Interesting."

"Don't try to go in there."

"I wouldn't think of it. So you got no idea what Thurman found?"

"How many times do I have to say it?"

"And you got no idea what the cops have on the girl in the first place?"

"You may have no idea. I've got plenty."

"Oh?"

"Aside from the traffic cop, they got her fingerprints in the apartment. Apparently the girl wasn't careful about it. There are none on the knife, but they're on everything else."

"Any chance they might wind up on the knife?"

"What do you mean?"

"I understand the cops lifted the prints."

"You understand that?"

"Well, that's what it looked like to me. Any chance a print gets mislabeled? A cop tryin' to write *doorknob* accidently writes *knife handle*?"

"No way. Thurman's dumb, but he's straight."

"Suppose the ADA asks another cop to slip one over on him?"

"Are you on your cell phone?"

"What about it?"

"I hate these goddamn radio waves bouncing around the city. You never know who hears what."

"It's the wireless bit that bothers you? A nice phone line you'd feel perfectly secure?"

"Fuck you. No one's framing anyone."

"Glad to hear it. What else they got on the girl?"

"That's not enough? They know where she works. They know she was payin' the guy off."

"How do they know that?"

"I don't know, but they do."

"That's still mighty thin."

"Yes, it is. That's why Sergeant Thurman's down at the Criminal Court Building runnin' a victory lap. He found something made an iffy case ice cold."

"And you got no idea what it is?"

"For the third time, I do not. But your insistence on asking begins to look suspiciously like a ploy. Which makes me wonder, do *you* have any idea what it is?"

"Thought you'd never ask. Grackle has a file system. Long about ninety-nine he switched over from manual to computer. And he's got nothin' about the girl in his computer files. Which is strange, since she's not old enough to have anything predate ninety-nine."

"So what?"

"Fuck you, shithead!"

"I beg your pardon?"

"Not you. Some son of a bitch just cut me off."

"Are you still driving?"

"I have an appointment. Life doesn't stop just because you have a case."

"I don't have a case. This is not my case."

"Of course not. And life didn't stop because of it. Anyway, the point is there's nothing on the computer, and don't ask me how I know. So he found something about the girl, it's gotta be in the file cabinet. Except the file cabinet's got the wrong dates."

"So what could he have found?"

"In the apartment? Hard to say."

Which was absolutely true. It was *very* hard to say. I didn't want to admit to not telling the police about finding two hundred and seventy grand in cash, for instance.

Not to mention throwing the file folder out the window.

Thirty-six

I FOUND A PARKING METER ON THIRD AVENUE AND STROLLED PAST THE front of Grackle's town house just to see if any oversized cops would come rushing out and beat me up. None did.

I walked back the other way, surveyed my options. The alley beside the town house was fronted by a rather formidable-looking iron fence, two stories high, topped with spikes, barbed wire, ground glass, razor blades, land mines, heat sensing devices, and a guided missile system. Maybe that's just how it looked to me. Anyway, my chance of getting inside it I put around zero.

The other side of Grackle's town house unfortunately abutted a townhouse, which abutted another town house, and another town house, and so on, and so on.

I continued on around the block and met with more success. The alley next to a fish store on Lexington was open, allowing easy access to the rather smelly dumpster in back. I detoured around it and found myself in a labyrinth of town house backyards, some of which had high fences, some of which had low fences, and some of which had none. It remained for me only to find Grackle's building.

There were no numbers, and the buildings didn't look anything like themselves from the rear. Fortunately, I had a clue. Grackle's town house was the one with the alley next to it.

I found it easily, slid over a six-foot fence, and dropped into the backyard, right into a pile of garbage can lids. Why the hell anyone would stack up garbage can lids was beyond me, but someone had, and I hit 'em all.

I staggered to my feet, ducked behind a garbage can, which of course had no lid, and looked to see if the police guard, if any, had noticed my approach. Apparently, none had. Either that or they'd been on to me ever since I passed the front of the building, and I was walking into an elaborate trap.

After a few moments of galloping paranoia, I crept out from behind the garbage can and worked my way down the alley.

The file folder wasn't there. Of course it wasn't. Not with Sergeant Thurman so happy. What else could he have found?

I gave the alley a good once-over, just to make sure I hadn't over-looked anything, and got the hell out of there.

I wasn't about to climb over the garbage can lids if I could help it, so I vaulted over the side fence into the neighbor's yard. And then into the neighbor's neighbor's yard, when that back fence proved too high.

Two houses down I stopped, blinked.

The house had an alleyway.

How was that possible? I'd only seen one alleyway from the other side.

The answer was simple. I'd started looking for alleyways when I'd got to Grackle's town house. His alleyway was the first one I'd noticed. There was no alleyway after Grackle's town house, but there was one before. The one before was the one I'd just inspected.

The one I was looking at now was Grackle's.

A silhouette in the upstairs window was a police officer.

I instinctively shrunk back into the shadows. But the cop wasn't looking out the window. He seemed to be flipping the pages of a mag-azine. I wondered if it was *Penthouse*. If so, he must be in the bedroom.

And the file folder must be right under the window.

Only, I couldn't see from there, because of the garbage cans in the way. I was having bad luck with garbage cans.

I crept along the side of the building. From his vantage point, the cop could only see me if he stuck his head out the window. There was no reason to believe he would do that. On the other hand, there was no reason to believe he wouldn't.

I kept low, worked my way around the garbage cans.

My cell phone rang.

It sounded loud as a fire alarm.

I dived back behind the garbage cans, fumbled in my jacket pocket, wrenched it out.

Tried to shut it off.

The only way I knew to do that was to answer it.

It was my wife.

"Hello," I whispered. For the benefit of those who sit next to me on trains and buses and in waiting rooms, Alice heard me just fine. These are technological advances, not tin-can telephones. You don't have to shout.

"Stanley," Alice said. "Where are you?"

I wasn't about to tell her. "Call you back."

I hung up, switched the phone off, and checked to see if I was in imminent danger of arrest. It appeared I wasn't.

When my blood pressure had dropped into the relatively comfortable range of twice normal, I checked Grackle's window again and crept around the garbage cans.

And there it was, the file folder, right where I had thrown it. I don't know why I was so surprised. I guess I felt like the coal miners in the old *Beyond the Fringe* sketch, who find a lump of coal and are delighted because it's the very thing they're looking for.

I wasn't standing there thinking this, by the way. I was creeping down the alley, grabbing the file folder, and hightailing it the hell out of there. I did stop somewhere along the way, after the third or fourth fence or so, to look in the file folder to see if it happened to contain Grackle's blackmail evidence. With my luck, it could just as easily have been some English professor's *Who's Afraid of Virginia Woolf?* term papers instead. But, no, like the coal miner, I had found exactly what I was looking for.

Okay, so now I had the porno pictures.

The only question was what did I do with them?

Thirty-seven

"OUCH!"

I peered over Alice's shoulder. "Don't try this at home."

"No kidding."

"Actually, I *was* kidding. If you'd care to try this at home. . . ."

"In your dreams."

Alice flipped to the next picture. "My, my!"

"How about trying *that* at home?"

"Stanley, you shouldn't even be looking at these."

"What?"

"You know the woman. It's an invasion of privacy."

"*You're* looking at them."

"I don't know the woman."

"Would you be looking if you did?"

"It's different. I'm a woman."

"For which I'm grateful."

"The point is, I'm a woman. So I wouldn't be invading her privacy."

"Suppose she's gay."

"Is she?"

"I don't think so."

"Then why suppose it?"

"Alice, it's a moot point. I've *seen* the pictures."

"I know. We're discussing whether you *should* have."

"Why?"

"Stanley, you're not going to ogle these pictures if you know it's wrong."

"Ogle?"

"That's not how you pronounce it?"

"I don't *care* how you pronounce it. I'm not pleased you think I'd do it."

"Give me a break. Any man would do it."

"Then why pick on me?"

"I married you."

"I can't believe you said that."

"Stanley, I don't give a damn how other men behave. It's your behavior that concerns me."

See, now that's why arguing with Alice is a no-win situation. Alice *does* care what other men think. And if that were her point—the fact her sensitivities were outraged by the proclivities of the male gender in general—she could argue it equally well, and my protestations that I was an individual, a special case, and no less than her husband, would fall on deaf ears. I avoid arguments with Alice like the plague.

I tried a simple deflection. "All right," I said, "if Thurman didn't find these photos, then what did he find?"

"How about the money?" Alice said.

"The two hundred and seventy thousand in cash?"

"Yeah. What about that?"

I shook my head. "Doesn't work for me."

"Why not?"

"Thurman's too happy. That would compute if he kept the money, but Thurman's straight. Not that he's a saint, I think he's just too dumb to steal. But he wouldn't keep the money. So I don't think he found it."

"Just finding it wouldn't account for his mood?"

"What he found clinches the case against the girl. The money wouldn't do that."

"Why not?"

"What connects it to her? If she was paying blackmail, some of that money might be hers. But if they can't prove it in court, it doesn't help."

"What if they could prove it in court?"

"How?"

"I don't know. But say they could."

I shook my head. "Doesn't do it for me."

"Why not?"

"If the money was hers, she obviously didn't pay him that night."

"How do you know?"

"Because the money was in the secret compartment. He's not going to put it in the secret compartment in front of her. And if he did, it wouldn't be there, 'cause she'd take it out."

"What if she doesn't care about the money? What if she kills him, panics, just wants to get the hell out of there?"

"Not a prayer."

"How come?"

"The money was under this file folder. She may not take the money, but she sure as hell is gonna take the blackmail evidence. I don't care how panicked she is, she's gonna stop for that."

"Yeah, but . . ."

"Yeah, but what?"

"So what did Thurman find?"

"We know he didn't find this file, because I've got it. But if he found evidence that implicates the girl, it wasn't in this file folder. So she's not takin' this file folder, 'cause it's not the evidence she wants."

"But the evidence she wants she leaves behind?"

I rubbed my head. Tried to follow. "Alice, wasn't all this predicated on the assumption Sergeant Thurman found the money?"

"Yes." Alice cocked her head. "That would seem to be a pretty shaky premise."

My eyes widened. "Alice, it was *your* idea in the first place."

"Yes, of course. I had to propose it in order for you to work out how illogical it was. Which you did very nicely, I might add."

"I did?"

"Absolutely. I think we can conclude Sergeant Thurman didn't find the money."

"That's what I said."

"Yes, and you were right. Tell me, did you discuss this with MacAullif?"

"Of course not. He doesn't know I found the money."

"Why didn't you tell him?"

"I didn't want to make him guilty of withholding evidence."

"It's not really evidence."

"Yeah. I'm sure that would be a comfort to MacAullif when he's suspended and sent to jail."

"There's no need to be sarcastic," Alice said. "Did you tell Richard?"

"Christ, no."

"Why not? He's your attorney. It's a privileged communication."

"Maybe."

"No maybe about it. He's your lawyer."

"It's a fine line when you start confessing to crimes."

"Stanley, you think there's any power on earth that could pry that information out of Richard?"

"That's not why I held out on him. Richard never met a buck he didn't like. If I tell him there's a small fortune in that apartment, his position is gonna be that's our money."

"Our money?"

"Not our money. His money. He's representing the widow. He'll take the position that she inherits as surviving spouse."

"What about the fact the money was illegally obtained?"

"How is he supposed to know that? There's no reason for him to make any such assumption. Grackle had money. Grackle's dead. The money belongs to the widow. A third of it belongs to Richard. Case closed."

"All right," Alice said. She turned her attention back to the file. "What else have we got?"

"I haven't looked."

Alice raised her eyebrows. "You looked only at the dirty pictures?"

"Alice, I came straight home with this. I didn't stop along the way. You tore it out of my hands the minute I got in the door."

"Tore it out of your hands?"

"The point is, I didn't have a chance to look at the other folders."

Alice reached for an envelope and dumped out Grackle's Starling IDs.

"See," I said. "There's proof the guy was Starling."

"I thought you didn't look at any other folders."

"Just this one."

"You saw it before the photos?"

"That's right."

"So after you saw the pictures, you couldn't look at anything else?"

I ignored the comment, reached for another file. "What have we got here?"

What we had there was a police report of a drug arrest for an Oscar K. Dowling III. I whistled, showed it to Alice.

"Something tells me Oscar K. Dowling the Third's parents don't know about this," Alice said.

"Either that, or their high-society friends don't."

"Really? I would have thought white-collar drug busts were almost fashionable."

"Maybe someone wasn't too happy about this one."

"Well, the police should know about it," Alice said. "How do you plan to go about telling them?"

"Beats me."

I looked at some more files. A DWI arrest of a young Yale student. A statutory rape conviction of a young stockbroker. I continued flipping through files, all remarkably similar, and suddenly stopped dead.

The name Joe Balfour leaped off the page.

I pulled it out, examined it, and whistled.

"What is it?"

"An arrest record for Joe Balfour dating back to nineteen-ninety."

"What's the charge?"

"Aggravated assault, and drunk and disorderly."

"Aggravated assault?"

"That's the charge. Let's see what happened." I flipped the page. "Here's the court disposition. The aggravated assault was dismissed. The drunk and disorderly was reduced to a misdemeanor count of public intoxication, which was also dismissed. "

Alice looked at me incredulously. "He was blackmailing him over that?"

"Wait. There's more." I flipped another page. "Uh-oh."

"What is it?"

"It's a death certificate. For a C. Fletcher Headly." My eyes widened. "Oh, my god!"

"What?"

"That's what the girl said. Just before she slapped me. She said, 'Do you know Headly?' When I gave her a deadpan, she let me have it."

"Gave her a deadpan? Stanley, you're beginning to sound like some film noir PI."

"Skip it, Alice. This is the payoff." I put up my hand. "And never mind the word *payoff*. The point is, Headly's important." I sucked in my breath. "And here's why."

"What is it?"

"The death certificate's dated the day after Balfour's arrest."

"The day after?"

"Sure. Balfour beats the shit out of Headly in a barroom brawl. The cops come. Balfour's arrested. Headly splits before they get there. Headly crawls off, collapses in an alley, and dies. Balfour's arraigned before anyone finds the body. Later that day the police find a drunk dead in an alley. There's no connection to the night before. It means nothing to anyone.

"Except Grackle. Or Starling. Or whatever you want to call him."

"So Balfour really did commit manslaughter."

"Sure. Which stands to reason. Most people aren't good at making up stories. They stick to the truth as much as possible. He committed the crime. But it wasn't twenty-five years ago, it was only thirteen."

"Why would he lie about that?"

"He didn't want to admit he was *wanted* for manslaughter. So he said he'd served time, but his family didn't know. He had to say it happened before he got married, because an astute wife would be apt to notice if her husband went away for three to five."

"You think *I* would?"

"But he was never in jail. Because he was never convicted. Because nobody knew he'd done it except Grackle."

"How did *he* know?"

"That was his business. Finding out things. He found this out. Instead of going to the police, he went to Balfour and turned the screws."

"Turned the screws?"

"Alice."

"It's not enough. That's the problem. You have a death certificate and a dismissed drunk charge. That's a far cry from a homicide. Why would Balfour pay?"

I flipped the page. "Here's why. Witness statement of Alan Rickstein, dated . . . let's see . . . three days after the incident. 'I was in Murphy's bar on the night of June 15, 1990. I saw a fight between Joe Balfour and Fletcher Headly. The fight broke up when the police arrived. Balfour was arrested. Headly ran off.'"

I flipped to the last page. "Here's another. Witness statement of Craig Keyson, taken a week later. 'I was in Murphy's bar on the night of June 15. I saw Joe Balfour beat up Fletcher Headly. Balfour beat him pretty bad. Fletcher was helpless, but Joe just kept hitting him. He only stopped because the cops came. Otherwise I think he would have killed him.'"

I looked up from the paper. "Well, that would seem to be enough."

"Yes, it would," Alice said. "So if Balfour killed Grackle, that's what he would have been looking for. And failed to find."

I frowned. "Maybe, maybe not."

"What do you mean?"

"Grackle was pretty smart—aside from getting killed—I would imagine he took precautions in case anyone ever broke in."

"So?"

"So what if he had a photocopy that was easier to find?"

"That might do it," Alice said. "Is that it?"

"That's it for this file. There's more."

"Let's check 'em out."

We ran through a number of files all remarkably similar.

It was the next to last.

I sucked in my breath.

"What is it?" Alice asked.

"Hospital admission form. For one Jennifer Balfour. Facial lacerations and bruises. Black eye. Broken arm. Sustained in a car accident. Admitted August third, discharged the next day."

"When was this?"

"Two years ago."

"She's healed rather nicely."

"Based on her picture in the paper?"

"Based on your hopeless infatuation. And why is that grounds for blackmail?"

"Let's see." I flipped to the next page. "Uh-oh."

"What is it?"

"Death certificate for a John Doe."

"Oh?"

"Dated the same day Jenny checked into the hospital."

Alice's eyes widened. "Well, isn't that interesting. What did he die of?"

"Trauma to the head."

"That's pretty wide open, isn't it? He could have been mugged. He could have just fallen down. Or—correct me if I'm wrong—he could have been a passenger in a car driven by a drunken teenager."

"You mean? . . . "

"There's gotta be some reason those pages are paper-clipped together. Here, let me see that."

Alice snatched the file out of my hands, flipped back to the admission form. "Hmmm."

"What is it?"

"The blank for 'Ambulance' is checked 'No.' There's also no police report. Wouldn't you expect one with an accident serious enough to put you in the hospital?"

"I suppose."

"So Jenny Balfour wrecks her car. The guy she's with is killed. It's a lonely road, no one around. Jenny calls Daddy, who rushes to the scene and takes charge. He removes all identification from the body and dumps it where it will be found as a John Doe. He rushes his daughter to the hospital and sends a tow truck for her car. The police are never involved." Alice shrugged. "Wouldn't that be lovely grounds for blackmail?"

"You're making an awful lot of assumptions," I said.

"Well, what do you think those papers mean?"

I had no idea. I just knew it wasn't good.

I was not a happy camper. Everything I'd found implicated the Balfours.

I picked up the last folder. Okay, Grackle. I could use a little help here.

I pulled the contents out of the folder.

It was a police rap sheet for one Herman Bertoli. It included convictions for such assorted crimes as receiving stolen property, sale of narcotics, promoting prostitution, aggravated assault, and rape.

The rap sheet was paper-clipped to a page from the newspaper. I removed the paper clip, unfolded the page.

It took awhile to find.

The page was from the *New York Post*, and it was actually a double page, which made four pages in all if you counted both sides. Two pages, the centerfold if you will, consisted entirely of celebrity photos, the kind of shots they love to get in the paper. Harrison Ford shopping in Barnes and Noble just like a real person. Jerry Orbach sitting on a park bench in between takes of *Law and Order*.

One of the pictures was a real coup. It showed a New York Knicks star—if they can be considered stars these days, considering the funk the team's in. The ballplayer was enjoying a laugh with a man identified as "Strip Club Owner Darien Mott."

As I say, I'm not good at faces, but I recognized Mr. Mott.

He was Greaseball from Midnight Lace.

Thirty-eight

Darien Mott's face froze the minute I walked in the door. He gestured to his bouncer, and the two of them headed me off.

"Guys, guys," I said. "Let's not make a scene. My business is brief. Let me state it and I'll get out of here."

"Who are you?" Mott demanded.

I smiled. "Well, that's just what I was gonna ask you. Would your name be Mott?"

"What about it?"

"Like the apple juice. Good name. Not too ethnic-sounding. Guy might change his name to Mott if he had a mind."

Mott looked at the bouncer. "Throw him out."

"Probably a bad move, Bertoli," I said.

Mott might have been playing poker. His face never changed. But he put up his hand. "Hold it, Bruno. What do you want?"

"I'd like to talk." I jerked my thumb at the stage. "If we could go somewhere where there aren't so many tits."

Mott considered. "Come on."

He led me around the bar into a small office with a file cabinet, a safe, and a desk. Mott didn't sit, however. He stood there, glaring at me. "What do you want?"

"How'd you know Grackle?"

"Who says I did?"

"That's not important. I'd just like to get the sequence."

"What do you mean?"

"You knew Grackle. Jenny Balfour knew Grackle. That's way too much coincidence. So did she meet him through you, or did you meet him through her?"

"Go fuck yourself."

"That's less than helpful. Could we try again?"

"No, I think you should leave."

"Then can we discuss your pseudonym?"

"My what?"

"Your alias, your nom de plume. The fact Grackle knew you were someone else. Do you think we could discuss that?"

"I don't know what you're talking about."

"Come on, give me a break. You've got a rap sheet as long as my arm. You think no one's gonna recognize you?"

"You think anyone's gonna care?"

"Just you. You're the only one I can think of who might. So when I see Grackle holding on to your rap sheet, I have to ask myself why."

His eyes narrowed. "When you see *Grackle* holding my rap sheet?"

"Oh, aren't you up to date on the murder? Well, I was arrested in Grackle's apartment. Apparently going through his files."

"And you found my rap sheet? Try again."

"Oh? Isn't it there?"

He smiled. "You run a good bluff, but that's all it is, a bluff."

"How do you know?"

Mott frowned. "I think we're done talking."

"How do you know your rap sheet's not in those files?"

"Go on. Run along."

"If I didn't find it, how do I know your name?"

"I'm done talking."

Mott reached over and pushed a button on his desk. The Hulk appeared in the doorway. He said something between a grunt and a belch.

"Show this gentleman the door," Mott said.

I didn't particularly want that to happen. But I didn't have another bluff, and I couldn't think of one, anyway, with two tons of malevolent muscle heading my way. I stepped nimbly toward the door just to show Bruno that force wasn't necessary. He must not have gotten the message, because in less time than it takes to tell, my right arm was rotated in its socket, jammed behind my back, and raised to within two inches of the ceiling.

The technique was quite effective. Not only did I find myself tripping daintily on my tiptoes, but entire portions of my life flashed before my eyes. I had just finished reliving my second year of grade school when I crashed unceremoniously in a heap next to a pile of dog shit by the curb. I remember being righteously indignant that some dog owners were so irresponsible—I always clean up after Zelda. I just had time to feel virtuous when a kick in the stomach made me forget all about it.

Thirty-nine

"You look like shit."

"Thanks, MacAullif."

"What happened to you?"

"A half a ton of bouncer used me for a soccer ball."

"Were you in that topless bar again?"

"I can't seem to stay away."

"It's that girl, isn't it? You just can't get enough of her tits."

"She wasn't there."

"That must have been a disappointment."

"I wasn't looking for her."

"Then why'd you go?"

"Chat with the owner."

"What about?"

"Dead guy named Grackle."

"He feel like talking?"

"Not really."

MacAullif pulled a cigar out of his drawer, began to play his desk like a drum.

"Do you have to do that?"

"Why, you got a headache?"

"I ache all over."

"The bouncer do that?"

"Yeah."

"You pissed at him?"

"Actually, I'm more pissed at his boss."

"You plan to get even?"

"Yeah."

"How?"

"I was hopin' to get him for murder."

MacAullif stopped in middrumroll. "Come again?"

I told MacAullif about Herman Bertoli/Darien Mott's rap sheet.

"So the guy's got a record," MacAullif said. "How'd you happen to see it?"

"I'm going to tell you what I told Mott."

"What's that?"

"I was arrested in Grackle's apartment."

"You mean that rap sheet's there for the police to find?"

"I didn't say that."

"But you saw it there?"

"I didn't say that either."

MacAullif snorted disgustedly. "Talking to you is a real workout. What the hell do you mean?"

"Once again, we're getting into hypothetical territory."

"God save me!"

"The point is, the guy's dirty and Grackle knew it. So the guy had every reason to kill him."

"That's mighty thin."

"It's the same case they have on the girl."

"Trust me, they got more than that."

"Oh? You find out what it is yet?"

"No, but I'm sure they do. For one thing, they can prove she was there."

"They could probably prove he was too if they knew how to go about it."

"And how would that be?"

"I'd tell you, but I don't wanna get kicked again."

"I beg your pardon?"

"It has to do with the doorbell. The one that didn't work."

"Oh, for Christ's sake."

"Which is why I'm not bringing it up. Which is why I'm not asking you if any progress has been made on that front. I do not wish to be used as a punching bag. I would rather just not know."

"What is it with you and the damn doorbell?"

"Someone put the buzzer out of commission. We know it's not Mommy, because Grackle called her and told her."

"So she says."

"Yes, but I think it's true. Otherwise, why bring it up? You see what I mean? If you cut the doorbell to get in, and the cops point it out, you say, 'Oh, yeah, Grackle called and told me it was out and he'd leave the door open.' But you don't call attention to it if you don't have to."

"What if the girl did it?"

"I'll buy you lunch. It's not her speed. The old man maybe, but not her."

"What if it's him?"

"Unlikely. If he's payin' off a crime over ten years old."

"A crime?"

"An alleged crime."

"The guy had no rap sheet. Are you telling me he was convicted under another name?"

"Not at all."

"What are you telling me?"

"As little as possible, MacAullif."

"Yeah, well what you do tell should make sense. You're washin' out the woman 'cause she brought the doorbell up? If she's claiming he was dead, she's gotta bring it up, otherwise, how the hell'd she get in?"

"She just says she found the door was open. She doesn't have to make up a phone call."

"What if there *was* a phone call? She knocks out the bell, Grackle calls and tells her the bell's out?"

I sighed. "MacAullif, you just doin' this to torture me 'cause you won't do the work?"

"The work? Like it's my job?"

"Right, right. It's not your job. You know where Thurman is now?"

"No. Is that my job? Keeping track of Thurman?"

"I just wondered if he was done bragging."

"What if he was?"

"I might try to find someone he'd been bragging to. See if they knew what the hell was going on."

"Not a bad idea," MacAullif said. When I said nothing, he added, "If I could figure any way to get the information myself without appearing too interested, I would."

I mumbled something under my breath that probably sounded less than pleased.

"What was that?" MacAullif said sharply.

"MacAullif, you're my friend. Or, at least, you know me. I was arrested in this case. You could probably evince a mild curiosity just on the strength of that, without anyone considering it unduly suspicious."

"Yeah, I suppose."

"So what's the matter?"

"The pills I been takin' got me all upset. I don't know whether I'm coming or going."

"Oh, for Christ's sake, MacAullif. These things got nothing to do with your head. They're all physical."

"Yeah, but . . ."

"But what?"

"Just takin' 'em has me upset."

"So?"

MacAullif drummed the cigar so hard it snapped in half. He didn't even notice.

"They got me on Prozac."

From the look on MacAullif's face the admission had nearly killed him, and if I said a damn thing about it he was going to rip my lungs out.

I couldn't help it.

"It's not working."

Forty

THE YOUNGER MILLSAP REGARDED ME WITH WARY EYES. "I'M NOT SURE
I should be talking to you."

"I don't know why not."

"You've been arrested in conjunction with the case."

"So's your client."

Millsap grinned nervously. "Yes, she has. But we've been cooperating with the police as much as possible. I don't think they'd like it if
they found out we were cooperating with you."

"And just how have you been cooperating with the police?"

Millsap winced like a golfer who'd just shanked an iron.

I grinned. "Yeah. Shouldn't have told me that, should you? So let me
guess. Jenny hasn't made a statement yet, or else the press would be all
over it. So any cooperation between you and the police means stuff you
leaked. There's probably a few key facts they'd like to know, a few key
facts you'd like to know. You're still adversaries, but you're willing to
trade. Highly unethical, I'm sure. What'd you do, talk in hypotheticals?"

"Damn it."

"Hey, nothing to be ashamed of. This case lends itself to hypotheticals. Anyway, I'm interested in the facts comin' back. Hypothetically,
the police give you any idea what they got on your client? In particular,
whatever Sergeant Thurman's treating as the most important discovery
since the wheel."

Millsap smiled nervously again. "I can't compromise—"

"Of course you can't. But, hypothetically, what might you be up against?"

He considered. "Say there were nude photos. . . ."

I stared at him. "You're kidding!"

"What's so surprising about that? My client's an exotic dancer."

"There's a nice euphemism."

"It's the one I'll use in court."

"If you get there. I'm tryin' to see you don't." I shook my head. "This makes no sense to me. For the reason you said. Your client's a topless dancer. So what if there's nude photos?"

"That, of course, will be my argument. But the cops don't see it that way. Just because she dances nude doesn't mean she does girlie mags. If she did one nude photo shoot just to get dancing work, she might want those pictures back."

"All right. If she killed him to get 'em, why didn't she get 'em?"

"She couldn't find them."

"Why not?"

"She didn't know where to look."

"And Sergeant Thurman did?"

"He had time. She was rushed."

"Oh? She had some appointment that was more important than finding the blackmail pics? I wouldn't like to be arguin' that in front of a jury. According to the prosecution's theory of the case, she killed the man to get the photos, but didn't take the time to find them."

"They'll claim she was interrupted."

"By what?"

"By someone else. Coming to see Grackle."

"Who caught her in the apartment?"

"No. Who scared her off."

"How?"

"They rang the doorbell. She got the hell out of there. She couldn't go down the stairs or she'd have met 'em, so she went up. She waited on the next landing till they went in the apartment, then crept down the stairs and got the hell out."

"That's what she says?"

"Hell, no. That's what they say."

"Then throw it back in their face. That doorbell wasn't workin' that night."

"How do you know?"

"Hasn't your client told you?"

He smiled. "*I* know what my client's told me. I wanna know how *you* know that doorbell wasn't working that night."

"I'm not in a position to tell you that."

"Then I'm not in a position to tell you what my client told me."

"Suppose I learned it from your client?"

"Did you?"

"Is that an admission your client knew it was broken?"

"No, just an attempt to find out how far you'll run your bluff."

I threw up my hands. "Fine, fine. May my house be safe from lawyers. The point is not who claims the doorbell was out, the point is it was. Now, that bit of information needs to be communicated to the police. If you're all palsy-walsy with this ADA, you might make the suggestion."

"And just why should I do that?"

I groaned. "Hey, I'm not trying to hustle you here. You should do that because it helps your client. The downstairs door was open because the buzzer was out. The buzzer was out because the killer disconnected it so the downstairs door would be open. I don't believe your client's the killer. That means the person who disconnected it was someone else. If the cops aren't too ham-handed about investigating it, they might be able to tell who that someone else was."

Millsap frowned, chewed on his lip.

"You gotta discount the fact the advice comes from me. You gotta say to yourself, if it were my investigator bringing me this, I'd think it was pretty good."

"Yeah, but it *isn't* my investigator, so I have to ask myself why. You're not working for me. You're not working for my dad. What's your vested interest in this thing?"

"I'm working for Richard Rosenberg, who's representing the Grackle's widow."

"Who, if my understanding is correct, hadn't seen the guy for years and didn't even know he was dead."

"Which would in no way negate her claim."

"No, but it certainly raises questions as to how she came to file it."

"Don't ask them."

"I beg your pardon?"

"Once again, you're missing the big picture by getting involved in things that don't concern you or your client. What's important is not why I'm involved in this case, it's the fact that I am. I was in that apartment. I took a look at those files. I didn't find those photos. Assuming your client was in that apartment and took a look at those files, *she* didn't find those photos. And whoever the hell killed Grackle didn't find those photos. This would tend to bring up the question, where were the photos?"

"I don't know."

"You know they exist, but not where they came from? Your friendship with the ADA is rather tenuous. I would think a simple, 'Bullshit, where'd you get them?' would suffice."

"Well, it didn't."

"Then I'd refuse to give his story any credence and take the position they didn't exist."

"Yes, that would be so clever, wouldn't it?" Millsap said sarcastically.

I studied his face. Realization dawned. "Of course. He showed them to you. No explanation needed. Just guy stuff. 'Hey, wanna see some pictures?' How'd she look?"

Millsap ground his teeth.

"So, that's the club he's holding over you. Cooperating, hell. If you don't do what he says, he'll leak those pictures to the press. How badly have you had to hurt your client's case?"

"It's not like that."

"What's it like?"

"I think this interview is over."

"That's what everyone says these days. I'm starting to get a complex. Just a few more questions. Does your father know about this? Does your father's client know about this? Have *they* seen the pictures?"

Millsap looked concerned.

"They haven't, have they? You told me more than you intended. Don't worry. I'm not a blabbermouth. Is your father in?"

"Now, look here—"

"No, *you* look here. The cops need to trace the doorbell. I don't care what it takes to get it. I just want it done. So you call 'em and make it happen. While you're at it, find out where those photos were. As soon as you have that information, phone it in to Richard Rosenberg of Rosenberg and Stone. He's the attorney for the widow. Have you got that?"

Millsap looked at me as if I were a blackmailing slimy son of a bitch.

That was a coincidence. I *felt* like a blackmailing slimy son of a bitch.

It didn't feel all that bad.

Forty-one

RICHARD ROSENBERG LOOKED PERPLEXED. THAT WAS GOOD. I'D seldom seen Richard perplexed. It was nice to catch him off stride.

Richard sat behind his desk, sipping some sort of concoction from Starbucks and eating a small sweet roll that looked like it must be all sugar. Richard often ate the most ostentatiously fattening of pastries. The fact he was as thin as a board could be attributed only to the enormous number of calories he burned up in the practice of his profession.

"Stanley," Richard said. "The reason I called you in here is there have been some developments in the case."

I figured there had. I was just about to leave home for an appointment in the Bronx when Wendy/Janet had beeped me into the office.

"What case?" I said innocently.

"The Starling case, of course."

Richard's choice of name for the deceased defined our relative positions in the affair. For me, the case was determining the identity of whoever killed Philip T. Grackle. For Richard, it revolved around the property of Paul Henry Starling.

"And what might those developments be?" I asked.

"I had a very strange phone call this morning from a Mr. Millsap. Jenny Balfour's lawyer. The gentleman felt as the attorney for the decedent's widow I was entitled to share some of the pertinent information in the case."

I nodded. "A most commendable position."

"A most inscrutable position," Richard said. "The guy's divulging information he doesn't have to, with no benefit to him."

"And lawyers never do that?"

"It's one of the first rules of law. Right after signing the retainer."

"Well, that's certainly lucky then. What did the attorney tell you?"

Richard frowned. He seemed extremely unhappy with my attitude. But he couldn't think of just what to say.

It was wonderful.

"He told me what the police have on his client, which is entirely out of place for any attorney."

"Oh? What's that?"

"It seems Sergeant Thurman found some naked pictures the decedent had been blackmailing her with."

"My, my."

"You don't sound surprised."

"Nothing Sergeant Thurman might do would surprise me."

"I was referring to the photos themselves. Not the fact he found them."

"I'm referring to the fact he found them. It is somewhat remarkable, since I searched the place myself."

"Yeah, well, apparently you didn't search well enough."

"Oh?"

"Which is why the good sergeant's so pleased. He came through when you fell down."

"So where were they?"

"In the file cabinet."

I sucked in my breath. "Is that right?" I said casually.

"You just looked in the files. Thurman took the files out, and looked in the bottom of the drawer. And there was an envelope that had slid down between the folders."

My relief was boundless. I nodded. "Good for him."

Richard frowned.

"Aren't those photos part of the estate you're attempting to conserve for Mrs. Starling? Shouldn't you be filing a motion to retrieve them?"

"I'm not in a position to admit I even know about them."

"Why not?"

"It would be betraying the confidence of a fellow attorney."

"And you wouldn't do that?"

"Of course not."

"I'll keep it in mind. If I'm ever on the other side of a case, I'll have my attorney tell you everything he knows on the theory you won't use it."

Richard scowled and picked up his coffee.

"Did Millsap say anything about the doorbell?"

Richard's coffee cup froze on the way to his lips. He set it down on the desk, laced his fingers together, leaned on his elbows. "What a coincidence, your asking me that. As a matter of fact, he did. According to Millsap, late yesterday afternoon the police investigated the buzzer system in the building and determined the bell in Starling's apartment was out. Further investigation revealed that the reason it was out was that someone had cut the wire just under the cellar stairs. Not that difficult to do. Anyone leaving any of the apartments in the building would have access to the stairs. It would merely be a question of knowing which wire to clip. Luckily for the perpetrator, the wires were labeled, making it an extremely simple job."

"Well, that's interesting," I said. "Anything else of note?"

"Yes. To reach the wire, a person would have had to lean out over the stairwell. The easiest way to do that would be to hold on to a water pipe."

"Don't tell me."

"That's right. The police got three clean latents off the pipe. Not perfect, but good enough to get a match."

"With who?"

"I don't know. But it's not the girl, and it's not her old man."

"How about her mother?"

"I doubt if they tried. She's not a suspect, and they don't have her prints. The father and daughter were both booked."

"And it's not them. That must throw a bit of a monkey wrench into their case."

"The police aren't treating it as if it were that important. They only looked because he asked them to."

"Even so, it's a huge point in her favor."

"One you seem to have anticipated."

"Well, I know the girl's innocent. So it had to be someone else."

"No, doofus. I mean the fact the bell was tampered with. You asked me about it before I even brought it up."

"Did I?"

"You know you did."

"Well, then, if I could make another suggestion. It would be awfully nice to have copies of those fingerprints the police found. I bet Millsap could get them for you, what with him feeling so cooperative and all."

I don't think I've ever seen Richard quite so exasperated. He looked at me sideways. "Let me tell you something. You seem to be having a very good time here. Perhaps a little too good. As if that girl bewitched you somehow. Got you acting all out of character. Some macho detective fantasy you saw on TV. If you wanna do that, fine. But do it on your own time. Don't involve me in it. Particularly as an unwitting dupe. That's really no fun. It's not the part I want to play. Unless . . ."

"Unless what?"

"Unless there's money in it. I'd be perfectly happy to help you act out your fantasies if we pocket a bundle. So far, we got zip. The late Mr. Starling/Grackle or whatever had only two known bank accounts—one checking, one savings—for a grand total of six thousand, three hundred twenty-two dollars and forty-five cents. The thought of dragging that amount through probate does not thrill me. Plus, the guy was renting his apartment and didn't own a car. So, much as I would love to pursue the somewhat tenuous claim of the so-called widow, I find very little reason for doing so, outside of keeping you out of jail. So if you expect me to continue to concern myself in this matter, I expect you to either let me in on the fun, or come up with a sizable amount of cash."

"Which would you prefer?"

"I would prefer both. I would accept one. I will not tolerate neither."

"That's quite clear."

"Care to tell me what you're doing?"

"No."

"Then you better have a lot of money."

"I'm working on it."

Forty-two

I WAS LUCKY. I ONLY HAD TO SIT AT THE BALFOUR HOUSE TWO AND A half hours before Jenny came out. I followed her far enough to make sure I wouldn't run into Mom and Dad, then honked her over.

Jenny looked good in a nubby pullover and tan pants. She'd have also looked good without a nubby pullover and tan pants, but I tried to keep such thoughts at bay.

"What is with you?" Jenny demanded, as she slammed the car door. Her chest bounced fetchingly. I concentrated on my task. "You come in, push my lawyer around, get him all upset. Can't you leave anything alone?"

"You're pissed off?" I said. "Unbelievable. All I did was prod your lawyer into prodding the police into finding another suspect in the case. That helps you. It also helps your dad, since it isn't him. As a matter of fact, I would think the police are pretty close to rethinking the whole affair."

She opened her mouth to speak.

I held up my hand. "But your lawyer will tell you that. Talk this over with him. Personally, I don't wanna get into it. All I want is the answer to a few questions."

"Oh, yeah?"

"Yeah. Your lawyer would tell you not to answer them, but I want you to anyway. For starters, the police found nude pictures of you. They

think that's real cool grounds for blackmail. I think that's bullshit. I
don't think that's what you were paying Grackle for. Not for any nude
pictures of you."

She said nothing, glared at me.

"Okay, we'll hold that question in abeyance for a moment. Two years
ago you checked into the hospital for injuries sustained in a car accident.
You care to tell me about that?"

Her surprise was genuine, but she wasn't relieved. Quite the con-
trary. "What's that got to do with anything? I'm not talking about that.
You talk to my lawyer."

I shook my head. "Bad way to play it, Jenny. Simple automobile accident and you refuse to talk? Makes it look suspicious. Like you got
something to hide."

Jenny said nothing.

"Someone in the car with you?"

"No."

"You're pretty sure about that one. I almost tend to believe you. But
everything points to the fact you weren't alone. If someone died and
your father dumped the body, wouldn't that fit in pretty well with a dead
John Doe?"

Her lip trembled. "You think . . . you think my father? . . . "

"Go on."

She seemed horrified. "No. No. I'm not talking to you. You talk to
my lawyer."

I nodded. "Very protective. Interesting."

"Will you please leave me alone?"

"You're more protective of each other than of yourselves. That's why
it fits so well. Your father covering up for you. Like you're covering for
him now."

She gazed at me pityingly. "You're mental, you know it? You haven't
got a clue."

"Your father didn't do that?"

She started to answer, then realized I was goading her, and clamped her mouth shut.

"Okay, no more questions. I'm gonna tell you something. You just tell me if I'm wrong. Grackle wasn't blackmailing you about your naked pictures, or your hospital visit, or anything else you ever did. I'll bet you dollars to doughnuts Grackle was blackmailing you about someone else in your family. It's just a question of who. So it's a toss-up. You got your mother's dirty pictures, and your father's barroom brawl."

"Talk to my lawyer."

"I don't think your lawyer knows. I don't think you told him. Which is good. I wouldn't tell him either. Let him think the pictures are it. The pictures of you. The ones the cops are so happy about. The way I'm guessin', you were payin' off your dad's manslaughter, just like you said you were way back in the beginning. The simplest explanation turning out to be true."

She heaved a sigh. She looked good heaving it.

"One question and I'm out of here. Was Grackle alive or dead when you left?"

She said nothing.

"I know. Tough choice. Either answer hangs a parent out to dry. But you gotta pick one. What's it gonna be?"

"Talk to my lawyer."

I nodded. "Good girl. Just keep sayin' that."

Forty-three

ALAN RICKSTEIN HAD MOVED, DIED, OR OTHERWISE CEASED TO EXIST, but Craig Keyson was still hanging out at Murphy's Pub. He was a little old man who chugged draft ale like water and chain-smoked nonfiltered Camel cigarettes. It was amazing not that I had found him after all these years but that he was still alive. Icy at first, Keyson warmed up when I bought a round.

"Fights? I tell you somethin', sonny. I seen some fights like you wouldn't believe."

"This is one particular fight."

His eyes twinkled. "They all are."

"I'll buy you another draft if you can recall the one I want."

"Which one is that?"

"It goes back to 1990."

He smiled. "No problem. So do I."

"Man by the name of Balfour."

"Joe Balfour?"

"That's the one. Remember that fight?"

"Which fight?"

"He had several?"

"Oh, sure. Real hothead, Joe."

"This would be with a Mr. Headly."

"Thought it might."

"And why is that?"

"Only fight of Joe's I can remember where someone wound up dead."

"Oh?

"Plus I signed a statement. No one gonna find me if I hadn't signed a statement."

"Why'd you do it?"

He grinned, smoke pouring out through the cracks between his teeth. "Good samaritan. Just doin' my duty."

"You got paid?"

"Says you. Try and prove it."

"So tell me this. If Headly died, how come the police didn't make an arrest?"

"They did. They made the arrest. They just didn't make the connection. Not very bright, the police."

"You didn't straighten them out?"

He looked offended. "Hey, you ask me, I tell ya. They didn't ask me."

"And you weren't about to go running to the police if they didn't come to you?"

"Go running to the police with what? Barroom brawl? They *know* about a barroom brawl. They were there. They made an arrest. You want I should go running to the cops, say, 'Hey, stupid, you got your charges wrong?'"

"What if someone paid you to?"

He looked offended again. "Hey, what I tell you? I'm a good samaritan." He drained his beer. "A good, thirsty samaritan."

I signaled the bartender. I needn't have bothered. He was already filling another draft. Keyson accepted it, took a huge gulp. "So, you finally here to do something, great. Usually it don't take this long, but what the hey. What's your angle?"

"You read the paper much?"

"Why?"

"No reason. Just wonderin' how you pass your time."

"What are you, a comedian? You care a rat's ass how I pass my time? What's your pitch?"

"How well do you remember the incident?"

"How well would you like me to?"

I gave him a look.

He cackled into his beer. "That was a joke. Can't you take a joke?" He tapped another Camel out of the pack, lit it from the butt of the last and stubbed the butt out. He puffed mightily on the new cigarette to keep it lit, and hissed the smoke out like a steam engine. After that, he took a slug of beer, snuffled twice, pulled out a disgusting-looking handkerchief, and blew his nose. When he was done, he jammed the cigarette back in his mouth, picked up the glass of beer, and looked at me. "I remember it well."

Keyson spun around on his bar stool and gestured toward the area in the back. There was a small pool table in the open space between the bar and the rest rooms. A cue stick and cue ball lay on the table. None of the half a dozen patrons of the bar showed any interest in wanting to play.

"See the pool table?" Keyson said.

I trusted it was a rhetorical question. If I couldn't see it, I could never have found the bar.

"Well, that's where it started, right there. Over a game. A game of eight ball. Lots of fights over eight ball. Guys play for money. Usually just a small draft, but you'd think it's the family jewels. The arguments start up. You gotta call the kiss. No combinations off the other guy's balls. Do you lose if you scratch on the eight?"

"In this case?" I prompted.

"Beats the hell out of me. First thing I know they got cue sticks in their hands and talkin' loud."

I frowned judiciously. "It might be important to know what they fought about."

"That's why I took pains to remember," Keyson said, without skipping a beat. "Balfour was shootin' the eight. Headly scratched. The eight ball was behind the line. Balfour claimed he got to spot it. Headly said, no, he had to leave it where it was, bank the cue ball the length of that table. You know what I mean?"

Having played pool in my reckless youth, I did. I could even recall arguments of a similar nature.

"It wasn't the other way around?" I said. "It wasn't Balfour who scratched, and Headly who wanted to spot the eight?"

He side-spied up at me. "Would you like it to be?"

"No, I just want the facts."

"You got 'em."

I sized up Keyson for a moment. Then I reached out, took the beer out of his hand, set it on the bar. "Cut the bullshit. The fight wasn't about a pool game. Balfour and Headly wouldn't play pool. Balfour and Headly didn't like each other. That's why they fought. Now, what did they fight about?"

Keyson looked like he'd just lost the winning lottery ticket. "Damn!"

"What's the matter?"

"You're the guy. After all these years, you're the guy, and it ain't worth a damn."

"What you talking about?"

"You're the guy needs to know. Well, you're way too late, damn it. What kept you?"

"I'm here now." I signaled the bartender. "Gimme a pitcher."

Keyson's eyes brightened slightly, but instantly dimmed. "Why not? Drown your sorrows."

"I'll drink to that," I said. I wasn't going to, but it seemed the thing to say.

The bartender set down the pitcher with an extra glass. I handed it back to him and said, "Diet Coke." I poured Keyson's glass full, clinked it with the pitcher and said, "Cheers."

As I had hoped, the activity distracted him from his morass. It also distracted him from the subject. That was okay. I talked baseball with him for a few glasses. He hated the Yankees, liked the Mets. As a Red Sox fan, I'd found it hard to like the Mets since '86, still I played along.

Three glasses of beer later I steered the conversation back to Balfour. I must have been doing something right, because this time Keyson didn't look like he'd lost his best friend.

This time he was pissed.

"Yeah, I signed a witness statement. What's it to you?"

"I'd like to know how it happened."

"How what happened?"

"How you signed a statement."

"I was there. I was a witness."

"The witness statement—you give it to the cops?"

"Sure, I told the cops."

"I know you told the cops. I'm talking about your signed statement. You give that to the cops?"

"Didn't ask me. What's it to you?"

"Who'd you give the statement to?"

He shrugged. "Some guy."

"Grackle?"

He said nothing, sipped his beer.

"Was it Grackle?"

He shrugged. "Guys have a lot of names."

"For example?"

He shrugged again.

"I notice nothing in your statement about why Balfour and Headly fought. So I guess you didn't know."

He thrust out his jaw belligerently. "Who says so?"

"Well, it stands to reason. If you knew, it'd be in there."

"If it was in there, I wouldn't get paid."

I don't know how long the silence was that followed that remark. I was afraid to speak for fear I'd blow it somehow, make him clam up. Which he already had. From his point of view, he'd stopped talking with the sudden realization that he'd gone too far. We sat there on our bar stools, as if frozen in time, neither one of us wanting to break the spell.

I picked up the pitcher, filled his glass.

He drained it dry.

I filled it up again.

He picked it up again. Seemed to have forgotten his faux pas.

"How come you're so pissed off?" I ventured.

He shook his head. "Ain't goin' to trial."

"What's that got to do with it?"

"Ain't *never* goin' to trial."

I sat there, trying to piece together the fragments of the man's story from what he was and wasn't telling me, trying to figure out which button to push to make him talk.

"No, it's not going to trial," I agreed.

He nodded. " 'Course not. No way now."

"How come?"

Wrong button. He seemed to steel himself for the interrogation.

I abandoned questions, tried conversation. "Yeah," I said. "It's too bad there won't be a trial. But that's how things worked out."

"Not fair."

"No, it isn't."

"After all, you did your part. Signed the paper."

"Damn right."

"And what did it get you? Lotta hassle, no reward."

He nodded emphatically. "Right. And I remembered everything."

"I'm sure you did."

"Damn right I did. Hell, I saw the pictures."

My voice faltered slightly while my mind maneuvered over that speed bump. "Damn right," I said, "and how many people saw them? You were *important*."

"Damn right," he said. "Fucking cops."

"Didn't even ask you."

"Didn't even *know*."

It was all I could do to keep from asking a question. "Some pictures," I ventured.

"I'll say."

"What a beauty."

"What a slut."

"Sexy stuff."

Keyson tried to say pornographic, but stumbled over several of the syllables.

"Pissed Joe off," I told him.

"I'll say."

"Is that what they fought over?"

Oh, dear. There I was, Orpheus, almost out of the gates of hell, looking back to make sure Eurydice was behind me, and, bang, she was gone. The one mistake, the one error, the one thing I knew was fatal. In spite of myself I went ahead and did it.

This time the door slammed shut with a note of finality.

Keyson steeled himself against any entreaty.

The interview was over.

Forty-four

ALICE WAS IMPRESSED. PREDICTABLE, SINCE I'D BASICALLY BLOWN IT. She tilted back in her computer chair and nodded in satisfaction. "Great. You confirmed the fight and dragged in the photos. It's gotta be what he fought over."

"He didn't confirm that."

"No, but it's a fair inference. And what you did get is interesting. Particularly the fact the guy expected to be paid."

"Or *didn't* expect to be paid," I pointed out. "He did at one time, but not anymore. He kept bitching that I was too late."

"That's hardly your fault."

"Thanks for your assurance. Anyway, the guy's pissed off he didn't get to be a witness. Even though he'd be a terrible one."

"How come?"

"Are you kidding? He oozes prevarication."

"Can one ooze prevarication?"

"I have no idea."

"You're a writer."

"Alice, stick with me here. The guy's a liar. He comes across as a liar. A child of five would look at him and say, 'Liar!' He's not the type of guy you build a case around."

"Yet someone did."

"No, someone *threatened* to. They took his witness statement. It never got to the police. Because it was never intended to. It was just a club to hold over Balfour's head to bleed him dry."

"It worked?"

"Of course it did."

"Why, if the guy's so unreliable?"

"Doesn't matter. He's the connection. Between the fight in the bar and the man who died. Plus he saw the dirty pictures. So he knows the motive too. The guy is *real* bad news."

"You like some *good* news?"

"Alice. What is that, a segue?"

"Sorry. I've been dying to tell you."

"What?"

Alice gestured to the desk. Next to our computer was the Mac PowerBook she had gotten "me" to look at Grackle's files. I was yet to use it.

"Grackle's disk. I ran some word searches."

"Bet the name Balfour came up."

"Actually, it didn't. But Herman Bertoli did."

"Oh?"

"I ran the names Herman Bertoli and Darien Mott."

"Yeah? And?"

"Well, Darien Mott's clean as a whistle, but guess what Herman Bertoli does every single month?"

"I give up. What?"

"He writes a check for a thousand dollars payable to Philip T. Grackle."

"You don't say."

"I do. And so do Grackle's records."

"Grackle was a blackmailer who took checks?"

"Evidently. Unless the guy was indebted to him for something else."

"Like he was a silent partner in the strip club?"

"That wouldn't be a personal check."

"No, it wouldn't."

"And when you put it together with the alias and the rap sheet, it's gotta be blackmail."

"So it seems. Is that the only one?"

"The only one like that. The Balfours must have been paying cash."

"That is the approved method."

I noticed Alice's eyes twinkling. "What is it? You holding out on me?"

"Not at all. I've answered all your questions and given you all the information you asked for."

I thought that over. "All right. What *didn't* I ask for?"

Alice grinned. "Similar deposits. I got one, thousand bucks a month, dating back to the end of time. Or at least to the end of the computer's memory."

"Who would that be?"

"Mr. Headly."

"What are you talking about. Headly's dead."

"Yeah, but nobody told his bank. According to Grackle's records, Headly's bank been cuttin' a check for a thousand bucks once a month, regular as clockwork."

"How can that be?"

"Pretty damn simple if no one knew about the account." Alice's eyes gleamed as she laid it out. "Here's how I see it. Headly dies in a barroom brawl. Grackle immediately sews up the witnesses and starts bleeding the guy who killed him dry. So Grackle is on the scene, Grackle leaves before the cops arrive and sees Headly crawl off and die. Grackle, prince that he is, riffles the guy's wallet and takes his bank card."

"Unnoticed?"

Alice shrugged. "If Headly is as slimy as Grackle, which is almost a given, I'm assuming he had at least two bank accounts, one of which was full of dirty cash. His regular bank account is closed, but the one that no one knew he had remains open. And the guy with the ATM card proceeds to bleed the account dry a thousand bucks at a time. Till when? Two years ago, when the account got small enough to close without attracting attention. Which Grackle did, cashing a check on the account for sixty-two grand."

I whistled. "You have all that on disk?"

"Absolutely."

"Then the police have it too."

"If they know how to look."

"Why wouldn't they? Isn't it in Grackle's bank account?"

Alice waggled her hand. "It was *funneled* through Grackle's bank account. But Grackle had a very small balance."

"You're telling me that's part of the money in the bottom of Grackle's file cabinet?"

"I would say that's a pretty good bet."

Alice turned back to the desk and began banging on our computer. I can't watch her when she does that. We have no extra chair, so I have to lean over to look at the screen. Even if we had a chair, I wouldn't want to watch her.

I walked across the room, sat down on the couch.

Zelda came, put her head in my lap, and whimpered softly.

"Does she need to go out?"

"Oh, hell, I didn't walk her," Alice said. "I got caught up on the computer."

"Where's Tommie?"

"Don't bother him. He's got a book report due tomorrow."

"Okay, Zelda," I said. I got up and got some plastic bags from the kitchen. I took the leash out of the drawer in the foyer, slipped a Baggie of Cheerios in my pocket to use for treats, put the leash on Zelda, and headed out.

On my way to the door, I snapped my fingers, turned back. "What's the date?"

"What date?"

"The date of the transaction. The transfer of the sixty-two grand."

"Let me see." Alice moved over to the PowerBook and called it up. "That would be two years ago, on August fifth."

"Is that the date Jenny went to the hospital? The date of the dead John Doe?"

"I have no idea."

"Wasn't it around then?"

"I don't know. It was a couple of years ago."

"Look it up, will you?"

Zelda voiced her displeasure at our interrupted progress. I dug a Cheerio out of my pocket and fed it to her. She ate it, but continued to indicate a strong preference for the front door.

"Here it is. That would be Saturday, August third."

"Two days before the final withdrawal?"

"That's right."

"Woof!" Zelda said.

I couldn't argue with that. I took the elevator to the lobby, ran her down to Riverside Drive.

The urgency of Zelda's need can be measured in easily recognizable increments. She will not use the sidewalk, so the direst of emergencies would be the street outside our front door. A standard emergency would be the mouth of 104th Street on the other side of West End. A slightly less pressing need would be the space by the fireplug halfway down the block.

Zelda, who likes the grass, will attempt to hold on till Riverside Drive. When we reach Riverside, an emergency ceases to qualify as an emergency if we queue up to cross the four-lane avenue. But if time is of the essence, we veer right to visit the tiny grassy knoll on the east side of Riverside. I do so with some reluctance. Dog owners are required by law to clean up after their pets. The grassy knoll north of 104th and Riverside Drive is one of the few places in the city where this law is flouted daily by daring daylight poopers, those shit-and-run dog owners who come and go and leave their mark behind.

At any rate, as I walked Zelda on the bank, my mind wandered from my appointed task of watching my feet.

Because it all fit so well. Balfour kills Headly, winds up paying off Grackle, who has seized Headly's checking account, and is bleeding it dry. Grackle is also bleeding Mott/Bertoli/topless bar owner, which is a less irregular arrangement and allows for the cashing of checks. However, it is enough of a hold that Grackle is able to request a favor now and then. Such as—and here I am getting brilliant, I really better watch my feet—hiring Balfour's daughter to dance in the bar, to earn enough to pay off the money he was squeezing out of her.

I glanced down and saw that Zelda had accomplished her mission. I whipped out a plastic bag and accomplished mine.

"Good girl," I said. "Let's go get a bagel."

Zelda gets a piece of frozen bagel after her last walk. Kind of a nightcap. The suggestion gets her home on chilly evenings. Or when I have something on my mind.

I walked her home, dotting the *I*'s and crossing the *T*'s.

I was halfway up the block when it hit me.

Alice was wrong!

What a revelation. Alice was never wrong. At least, not so far as I could remember. There were times I had *thought* she was wrong, and even times I had attempted to *point out* to her she was wrong. On such occasions she had assured me she was right. And not only had she been capable of demonstrating that fact, but before she was done I would have been hard pressed to state my own name with any degree of certainty.

Except now. I was right, and Alice was wrong. Granted, Alice was not privy to all the facts as I knew them. And Alice had not had time to think it out. And when she did, she would surely do better. But she was wrong about Jenny Balfour's car accident.

Grackle cashes a thousand-dollar check every month for years, until Jenny Balfour winds up in the hospital the same day as the John Doe, at which point he closes the account.

Quite a coincidence.

Grackle was a clever blackmailer. Careful not to get his hands dirty. He has a stooge. The stooge's job is to keep the bank account open and write the checks. The stooge takes a shine to Jenny Balfour, beats and rapes her. Daddy flips out, kills the stooge with his bare hands. He dumps the body where it's found as a John Doe, and takes his daughter to the hospital, claiming she's been in a car accident.

Grackle, who knows better, gathers grounds for blackmail, and, with his check writer gone, closes Headly's account.

That had to be right. That had to fit.

I marched Zelda triumphantly across West End Avenue, took the elevator upstairs, and burst in the door.

"Alice!" I cried, before I'd even taken off Zelda's leash. "There was no car accident. The John Doe is Grackle's accomplice. Balfour killed him for raping his daughter."

Alice turned away from the computer, raised her eyebrows in surprise. "You thought all that up walking the dog?"

"Yeah. Why not?"

Alice shrugged. "Well, for one thing, you're wrong."

Forty-three

THE FINGERPRINT EXPERT COCKED HIS HEAD. A PUDGY GUY WITH thick-rimmed glasses, a mustache, and not much hair, he clearly wasn't comfortable dealing with anything out of the ordinary. "You don't want a written report?"

"No."

"I always write a report."

"Go ahead and write one. I just don't want it."

"This is most unusual."

"Not really. Just tell me if the fingerprints match."

"To what degree of certainty? Eighteen points of similarity will stand up in any court."

"This doesn't have to stand up in court. I just want to know."

"Yes, but surely you want to be certain."

"Hey, man," I said. "I'm in a bit of a bind. Just tell me if they match. You'll know if they do. I don't care if you find four points of similarity or forty. Just tell me."

He picked up the two papers. The first contained Herman Bertoli's fingerprints, which I had copied from his police record, carefully removing his name. The second contained the fingerprints taken from the water pipe in Grackle's basement.

He frowned. "Is this a police exhibit?"

"Absolutely not," I assured him. It was, in fact, a photocopy of a police exhibit. A fine distinction, but one's own. "Anything I can do to help?"

"Yeah. Go out there and read a magazine. What you want shouldn't take long."

"If you only knew," I told him.

I went out in the waiting room, where no one else was waiting. I wondered how the guy made a living. I wondered less when the hundred bucks he was charging me turned out to be for five minutes work. Of course, I hadn't wanted a written report, but that probably would have been extra.

"It's a match," he said, sticking his head out the door.

"You sure?"

He grimaced. "I'm as sure as you wanted me to be. You want me to look again?"

"No, that's fine," I told him.

"Good. Here're your prints. You mentioned this would be cash?"

"It seemed appropriate."

I came out on Broadway feeling good. The prints had matched up. I'd figured it was a pretty good shot, what with Mott/Bertoli's rap sheet in Grackle's files, but the god of Dork visits me so frequently I tend to expect him.

Not this time. I had a match.

Onward and upward.

I set my briefcase down on a newspaper vending machine and popped the lid.

I pulled out an envelope, addressed it to Darien Mott at Midnight Lace.

I took out a sheet of paper and wrote on it, THIS IS WHY THE POLICE MISSED YOUR FILE.

I folded the piece of paper, stuck it inside the instruction manual for Grackle's file cabinet.

I put the manual in the envelope and sealed the flap.

I took it down the street to the Speedy Day Messenger Service.

Forty-four

MOTT/BERTOLI SHOWED UP AROUND 11:30. HE CAME CREEPING DOWN the street as furtively as if he were about to rob the place. If I were a cop, I'd have been watching him on general principles.

Mott came down the block, scoping out every passerby as a prospective cop. These included a sixteen-year-old boy, an elderly woman, and a man with a Saint Bernard. The dog didn't look suspicious to me, but what do I know?

Mott passed the dark alcove where Jenny had ducked in to avoid her mother. Luckily, Mott's mother wasn't coming, so he didn't have to do that. He kept going, reached Grackle's building.

Where he proceeded to have an anxiety attack. He whipped out a pack of cigarettes and lit one, cupping his hands against the wind. Then he strolled slowly across the alleyway, side-spying up at the windows on the second floor. No lights flickered behind the drawn curtains. The apartment was dark.

Mott walked all the way to the corner, turned around and walked back, smoking as he went.

Calming himself.

This time he slowed as he passed the darkened alley, stopped, flicked his cigarette butt into the street. He glanced up and down the block, then went up the front steps.

Mott tried the front door. It opened easily. That surprised him. He hesitated a moment, then went in.

For thirty seconds nothing happened. No sound, no movement, no lights switching on. I wondered how he planned on getting through the apartment door. Not my problem, still I wondered. Particularly when nothing happened.

Then, very faintly from the back alley, nestled among the city street noises, came the sound of a window sliding open. Moments later, in the rear of the alley, a silhouette appeared on the fire escape. A hand gripped the side rail. A leg slung over. Then the other. The shadowy figure stood outside the fire escape, a foot on the edge, a hand on the rail. In the dark the other foot reached out along the side of the building to the window of Grackle's apartment. The foot reached the sill, slipped once, then found a foothold.

The window was open a crack. The climber's hand reached out toward it. Rested, pushed up. The window slid easily.

The figure stood for a moment spread-eagled in space, then pulled himself over to the window and hopped inside.

A light flickered on. A dim light, like the beam of a flashlight. It moved away from the window, played around the walls.

Then all hell broke loose.

There came the sound of a crash. Every light in the place came on. A curtain in the open window was yanked aside, and a leg thrust over the sill. Mott's head followed, ducking under the window to the open air. His eyes were wide, desperate. He might have been trying to reach the fire escape again, but he might have just been trying to jump.

It was a moot point. Arms grabbed his shoulders, yanked him inside.

A police car screeched to a stop in front of the town house. Two cops erupted from it, rushed inside.

They were out minutes later, ushering a handcuffed Darien Mott. One cop marched on either side. A third cop marched behind, holding Mott's shoulders.

As they came down the steps, Sergeant Thurman roared up. The good sergeant looked utterly confused, horribly conflicted. He was delighted, of course, to have his trap work, but baffled by what he'd caught. Clearly whoever'd radioed him hadn't mentioned the identity of the intruder. He'd been hoping for Jenny Balfour. Darien Mott wasn't nearly as good.

After a few minutes of farbling around, during which Thurman posed a number of questions, the answers to which none of the policeman knew, Mott was loaded into the police car and driven off. Thurman and the cop from the apartment followed along behind.

The minute they were gone I crept out of my hiding place, hurried back to my parked car, and woke up Leroy Stanhope Williams.

"Showtime," I said.

Leroy rubbed sleepy eyes. "Cops gone?"

"Yup."

"All of them?"

"I hope so."

Leroy snorted in disgust. "Couldn't you have just said yes?"

"Sorry. Yes, the cops are gone."

"That's less than comforting."

"You're a hard man to please."

We reached Grackle's town house and went up the steps. The front door was still unlocked like we'd left it for Mr. Mott. We pushed it open, went inside.

"Come on," I whispered.

I led Leroy up the stairs. He followed reluctantly. I marched straight to the door of Grackle's apartment. Leroy gave me a look, whipped out a set of picks, and inserted them in the lock. Seconds later it clicked open.

Without a word, Leroy turned and walked down the stairs.

As we'd agreed, I waited until he was outside. Then I pushed the apartment door open and stepped in.

I half expected to be handcuffed by cops, but, no, Sergeant Thurman was running true to form. His trap having worked, it hadn't occurred to him to set it again. The apartment was empty.

Well, in for a penny, in for a pound. I switched on the light, went to the file cabinet, pulled out the drawer. Lifted the false bottom.

The money was still there.

I set my briefcase on the floor, popped it open.

I pulled out the documents I wanted, put them in the file cabinet on top of the money. I closed the false bottom, replaced the drawer.

And got the hell out of there.

Forty-five

SERGEANT MACAULLIF HAD HIS PILL BOTTLES LINED UP ON THE DESK in front of him. "Which one should I take?"

"Why do you ask?"

MacAullif cocked his head. "There's been some developments in the case."

"Oh, is that right?"

"Yeah, that's right. I thought you might be interested."

"Oh, absolutely. It's got nothing to do with me anymore, but I'd still like to know. So what's the big news?"

"I think I'll try the stomach pill," MacAullif said. "I have a feeling I might need the stomach pill."

"How come?"

MacAullif poured a glass of water, popped the pill in his mouth, swallowed it down. "The police have made an arrest."

"In the Grackle case?"

"That's right."

"They arrested someone *else* for killing Mr. Grackle?"

"That they have."

"Who is it this time?"

"A Mr. Darien Mott. The proprietor of Midnight Lace."

"Hmmm," I said. "You know, I wouldn't want to tell the police their

247

business, but wouldn't you think the more people they arrest for this crime, the harder it's going to be to get a conviction?"

"That's undoubtedly how the ADA sees it. However, from Sergeant Thurman's point of view, all arrests are good."

"What do they have on Mr. Mott?"

"Quite a bit, actually. He was arrested trying to break into the apartment. Some incriminating documents turned up in Grackle's files. Files concealed in a false compartment of the file cabinet, no less. The police theory is if he'd break in to get them, he'd kill to get them."

"Can they prove it?"

"Yes and no. Thurman thought he was being smart putting a cop in the apartment. But as a result they nabbed our boy before he could ransack the file cabinet."

"Too bad."

"Yeah, but the guy had an instruction manual on him, showing how to get into it, which sort of cooks his ass."

"Where would he get that?"

"I have no idea. But the point is, he had it."

"What a moron. He couldn't remember the instructions?"

"Evidently not. The other thing that nails him is that his prints were found in the cellar, right next to the doorbell wire that was cut."

"Now, that's bad," I said.

"Yeah, terrible." MacAullif waved the pill bottle at me. "Weren't you the guy pushing that idea?"

"I dislike the characterization pushing."

"I dislike a lot of things. But they keep walking into my office."

"Hey, low blow. This arrest helps you as much as me."

"Don't be too sure," MacAullif said. "Like I say, it's an iffy case. All it really does is fuck up the case against the girl. Just like the girl fucks up the case against him. She's his reasonable doubt and he's hers. No jury's gonna convict the one when there's so much evidence against the other."

"Any chance of collusion?"

"None. They didn't like each other, and everybody knew it. Plus the cop who tagged her car knows she was alone. So the Grackle case has suddenly moved from nearly solved to wide open."

"Too bad."

"Which leaves me twisting in the wind."

"Not at all, MacAullif. Your only connection was the girl. If she's out of it, you're clear."

"Maybe," MacAullif grumbled. He didn't sound happy.

"What's your problem, MacAullif?"

"It's a little too pat. The guy breaks into the apartment, he's got an instruction manual in his pocket—where the hell'd *that* come from?— the manual is to a false bottom in the file cabinet. Thurman tumbles to what the manual is, goes back and searches the hidden recess, and finds a fortune in small bills and this guy Mott's alias and rap sheet."

"Anything else in the drawer?"

"Yes, there was something else in the drawer."

"What was it?"

"Why do I have a feeling you could tell me?"

"You give me too much credit, MacAullif."

"I give you very little credit. I give you gall, moxie, and chutzpah, but little credit indeed."

"So what was in the drawer?"

"Two things. Police report of an aggravated assault complaint stemming from a fight in a bar—where have I heard that before?—and a death certificate for a Mr. Headly on that same day, and a witness statement signed by a patron in the bar to the effect that he saw Balfour beat Headly to within an inch of his life."

"Interesting," I said.

"Somehow I knew you'd say that. You got the word *interesting* sort of filed away in a box of all-purpose words that piss me off."

"I can't even follow that, MacAullif."

"You're damn right, it's interesting. Here's the girl charged with murder, and the only things in the drawer are evidence pointing to the motives of two other men."

"Lucky there."

"Very."

"So they gonna dismiss the charges?"

"I don't know what they're gonna do. All I know is nobody's happy. Except maybe Thurman, 'cause he's too dumb to know better."

"You say there was money in the drawer?"

"There was a lot of money in the drawer. And your buddy Rosenberg's already laid claim to it. On behalf of the quote 'widow' unquote."

"She *is* the widow, MacAullif."

"Who gives a shit? The point is Rosenberg claimed the money practically before anyone knew it was there."

"Richard has a nose for money."

"And a head for figures. He asked for the exact amount. Which the cops swear up and down they didn't give out."

I nodded. "If the widow knew the right amount, it's a pretty good indication the money's hers."

MacAullif rolled his eyes. "Oh, sure. The woman hasn't seen him in six years, but she knows what's in his cash drawer."

"So she loved his money. Is that so rare?"

"Save it for someone who wants to hear it. All I care is the girl stays off the hook so no one gets to me. As for the rest of it, frankly I could care less."

"Yeah, I know, MacAullif. I'll tell you anyway, when it's all over."

I could hear MacAullif's stomach erupt all the way across the room.

"You don't think it's over yet?"

"Not by a long shot."

Forty-six

RICHARD ROSENBERG WAS SMILING ALL OVER HIS FACE. "TWO HUNDRED seventy thousand dollars. I *like* that. You know what I like most about it? I like the way three goes into it. No small change. No decimal points. No rounding it off to the nearest penny. No, a third of two hundred and seventy thousand dollars is ninety thousand dollars. Which is a nice, round figure that I can deal with. My god, when I think of the amount I'll save on bookkeeping costs alone."

"Yeah, you'll almost be able to offset your finder's fee," I told him."

Richard sputtered into his coffee. "My *what*!? What are you talking about?"

"My fee for finding the money. I was talking about that."

"You didn't find the money. Sergeant Thurman found the money. I'm damned if I'm paying him."

"Right," I said. "I didn't find the money. I just pulled the figure two hundred seventy thousand out of a hat."

"And very nicely too," Richard agreed. "You could work as a psychic."

"Great. I'll be sure to give you as a reference. Richard, as far as this deal is concerned, I consider myself your agent. I found you the money, and I found you the client. If you manage to put the two together, I want ten percent."

Richard gagged. "Ten percent! You want twenty-seven thousand dollars!"

"No, Richard. I said an agent's fee. Ten percent of your end. Nine thousand dollars. If you think that's excessive, I can tell you a dozen reasons why it isn't."

"Tell me *one*."

"The woman's claim to the cash will be predicated to a great deal on my recollection of events."

"I fail to see how that could be true."

"Okay, how about if I made you a party to the illegal steps I took in order for you to procure that money, you could go to jail?"

"That's pretty persuasive."

"Glad to hear it. If you get the dough, cut me in."

"I certainly will," Richard said dryly. "Tell me, was that on your list of things to do today? Get the morning paper, take out the garbage, blackmail your employer?"

"Absolutely. So what are the chances of our procuring this money?"

"I was on the phone with ADA Kinsey today. I must say he's not happy."

"How come?"

"The Grackle case. He'd like to prosecute someone for it."

"Why doesn't he?"

"Too many suspects. All of them good. It's hard to choose just one."

"Who's his favorite?"

"The strip club owner. By a wide margin. He's convinced he did it. The fingerprints prove he cut the wire. The records prove he was paying the guy off. A copy of his rap sheet was in the file along with the cash. Plus he was caught postmortem, trying to remove the evidence and/or the money."

"Why didn't he take it when he killed him?"

"He didn't know where it was. He went in there, stole a mess of papers from the file. He didn't get what he wanted, but among the stuff he took was a manual telling him about the trick drawer."

"If they got that much on him, why don't they prosecute him?"

"Little problem with the time of death. Guy was at the strip club all night. Confirmed by his bouncer and a bunch of the girls as well." Richard made a face. "Now, you know what an alibi is like. Perfectly possible the guy snuck out long enough to do the deed. But you put the alibi witnesses together with the fact he'd be the third suspect charged, there isn't an attorney fresh out of law school who couldn't raise reasonable doubt. From my understanding, unless someone confesses or someone rolls over on him, this one ain't getting solved."

"A shame," I said. "How's the ADA feel about that?"

"Justifiably pissed. And looking for other game."

"Such as?"

"The evidence in the file against Darien Mott was rather straightforward. He had a record, was paying to suppress it. The evidence against Joe Balfour, however, is a little different. It would tend to indicate he had something to do with the death of a Mr. Headly some years back."

"Is that right?"

"Yes, it is, and the guy thinks he can prove it. Balfour was arrested for a barroom brawl, the guy he fought with wound up dead, and a witness confirms the fight."

"Isn't that over ten years old?"

"Murder never outlaws. I understand the ADA's looking for a grand jury indictment."

"What's Balfour's lawyer say?"

"He says it's a crock of shit. They're proceeding out of spite, they haven't got the evidence, it will never come to trial, they're just going through the motions, et cetera, et cetera."

"Is that all?"

"Well, the guy was caught by surprise. I'm sure he'll come up with something better when he's had a chance to think it over."

"Maybe. On the other hand, maybe he'll plead him out."

Richard gawked. "What, are you nuts? The prosecution's got no case. No lawyer in his right mind would plead it out."

I shrugged. "Wanna bet?"

Forty-seven

THE SENIOR MILLSAP WASN'T PLEASED TO SEE ME. HE SAT BEHIND A mahogany desk covered with a confusion of papers, inbox, outbox, telephone, ashtray, cigar box, and various objects the function of which I could only guess at. It looked like it hadn't been cleaned in twenty years.

Millsap, on the other hand, looked like he'd just had a haircut. He was one of those guys who always looked like he'd just had a haircut. Today, he looked like he'd just had a haircut and swallowed a bottle of castor oil.

"You're a menace," he said, putting as much authority as he could behind the word.

"I'm certainly sorry to hear that," I said. "I'd like to apologize for everything I've done. I'm here to offer any help I can."

"I've frankly had enough of your help."

"Hey, don't be such a grouch. Your son's client's off the hook. Doesn't that count for something?"

"I don't find that funny."

"Oh, sorry. I forgot the family infighting. You're pissed off I helped your son out too."

"Don't be dumb."

"Oh, am I in error? I'm sorry. Gee, I just can't stop apologizing today. And I haven't really done anything wrong."

"Will you get out of my office?"

"Absolutely. But I have a few things to say first. I understand your client's been indicted for the murder of Mr. Headly."

"Oh, you understand that, do you?"

"Well, it was in the paper."

"I'm *aware* it was in the paper." He said it through clenched teeth. "What *wasn't* in the paper was the fact a great deal of this evidence was uncovered by you."

"Almost none of it," I said. "The strip club owner who got arrested—"

"Yeah, I know. He claims he was set up. He makes a fairly good case. So good they aren't going to prosecute him. They're coming after my client instead."

"Exactly. And that's what I want to talk to you about."

"Why is that?"

"I'd like to help you."

"You've uncovered some evidence that gets my client off?"

"Not exactly."

"Then how could you be of help?"

"Actually, I was going to suggest a legal strategy."

Millsap's face purpled. One could practically see steam coming out his ears. "*You* are going to tell *me* a legal strategy?"

"I didn't say tell. I said suggest."

"I suppose you're going to instruct me on the legal distinction of those words?" he said sarcastically.

"That wasn't what I had in mind."

The door opened and the younger Millsap came in. He saw me, stopped, and said, "Oh, should I come back later?"

"Not on my account," I said. "Come on in. We were just talking about you."

The elder Millsap sputtered indignantly.

His son smiled. "No, no, Dad. I'm sure you weren't. So what's up?"

"I was coming to see you next, but we might as well talk here."

"In front of my father?"

"Why not? The cases seem to have diverged. Your dad's defending a whole different homicide."

"Funny how that happened."

"You're in a good mood. Charges dismissed yet?"

"No, but it's just a formality. What with this new arrest."

"That's what I wanted to talk to you about. The ADA offered your client anything to roll over on the guy?"

Young Millsap frowned. "That's hardly likely. My client knows nothing about the activities of Mr. Mott."

I smiled. "Give me a break. Your client was in the apartment. If she's willing to testify Grackle was dead when she got there, that would tie in with the theory Mott killed him earlier. Before his so-called alibi."

Millsap frowned. "Even if the police *were* pushing that theory, there'd be no reason for us to go along, since the cops have nothing to trade."

I thought that over. "I see. You're telling me your client wants to make that deal, but you won't let her."

He flushed. "That's not what I said."

"I know. I find it interesting all the same. What does she say about this new murder charge against her father?"

The elder Millsap waved his arms. "Hey! Hey! You're not discussing the case in front of my son."

"Of course not," I said. "Your son and I are discussing the case in front of you. Feel free to jump in if you like." I turned back to Junior. "What's her take on it?"

"It's absolutely absurd, her father never killed anyone, it didn't happen."

"That's pretty emphatic. How would she know? She was just a child at the time."

"She's grown up now. She knows what's what."

"That she does," I said. "Well, I was just about to give your father some advice on the case. You wanna stick around and hear it?"

"You got a lot of nerve," Millsap senior said.

"It makes up for a lack of brains," I told him. "Look, here's the situation. I feel bad about the position you're in. I'd like to help you out. So here's a friendly tip. If I were you, I'd hunt up the ADA, see if he wants to plea-bargain."

Millsap couldn't have looked more shocked had he been run over by a Mack truck. "Plea-bargain? Are you nuts? Who wants to plea-bargain?"

"You'd be surprised," I said. "The ADA can't be all that happy about the case. I bet if you played your cards right, you could get him to offer manslaughter."

"They won't talk manslaughter. They're pushing for murder."

"They'll never get it."

"I'm glad you're so sure. They got this witness who saw the fight."

"He's a bad witness. You'll eat him alive."

"He did okay in front of the grand jury."

"Of course he did. You weren't there. Just the ADA holding his hand. On cross-examination the guy's dead meat. A jury hears his account, they won't get murder."

"I hope you're right."

"Don't hope. Make it happen. Get the ADA to agree to manslaughter, three to five."

"Even if I wanted to, he wouldn't go for it."

"Yes, he would. You don't know how bad this witness is."

"If he's that bad, why shouldn't I fight it out?"

I turned to the younger Millsap. "If you have any influence with your father, maybe you can get this through his head. His client's sweating a murder rap. He should be apprised of his options. I'll tell him myself if I have to, but I'd rather it came from his lawyer. So ask him if he'd like to plead it out three to five manslaughter, right now, bang, it's all over, and the case never goes to trial."

The older Millsap frowned. "That's a strange way to put it. What are you getting at?"

"Just ask him," I said, and walked out.

Forty-eight

IT MADE THE FRONT PAGE OF THE *NEW YORK POST*. DELAYED JUSTICE was the headline. Underneath was a picture of Balfour and a picture of Jenny in a bikini. The paper justified the leg art by pointing out that they had both been suspects in a recent murder. The fact she had been practically a toddler when *this* crime occurred was somehow glossed over.

BALFOUR COPS PLEA the subheadline read.

The lawyer for Joseph Balfour, who was indicted last week in the 1990 murder of Fletcher Headly, today reached an agreement with the district attorney's office to plead his client to a lesser charge. Balfour entered a plea of guilty to a count of manslaughter stemming from the death of Headly and was sentenced to three to five years in the state penitentiary. With good behavior, Balfour could be eligible for parole in as few as eighteen months.

The plea effectively disposes of one of the most unusual murder cases in recent memory. Headly's murder took place on June 15, 1990. Balfour was arrested on that date and charged with assaulting Headly. However, through a bizarre case of miscommunication between the police force and the medical community, it was not known that Headly had died. As a result, when Headly failed to appear in court to press charges, the assault charge was dropped. No one at the time knew Balfour was actually guilty of murder.

With one exception: Philip T. Grackle, a man with a history of blackmail and extortion.

Grackle made a point of obtaining sufficient evidence to convict Balfour of the crime. In short order, he obtained: Balfour's arrest record; Headly's death certificate; and a signed statement of a witness to the altercation between Balfour and Headly. On the strength of this evidence, Grackle had been extorting money from Balfour for years.

It was also on the strength of this that the police originally arrested Balfour for the murder of Grackle, a charge they have subsequently come to realize was without foundation. However, on the basis of the conclusive proof that Balfour had killed Headly, the prosecution went ahead and had the grand jury indict him for murder.

Yesterday afternoon Balfour pled guilty to the lesser charge.

The article was continued on page 12.
I didn't turn to page twelve.
I hopped in my car and headed for the office of Millsap & Millsap.

Forty-nine

MILLSAP SENIOR WAS SMILING ALL OVER HIS FACE. "MANSLAUGHTER," he said. "I thought you were nuts with that manslaughter stuff, but damned if it didn't work."

"You're mighty happy."

"Well, who wouldn't be? Yesterday I'm facing countless legal hassles, and suddenly they all went away."

"Yes, they did. But you weren't that happy with the prospect when I laid it out. I wonder what changed your mind. Your son wouldn't be having problems with *his* client, would he?"

"What makes you say that?"

"The famous Millsap family rivalry. How's Junior doing this morning?"

"Pulling his hair out, last I saw. And trying to calm his client down." He shook his head and grinned. "It wasn't a pleasant sight."

"Well, I guess I better go let the boy off the hook."

"Hey, you're not going to put me back on it, are you?"

"Never fear."

"You sure you wouldn't wanna let him twist in the wind a little?"

"I think he's suffered enough for one case, don't you?"

"You weren't around when he was gloating before."

"Maybe not. But look at it this way. If he can't control his client, she could get us all in trouble."

"Good point. Go straighten him out. Can you make him feel dumb while you do it?"

"I think that's a given."

The door flew open and Jenny Balfour burst in. She was a fright. She had been crying, and mascara was running down her cheeks. Her hair was a tangled mess. Her frumpy smock was as attractive as body armor.

"You son of a bitch!" she yelled. "You did this. You set my father up and let him take the fall."

Jenny lunged for me.

Millsap junior tried to stop her. He might as well have thrown himself in front of a speeding truck. Jenny pushed him backward as if he weren't even there.

I suppose I could have helped him make a goal-line stand. Instead I stepped out of the way and let Jenny push him over. She fell on top of him, twisted free, and staggered to her feet with some of the steam knocked out of her.

"You have a right to be angry," I said in a preemptive strike. "I was coming to tell you about it. I got something to say. Then you can be as mad as you like. But physically assaulting your attorney is not the way to go."

Her eyes blazed. "You put my dad in jail."

"Who told you that?"

"Everyone keeps giving you credit." She snorted. "*Credit.* How do you like that? As if you'd done something good."

"Yeah, it is ironic," I said. "Junior, can we use your office?"

The younger Millsap had recovered his balance, if not his composure. "Could you *what*?"

"I need to talk to Jenny alone. Your office seems a good place, since you don't happen to be in it."

He couldn't quite believe I'd asked him that. His face was so red I couldn't see his freckles. "No, you may *not* use my office. No, you may *not* talk to my client alone. No, you may *not* whatever else you might be asking for. Haven't you meddled in this case enough?"

"Fine, I'll butt out," I said, and walked out the door.

He stopped me before I got to the elevator. Actually, it was a dead heat between him and Jenny. Neither looked happy.

Moments later, I ushered Jenny into his office. "Sit down," I said, closing the door.

"I don't want to sit down."

"All right," I said. "Stand up. Stand up the whole time. Don't sit down no matter what you do."

She frowned at me. "What the hell are you up to?"

"Just trying to show you if your purpose is to defy me, you can't manage it a hundred percent. So I'm going to sit down behind this desk pretend I'm a lawyer for a minute. I suggest you sit in that chair."

"Why?

"Well, the desk between us would make it harder for you to scratch my eyes out."

"You're not funny."

"I know. But I'm not the bad guy, either. Let's have a little talk. When we're done, if you still think I'm the bad guy, slap me in the face again and our relationship will end the way it began."

"Start explaining, damn it. My attorney says copping a plea was your idea."

"It seemed like the right move."

"Are you nuts? Are you crazy? You don't even know the facts."

"I know more than you think."

"You couldn't. Or you wouldn't be so stupid."

"Hey, don't sell me short. Trust me, I can be pretty stupid."

She threw her hands to her head. "Stop. I'm going nuts. Nothing makes sense. Tell me, please. What the hell is going on?"

"Okay," I said. "Here's what it's all about. Basically, it's all about you. Two years ago you were hospitalized for a car accident. Broken bones, facial cuts and bruises. Grackle had that hospital record attached to a police report of a John Doe. Just the way he had your father's arrest record attached to the police report of the death of Mr. Headly. The inference was obvious: The John Doe died in your car. But there was another possibility. The gentleman in question had put you in the hospital; your father had beaten him to death."

Jenny started to protest.

I put up my hands. "Please, let's not argue it now. Or we'll never get done. Just let me lay out the facts for you. Your dissenting opinion is noted.

"Okay, why was this such a good possibility? First of all, because your father has a history for violence—and, please, let's not argue that either. And second of all, because your family has a history of protecting each other." I rubbed my forehead. "Which is what drove me nuts from the beginning. Everyone's being blackmailed, and everyone's payin' it. Why? These are a bunch of stand-up people. These are the type of people who'd tell the blackmailer to go to hell. So why are they such wimps? Mommy's payin' off her dirty pictures. Daddy's payin' off his manslaughter rap. And you're payin' off your dancing gig. How can that be?

"Well, it has to do with these Balfours protecting each other. *Daddy's* payin' off the dirty pictures. *Mama's* payin' off the manslaughter rap.

"And who's payin' off the homicide rap when you went to the hospital? Could it be you? Could you be protecting your father? Could that be the source of your blackmail? Could your job at Midnight Lace have nothing to do with it?"

"You're so off base," Jenny scoffed.

"Maybe. But these are just suppositions. I'm throwing out possibilities. Of course, some of them are going to be wrong."

"They're all wrong."

"Not entirely. Here's the way I piece it together. A long time ago, in a galaxy far, far away, a young girl fell on hard times and posed for some pictures she probably shouldn't have. That girl was your mother. Those pictures fell into the hands of a man by the name of Headly.

"Now, Headly was not your everyday, ordinary blackmailer. He had his own philosophy: Don't blackmail the victims, blackmail their loved ones. So Headly took the pictures of your mother and blackmailed your father. Bad move. Your father paid Headly off. But as soon as he destroyed the pictures, your father confronted Headly. They had a fight in a bar. Your father beat Headly senseless.

"Your father was arrested, but Headly managed to crawl off into a back alley, where he collapsed and died.

"This evidence was put together by a Mr. Grackle, who proceeded to blackmail your father.

"These facts are very well known. It is, in fact, the crime your father has just confessed to."

Jenny let out a soft moan.

I nodded sympathetically.

"What's killing you," I said, "is the fact he didn't do it."

Fifty

JENNY'S MOUTH FELL OPEN. SHE BLINKED AT ME.

"That's the problem, isn't it?" I told her. "And you know it better than anybody. It never happened. Oh, they had the fight all right, and Headly beat it before the cops got there. But Headly didn't crawl off to die. Headly hightailed out through the back alley and started home. When what should he happen upon but a John Doe. Some poor vagrant son of a bitch cashed in his chips in the alley. Well, Headly's a clever sort, and Headly has it in for your dad, and Headly knows the cops just picked him up. So Headly sets the stage to frame him on a murder rap.

"I don't know how much staging was required. Headly had to kick the guy around some to make it look like he'd been in a fight. But the main thing Headly did was drop his ID on him. Nothing major, you understand, and certainly nothing with a picture on it. But just sufficient he'd be taken in and buried under that name.

"So what happens then? Headly takes the evidence of his own death, and makes your *mother* jump through hoops. And why not? *She's* never met him before. *She* has no idea he's the guy who's supposed to be dead. Your father was the one payin' off the porn pictures. But he's not gonna deal with your father. What could go wrong?

"Well, for one thing, a man by the name of Starling, a man you subsequently knew as Grackle. He found out, and what a sweet deal that was. Here's a man takin' money on the theory he's dead. Starling shakes him down for a cut not to say he's alive.

"This very nice arrangement goes on until two years ago. What happens? Your mother gets elected to the city council. It's too good an opportunity to pass up. Headly gets greedy. He still has the porno pictures. He goes to Grackle, says, 'Hey, I'm tired of payin' you the vig every month. But here's something better. The husband who thinks I'm dead. This would be a neat time to shake him down.

"So Grackle makes a pass with the pictures. Your father is dumbfounded. Where the hell did these come from? He thought he'd killed the man who had them. And he thought he'd bought the pictures back. Of course, Headly kept a set, and Headly wasn't dead. So Grackle moves in on your dad. Which might have worked.

"Except for you.

"Time has passed. The little girl has grown up. She's noticed that certain things about her family life are strained, to say the least. She's investigated. She's followed her mother. She's followed her dad. She's seen Headly. She's seen Grackle. She's seen Headly meet Grackle.

"Which brings us to the night of August third.

"She meets with Headly. She's young, pretty, full of the naive arrogance of youth. She thinks she can make him stop just by asking him to.

"Big mistake.

"Headly isn't taken in by her charm. Headly beats the shit out of her. Her father, in a murderous rage, finds the man who beat up his daughter. It's the man he thought he killed. He loses it. In a blind fury, he kills him again."

Jenny was practically jumping out of her chair.

"Yeah, yeah, I know. It's absolutely ridiculous. Farcical. I feel like a fool just saying it. It's too stupid. It simply can't be. You needn't make that argument. I'm in complete agreement.

"It didn't happen.

"Here's what did.

"As I say, the daughter found out everything, confronted the man. Who laughed in her face. Taunted her. Perhaps even showed her the blackmail photos. The ones of her mother.

"The girl was outraged. She followed Headly that night. Followed him in her car. Followed him until he parked his. Followed him until he was crossing the street.

"She gunned the motor, ran him down.

"The car went out of control, slammed into a light pole.

"The girl sustained cuts, bruises, and a broken arm.

"The girl had her cell phone. She called her father. He raced to the scene. Imagine his shock at finding the man he was supposed to have killed years ago. There was no time to dwell on that. He searched the body, removing any means of identification. He dressed it in rags, dumped it in the bowery, just another John Doe.

"He took his daughter to the hospital, told them she had been in a car accident. But he didn't report it to the police. He had the car towed, had the body work done the next day.

"He did a good job. No one suspected a thing.

"Except Grackle.

"Grackle put it all together. Probably even ID'd Headly. Not to the police, just for himself. Went down, took a look at the body, said, 'No, I don't know him,' while dollar signs flashed in his head. He proceeded to clean out Headly's bank account and start blackmailing you.

"Of course you were a kid, you had no money to pay, but, no problem. Another of the men on his hook was Darien Mott, owner of Midnight Lace. Easy enough to get you a job there to get the money to pay off. You've been dancing to Grackle's tune ever since."

Tears were streaming down Jenny's face. "You see? You see now? You see why I have to go to the police? You see why I have to confess?"

"Actually, I see why you don't."

"What?"

"You're young, you're emotional, you haven't thought this through.

Your father's caught a good deal, light sentence, he'll be back before you know it. You're free of a blackmailer. So is your mom. The Grackle killing is as good as closed. The police know Darien Mott did it, they just don't have enough evidence to convict. But Mr. Mott is no longer a factor in your life.

"And neither is Mr. Grackle.

"You're young, you got your whole life in front of you, you got a chance to start over. You can go back to college. I suggest one on the West Coast. Or, at least not in New York.

"Now, I know you'd like to go all noble and save your father, but the fact is, you can't do it.

"On the other hand, there is enough evidence to convict you of vehicular homicide, maybe even murder, if the true facts came out. Given time, the police may be able to put it together from Grackle's files. I did, and I'm not the smartest private eye on the block."

That was a bit of a fudge. Actually, Alice had put it together, from Grackle's files and her search of the Internet. She'd found evidence of a Mr. Fletcher Headly living at an address in Glen Cove, Long Island, up until two years ago.

I felt guilty taking credit for it.

I felt more guilty the reason I was taking credit for it was so I wouldn't have to say "My wife."

Because MacAullif was right. I wanted to be the hero. And not because I had the hots for the girl. I just wanted to be Mike Hammer. Just for once.

Jenny was devastated. "But I didn't . . . I didn't . . ."

"Kill Headly?"

"No, I did. But it wasn't like that. He assaulted me. Grabbed me through the window. Tried to pull me out of the car. I gunned the motor. The car hit a tree."

I shrugged. "Maybe. You've told so many stories. No one's apt to believe you now."

"You mean . . . you mean they may prosecute me?"

I shook my head. "Not as things stand. Headly wasn't run over by a car two years ago. Your father killed Headly in a barroom brawl in 1990. You got the court papers to prove it. You can be pissed off at me as you like, but it's something he wanted to do for you. He felt very strongly."

"You spoke to him about it?"

"Of course."

"You suggested he do it?"

"Gonna hit me again if I say yes?"

"Why did you do that?"

I sighed. "Because it works. Because it fulfills some childhood fantasy of saving a damsel in distress. Though you're not a damsel in distress, you're probably a cold-blooded killer. I don't condone it, but I can't fault you on it. I'm rather conflicted myself.

"Anyhow, that's the way this one plays out. Everything's not neat and tidy like in a book. The Grackle murder doesn't get solved. The Headly murder gets solved wrong. And that, believe it or not, is the best I can do."

I reached in my jacket pocket, pulled out an envelope.

"What's that?" Jenny asked.

I handed it over. "The blackmail photos. Of you. And of your mother. I suggest you burn them."

Jenny clutched the envelope. She blinked at me in amazement through eyes caked with tears. "You did all this for me?"

"To a certain extent."

"Thank you."

"Don't mention it."

"Wow. And I was so angry. Listen, if there's ever anything I can do for you."

"Well, you could take your clothes off and let me shoot you in the stomach."

She drew back, shocked, repulsed. "What?"

"Sorry," I said. "A Mickey Spillane reference. Totally insensitive under the circumstances."

She frowned. "Mickey Spillane?"

I sighed. Ah, the difference in our ages.

The white knight, private eye, and romantic leading man got up, walked around the desk, and opened the office door to let the fair maiden, femme fatale, and possible murderess he had just saved from the dragon, police, and prosecuting attorney out.

Fifty-one

"YOU HAVE NO PILLS ON YOUR DESK."

MacAullif beamed. "You are correct, sir. I don't need any. At least not now. Things have worked out remarkably well. The Headly case is closed. The Grackle case, while not closed, is solved, and the perpetrator, god bless him, has nothing to do with me."

"Some days you get lucky."

"Hey, they can't all be losers. So, you just come by to celebrate?"

"I thought you might like to wrap up the case."

"What's to wrap up? It's wrapped."

"Wouldn't you like to know what really happened?"

"Will it upset me?"

"It shouldn't."

"Then, sure. What details would you care to add?"

"Balfour didn't kill Headly."

MacAullif stared at me. I probably could have played handball on his face and he wouldn't have blinked. Without looking, he jerked his drawer open, pulled out his pill bottles, and began arranging them on his desk. When he was done, he said in a voice so low it was almost inaudible, "Care to run that by me again?"

I laid it out for MacAullif the way I'd laid it out for Jenny. While I talked, MacAullif's face grew darker and darker. When I was finished he exploded, "You son of a bitch! How can you do this to me? The case was closed. Closed!"

"It is closed, MacAullif. Everything I just told you was off the record. Consider it hypothetical."

MacAullif hurled a bottle of pills at me. It popped open. Green-and-white capsules rolled around on the office floor. So much for safety caps.

I got down on my hands and knees and started picking up the pills. "Anyone pee on this floor recently?"

"Shut up," MacAullif said. He crawled by me, reached under the desk. His head was practically in my lap.

I prayed no one would open the office door.

We finished picking up the pills. MacAullif heaved himself into his desk chair, breathing hard. He pointed a finger at me. "You say the 'H' word again, I'll take out my service revolver and shoot you. Just tell me what's going to happen when this whole fucking mess gets straightened out."

"It isn't, MacAullif. The case is over. Balfour pled guilty to manslaughter. It's what he wants to do."

"But he didn't commit it."

"Let's not get hung up on technicalities. The point is, the case is closed, no one's gonna reopen it, and no one's gonna bother you."

"But—"

"You're the only one arguing, MacAullif. Do you hear Balfour arguing? Do you hear Balfour's attorney arguing? Do you hear the ADA arguing? No. Everybody's happy, everybody's gonna leave it alone."

"If you say so."

"I know so. No one's gonna touch it any more than they're gonna touch the Grackle case."

"That's what I thought a half an hour ago. Now I'm not so sure."

"Believe it, MacAullif. No one will touch it. The facts aren't there."

"How do you know?"

"Because I know what they are. I know exactly what happened. If you'd like me to tell you without using the 'H' word, I will. Just don't jump over the desk and try to kill me."

"You know how Mott killed Grackle?"

"No."

MacAullif snorted in disgust. "Then what *do* you know?"

I held up a finger. "No jumping."

"Hey, schmuck."

"Okay, I'll tell you what I know. Mott, tired of payin' Grackle off, made a play to get the evidence back. On his way out of the building one day, he traced the doorbell wires and found a place they could be cut that wouldn't readily be seen. He also scouted out a fire escape in the back hall. It was possible from that fire escape to reach a window that Grackle was in the habit of leaving open.

"So, Mott laid his plans. One night when he came to pay off Grackle, on his way out he detoured down the basement and clipped the buzzer wire. Sure enough, when he wandered by the next day, the downstairs door was unlocked. He waited till Grackle went out to dinner and let himself in the outer door. He went up to Grackle's floor, climbed out on the fire escape, and swung over to Grackle's open window. He climbed in and proceeded to ransack Grackle's files."

"So," MacAullif said, "Grackle came back from dinner, caught him going through the files, and he killed him. Earlier that night. Before the people at Midnight Lace gave him his alibi."

"Nice theory, but wrong. When Mott couldn't find what he was looking for, he got the hell out of there. When Grackle returned from dinner he had no idea the apartment had been searched."

MacAullif blinked. "How can that be?"

"Perfectly easy, MacAullif. You saw the medical report. Grackle wasn't killed that early."

"Those things aren't ironclad."

"I don't want to argue. It's just my theory, and you don't have to buy it. But say Grackle was alive when he left."

"And someone else came by and killed him? After he'd coincidently cut the doorbell wire? You expect me to buy that?"

"Not at all, MacAullif. The wire is cut. Which means anyone could get in the building. If you were planning a murder, that would be the time to do it. When someone else will be suspect."

"And how does the killer know the wire's cut?"

"Grackle called them. He had to. He called everyone who was coming to see him."

"You mean? . . . "

I nodded. "Look what happens next. Mommy comes by to pay him off. Jenny comes by to pay him off. And Daddy comes by to pay him off.

"My theory was Jenny found him dead, but she said he was alive, because she thought if she said he was dead it would be the same as fingering her mother. Of course, once Mott entered the picture it .was a different ball game. She could say she found him dead, and it was all right.

"Which is the situation. According to Jenny, she walked in and found Grackle dead. She's not afraid to say it anymore. No one knows her mother was there. When I asked her just now, she told me quite definitely Grackle was dead."

MacAullif's eyes were wide. "You mean her *mother* did it? That's what it means if Mott's innocent. You expect me to sit on that?"

"You're not going to go running to the ADA with some half-assed theory."

"Half-assed theory? You just told me it's true."

"Well, you won't let me use the 'H' word, MacAullif. But, believe me, just because I tell you something doesn't mean it's true."

"God knows that's for sure. But from what you say, Mommy must have done it."

"Yes, of course."

"*Did* Mommy do it?"

"Do you wanna know for sure?" As MacAullif started to rage at me,

I said, "Sorry. In my opinion, and here again it's just my opinion, Mommy didn't."

"Then who did?"

"It's actually pretty easy with Jenny changing her story. Insisting he was dead."

"You mean she did it after all? She's a habitual killer? You're helpin' to cover up two murders just because she's got nice tits?"

"She does, MacAullif, but that's beside the point. I'm afraid you're missing the boat. If Jenny says Grackle was dead when she got there, it's not to protect herself. The Balfours all cover up for each other. It's one thing you gotta admire about 'em. They got a real sense of Family. If Mama's out of it, Jenny's protecting dear old Dad."

"You mean? . . . "

"I mean Jenny Balfour goes up there, finds Grackle alive. Gives him the money and gets the hell out. Which she ought to be able to prove by the cop she talked out of a ticket. A girl would have to be a pretty cool customer to stab a guy to death, then go downstairs and flirt with a cop."

"For Christ's sake."

"Balfour shows up later, finds Grackle very much alive. Balfour's not in a very good mood. His wife's bein' blackmailed. His daughter's bein' blackmailed. He's been set up to meet someone in a bar, and the meeting didn't come off. He's tired of being jerked around. He tells Grackle so in no uncertain terms. They argue. But Grackle is no pushover. He attacks Balfour. Balfour runs into the kitchen, grabs a carving knife. Backs Grackle into the living room. Holds him at knife-point, tells him to cease and desist."

"So?"

"Not Grackle's style. Grackle bats the knife hand away, attacks Balfour. Balfour stabs him in self-defense."

"*Self-defense?*" MacAullif said incredulously. "You're arguing self-defense?"

"No, and an attorney wouldn't either. It's hard to make a case for self-defense when you kill a man in his own home. According to Richard, it's very unlikely a jury would acquit on those grounds."

"You told Rosenberg?"

"Not everything, but, after all, he is claiming the widow's money. On the other hand, the facts bein' as they are, a jury isn't gonna wanna come back with a verdict of murder."

"You mean it'd be a hung jury?"

"Not at all. Most likely they'd bring in a compromise verdict. Find him guilty of a lesser charge."

MacAullif's eyes widened. "Don't tell me."

I nodded.

"Manslaughter."